THE QUILT JOURNEYS MYSTERY SERIES

DAWN D. BENNETT-ALEXANDER

RENÉE T. H. PATTERSON

THE WANDERING QUILT
THE QUILT JOURNEYS MYSTERY SERIES

iUniverse books may be ordered through booksellers or by contacting:

iUniverse
1663 Liberty Drive
Bloomington, IN 47403
www.iuniverse.com
844-349-9409

ISBN: 978-1-6632-4396-6 (sc)
ISBN: 978-1-6632-4398-0 (hc)
ISBN: 978-1-6632-4397-3 (e)

Library of Congress Control Number: 2022915157

Print information available on the last page.

iUniverse rev. date: 11/02/2022

Dedication

To:

The Ancestors
I cannot thank you enough for trusting me.

Renée Tracy Harris Patterson
whose boundless creativity and imagination finally found a true purpose.

Brian Alzue Thompson
Thanks for holding my hand—without even knowing it.
Now are you sure this is actually dedicated to you
since your entire middle name is there? ;-)

Sonia Choquette
I can't believe you knew this in 1994. You really are incredible.

DDB-A

To:

God
Thank you for continuing to cultivate all iterations of me.

Mommy and Daddy
You both allowed me to pursue my creativity no
matter how many times I reinvented myself.

Auntie Dawnie
You ALWAYS knew me. Working with you is
a private dream I am living out loud!

To the largest minority in the world I now call my
community: the disabled. I endeavor to enable us all.

RTHP

With That Moon Language

Admit something:
Everyone you see, you say to them,
"Love me."

Of course you do not do this out loud, otherwise
someone would call the cops.

Still though, think about this,
this great pull in us to connect.

Why not become the one who lives with a
full moon in each eye that is always saying,

With that sweet moon language,
what every other eye in this world is dying to hear?

14th century Persian Sufi poet, Hafiz

CHAPTER 1

"*U*nbelievable!!!" Camille sighed forcefully.

"Excuse me?" said the startled browser a few feet away.

"Oh! Did I say that out loud? Sorry!" laughed Camille.

"No problem."

"I just get kind of carried away. I was admiring the handwork on this quilt. It is incredible," Camille gushed.

"Yes, it's quite beautiful."

"I quilt. In fact, I am an avid quilter. And collector!" Camille said with obvious relish. "This is not just beautiful. It is incredible. So many pieces to deal with, such tiny, uniform stitches, so much detail that, as a quilter, I know took extra time, effort and energy. I know how much less work this quilt would have been if they had not made some of the choices that took it from gorgeous to extraordinary. That makes me appreciate it even more."

"Oh! Well I'm glad you told me that. I just saw it as a nice quilt. What you've told me makes me admire it even more. Thank you."

The shopper took the opportunity to move away to view other items in the pleasantly crowded little shop as Camille held part of the quilt nearer to her face for a closer look at the stitching and details.

Camille picked up the quilt, folded it back up neatly, took it in her arms, and nonchalantly meandered toward the counter, stopping briefly along the way pretending to look at this and that. She was relieved that the person behind the counter had not been nearby when she was gushing over her beautiful find. If he knew how she felt about the quilt, he might hike the price up on her. It was a tiny town and, from the looks of it, it seemed pretty obvious that she was not from around here. She had to remain calm and casual. Just because she found it in a rather charming little thrift store in rural South Carolina didn't mean that the owner was an uninformed hick who didn't know the value of what he was selling. The internet was the great equalizer. All the information you wanted and more, right at your fingertips.

She had no idea who the person behind the counter was, how much he knew about quilts or the shop's inventory, or his relation to the store, so she needed to play it cool to neutral. As an avid quilter and quilt collector, she probably knew more than he did, selling everything in the little thrift shop from used iron skillets to the spinners kids were crazy for a few years ago, resulting in them being banned from many schools. But that didn't mean he did not know, or could not quickly discover, the value of the quilt she held in her arms.

Camille knew that her best hope was that this little shop, well off the main roads, in the rural area of this southern state, was just rather glad to have a customer, and likely didn't think the quilt was a big deal since so many people in this rural area probably still quilted. As was her usual practice when on the hunt for great quilts, she also dressed down so that sellers did not take one look at her and think she was some high falutin' money bags willing to pay whatever crazy price they asked for some "quaint" find.

Camille actually had on a pale blue, cotton blend shirtwaist dress with a matching fabric belt. She knew it looked borderline crazy, fashion-wise. She knew she looked like something out of a 1950's or early 60's TV show like June Cleaver, the mother in "Leave it to Beaver." In today's time, it was rather like the equivalent of wearing a turn of the 20th century bustle dress with whalebone stays.

She'd found the dress once when scouring the finds during one of her omnipresent flea market or thrift store shopping trips and knew it would be just the thing for just such occasions. Who in the world wore shirtwaist dresses anymore? Didn't they even stop making them in the 1960s, at the latest?

But this was a great find, in just her size. In fact, there were three of them in perfect condition in pale blue, pale pink and pale green. Camille had bought all three. She knew she would buy even more if they'd had them. Of course, she'd gotten them for a steal because again, "Who in the world wears shirtwaist dresses anymore?" But, she knew that the dress was so unassuming, so casual-yet-informal formality, that it would put any seller at ease, even as she approached.

Camille casually made her way over to the counter, still glancing around at the wares, and put on a studied pleasant smile of interest once there. It was a smile that revealed beautiful straight, white teeth and a warm, unassuming disposition. A look that conveyed that butter wouldn't melt in her mouth.

"Hi! Are you the owner?" Camille asked pleasantly.

The man behind the counter was looking through what was obviously an outdoor sports magazine featuring things like fishing and hunting. Dressed in a pair of clean, loose-fitting overalls, with one of the chest straps undone, and a clean cotton shirt about the color of Camille's shirtwaist dress, Camille instantly knew she would be able to deal with him in a way that would make them both walk away happy.

"Yeah, I guess you could say that," he said with a chuckle. "Although sometimes I feel like the shop owns me rather than the t'other way around. Keepin' it goin', gettin' up early to open up, wantin' to make sure I have enough of what I'm sellin', keepin' things in stock, findin' just the right thing I want to sell, it's a lot," he said with a careworn but friendly smile and decidedly southern accent.

"Well, I've got something I'd like to take off your hands if we can come to an agreement on a decent price for it," Camille said lightly, with a shy-ish, side-glance smile.

"Is that it in your hands?" he asked, looking from Camille's face to the quilt she clutched to her chest.

"Yes. I have a room I think it might look good in; but since it is just a guest room, I can't afford to pay too much for it."

"Wellllll….." he said, looking steadily at the item and giving it some thought. "Would $150 be too much?" he finally asked.

Camille nearly fainted. She tried hard to keep a straight, neutral face as she said hesitantly, "Well…. Ummm…. if that's the best you can do."

The owner then hesitated, as if thinking it over. Finally, he said, "Well, since you seem like such a pleasant lady, I might be able to let it go for $125."

Again, Camille was stunned, but tried not to show it. She took a minute and acted as if she was thinking seriously about whether she could afford to spend that much out of her budget for a guest room purchase. Finally, she gave a resigned sigh and said, "Oh, OK. I guess I'll take it. We're just finishing up a major much-needed renovation for our home, so we're pretty tapped out, financially. It'll mean I have to go longer than I expected to without curtains for the windows; but it's a nice quilt that will fit the room, so I guess it's worth it."

He smiled as if he understood that she was giving him a hard time for no good reason since it was such a good price. He took the quilt from her, pulled out a long piece of brown paper from an old fashioned cast iron roller on the well-worn wooden counter that had clearly seen many a transaction in its day, and began to wrap it up for her. As he did, Camille saw a slight smile come to the corner of his lips. Curious, Camille said, "You seem tickled. What's so funny? Did you just sell it for a great price? I don't mind."

"Well, actually, it, —your quilt here?— has a name. And it also has a little history to it. That's what I was thinking 'bout," he said with what Camille decided was a cross between a smile and a bit of a smirk on his face. She decided to go with the smile.

"Oh, Please do tell! Especially since it brings a smile to your face! I love a quilt with a history! You were smiling. Is it a funny history?"

"Well, I wouldn't say it were *funny,* so much as sorta *peculiar.* You see, the quilt's kinda been 'round for a while. It keeps a' comin' back to the shop from different people who done bought it, so we calls it The Wanderin' Quilt. It's not even from 'round here. I think it was originally made in Mississippi. The Delta, maybe."

"How interesting! I love it! Thank you for telling me!"

"Yeah. I've heard quite a bit o' scuttlebut over the years about it. I've had this shop for the past thirty (which Camille noticed he pronounced "thuttie") years and even 'fore I owned it, they was stories. Just talk, really, small town gossip, you know…"

"What?! Really? About a quilt?! What sort of stories?!"

"Well, it's silly, really. Not even hardly worth passin' along. It's just small town talk. You know, people not having nothin' better to do."

"But, what were the stories about?"

"Well…." he said hesitantly, his face clearly reflecting his discomfort at passing along whatever it was he knew. "Wellll…" he said.

"Charlie," Camille said, finally realizing he had a name tag on his shirt. "Whatever it is can't be that bad. You were smiling. What was it?"

"I don't know what it is, but they's some what said it just acted peculiar, sorta."

"The quilt? Acting peculiar? That sounds strange."

"Well, it was sorta. Kinda weird. But I told you it were just talk from time to time. People saying' it just didn't feel, you know….quilt-y… whatever that is…."

"Oh, really? Like what? How?"

"Well, I don't really know as I know how. Some peoples think it's somethin' from the past. Some think it's 'cause o' bein' 'round other quilts or somethin', I don't know…." he trailed off.

"Oh!" Camille said, sucking in her breath. "Huh. That sounds really strange. I mean, it's just a quilt, after all. I have many of them *and* I make them. I don't understand how a quilt could not feel like a quilt unless you used a weird batting inside or a stiff or scratchy uncomfortable fabric for the outside. I don't get it. But, I guess we'll see now, won't we? If nothing else it makes an interesting story, Charlie!" Camille said laughing.

"I guess it does, at that," Charlie smiled. Charlie handed Camille the large brown paper-wrapped package tied up with twine that Camille watched him unroll from the cute string holder on the counter that looked like an antique cast iron cat. "Here you go, Mam', and we thanks you for your business. Come back anytime. We may not have a quilt for you, but we got lots of other things you can meander through."

"Thanks, Charlie, but my family and I are just passing through on vacation. We're from the midwest. I doubt if I'll have a chance to see you again, but I love your thrift shop."

"Well, you never know, Ms. Camille," Charlie said, looking down at her name on her payment information. "I put a card in the quilt package for you in case you want to come back or to see if I have anythin' in particular you might be a' looking' for. We're little and tucked away out here off the main road now that they built the other big highway, and people who live here tend to stay 'round for a long time. When they die, or get sick or go to live with their children and such, we get a lot of different things come through here that you don't see much nowadays; so you never know. You can even email me and ask if I got something you might be a' lookin' for and I can send you pictures. I'm tryin' to stay up with the times, you know. Tryin' to do what they calls 'e-commerce'."

"Well, thank you, Charlie. I appreciate you telling me that," said Camille, smiling, as she headed out the door. "Bye, Charlie! And thanks again!"

Camille was glad for the opportunity to smile because she was just bursting at the find she'd just made and the price she paid for it. She couldn't wait to tell Tristan, who was, she suspected, still sleeping at the motel with their kids. Camille couldn't help but continue beaming at the fact that she had made a purchase that she was prepared to pay so much more for, but Charlie seemed quite happy with the deal that he, himself, proposed. She practically skipped to her car with the precious new addition to her quilt collection.

As she had thought, when she got to the motel Camille wasn't surprised to find her sweetie pie husband, Tristan, and their kids were still sleeping. Of course, since this was a summer vacation trip, that made perfect sense. But the Thorntons needed to get their day started. As a mother who was also a professor, she was used to being an early riser in order to get things done, including breakfast, packing lunches and getting the kids off to school.

While they had a great division of labor for the family, Tristan was an emergency room surgeon and was often on call at all hours. So, they had decided that it made most sense for Camille to take on the morning shift in order to provide the stability and predictability of mornings so their kids got off to a good start. They were both firm believers that routine provided their kids with stability, stability provided confidence, and confidence provided a stronger armor with which they could meet the day.

Camille had no choice but to be an early riser. Her best uninterrupted writing time for the books and articles she needed to publish was often well before the household stirred awake. But rising early was a habit she got into long before all that came along. From high school on, she had held a job of some kind in addition to going to school, so fitting everything into her day required being sure to make good use of the time she had. Discipline was not an issue for Camille. Waking up early was part of that. With her being a law professor and having a husband who was an emergency room surgeon who seemed to be perpetually on call with uncertain hours, Camille's schedule was more flexible; so she had to be ready for anything. She did not take for granted the blessing it was to be able to have a job with flexibility. Although she appreciated it, she also knew that a regular 9 to 5 job would, at times, be preferable to the life of an academic whose workday was really more like 24/7.

Students thought of professors as just someone who stood in front of a classroom for 75 minutes pontificating. In truth, that was the easiest, most fun part of the job. The real work came in time spent outside the classroom in office hours, department meetings, college meetings, university meetings, speaking engagements, advising student groups, and interminable publishing schedules. This did not even include the pleasant and rewarding, though intense and unrelenting mentoring of faculty, staff and students, papers to be dreamed up, researched, written, delivered at professional meetings, and published, books to be published and consulting in her area of expertise. The latter was especially important to Camille since she eschewed the idea of stuffy academics publishing their findings in journals important for their career progression but rarely passed on to those out in the world doing the actual work academics wrote about who could most benefit from their findings. To reject that notion for herself, for virtually every article Camille published in such journals, she also published one in some vehicle geared more to everyday working people and she did speaking and consulting about her issues. Camille also co-authored the best selling textbook on the market in her discipline, and it meant daily check-ins with many sources that allowed her to keep up with the latest information for new editions on an ongoing daily basis. She not only enjoyed, but loved it all; but, she had to admit, it was a *lot*.

So, what, to students, looked like a piece-of-cake, leisurely job only requiring her to show up for class twice a week for 75 minutes at a shot, turned out to be much, much more.

Camille picked up the phone and asked the front desk for a later check out time. That done, she cheerily woke up Tristan and their son Luke, 6 and daughter, Leslie, 9, by loudly reciting noted poet Paul Laurence Dunbar's famous poem, "In the Morning." As usual, they groaned upon hearing it, but sleepily and slowly began their day.

It was going to be a long drive back home. Camille and Tristan agreed that starting to expose their children to travel at an early age was an important thing to do to broaden their world, but actually doing it was another story. Long hours on the road interspersed with hitting the sights and interesting shops, still made for a long haul. But, Camille thought to herself, it was worth it if it gave their children more of what they needed to be able to navigate a quickly and deeply changing world.

CHAPTER 2

*W*ow. Camille could swear that they did not take all these clothes with them when she had packed for their vacation ten days ago. It always seemed that there were more clothes when she did post-vacation laundry, than when they began the vacation, even though they purchased no clothes along the way. Tristan swore the same thing happened when he did the return laundry. It always seemed to be more than they packed.

The one thing that Camille knew she would have to launder all on its own was her exciting new quilt find. As beautiful as it was, there was no telling how long the quilt had been sitting in the store or whose hands had been on it, perusing it for purchase just as Camille had done, or even what the life of the quilt was before she received it.

All quilts had a story. All handmade quilts, Camille's favorite kind. After all, they were beautiful, decorative, comfortable additions to a home, but the reality is that they were also a huge piece of the quilt maker's life. It never ceased to amaze Camille when she thought about it. Each quilt was, quite literally, part of the quilter's life story. It also became part of the story of the owner who used it. It could instantly change an unfamiliar space into a comfortable one. Camille remembered her sister telling her of dragging along one of their mother's handmade quilts when she traveled to Europe one summer and using it to make long waits in strange airports more comfortable. She recreated a "nest" with the quilt and felt right at home wherever she was.

For the quilter, what started out as old clothes or scattered pieces of various fabrics or even newly-purchased crisp, new fabric, ended up, after the usually tedious process of choosing, measuring, cutting, and sewing, as a single, comfortable, beautiful covering that belied little of the true story of how it came to be.

Once the fabrics were in the quilt, once the quilt was carefully placed on a bed or cozily tucked around a TV watcher, or on the ground for a picnic or concert, or even forgotten in an attic, it really didn't show that this piece of fabric in the quilt square came from the maker's grown daughter's favorite skirt she loved to twirl around in when she was five years old. No one really thought about the fact that that little piece in the quilt is the same fabric in the large photo hanging on the wall of the now-grown daughters, then ages 2 and 4, in the matching outfits their Mama made them. Or that that beautiful blue piece was from the fabric from the matching dresses the quilter made for the wedding of her niece for her own three daughters and her niece's daughter. The quilt did not necessarily reflect any of that or that the pieces may have come from Egypt, Ghana, Russia, Budapest, Italy, England, Hawaii, Alaska, or Kenya, or other places the quilter picked them up from in her travels.

The quilt did not tell the story of how the quilt was made by the quilter to feel close to her Ancestors who used whatever scraps they could gather to make a quilt to keep out the mean cold air coming through the cracks of a sharecropper's rough wooden shack in the winter, little or no better than their Ancestors' slave shacks; or act as a pallet on the floor in the heat of the summer, or a message hanging on a clothesline or an isolated, innocent porch rail to those escaping to freedom on the Underground Railroad as to which was the safest route to take or house to stop in and ask for help; or act as padding on the floor of a covered Conestoga wagon making its way over new territory to parts unknown. It did not reflect an unbroken line of mostly women, who had taken up the craft to keep it going and to remember where they came from and what skill they brought with them whether from Africa or England, Egypt or Scotland, China or Japan, each with its own unique style.

It did not show the pricked fingers, weakened eyesight from doing the close work, the swollen ankles from sitting long hours to get the job done, the rough hands from handling fabric that stole the oils from those hands and robbed them of their smooth texture, or the calluses from tens of thousands of pushes and pulls on a needle through layers of fabric.

And, most of all, it did not show the countless hours and stolen moments used to create that beauty that would give comfort and never reveal its history as it lay there. No. None of that was there when that quilt was lying on a bed or tucked up around someone enjoying its comfort. All the viewer saw and admired was the beautiful, comforting, comfortable quilt itself.

Camille recalled her firefighter friend, Chela, emailing to tell her she was driving four hours to bring Camille nine quilts that she discovered in an old, dilapidated, abandoned house that the fire department had purchased to allow firefighters to practice and hone their skills. Chela liked to go through the house before they began their drills in order to be sure nothing of use was left. This time, she got to the attic and found a treasure trove of quilts that had clearly been there for years. They were pretty haphazardly made, with random fabrics and in such poor shape that her male colleagues questioned her sanity in even bringing them out of the house. "Why not just let them burn?" they'd said.

But Chela knew someone had spent time creating these quilts using what resources they had. She had gently washed them, dried them, and wanted her quilt-loving friend, Camille, to see them. Chela later even managed to track down the people who had owned the house and through them, had discovered the quilter and even had a copy of her funeral program. She returned the quilts to the thankful family who had in turn agreed to allow them to be put on display at a county facility as part of a community outreach exhibit.

As a quilter, Camille knew what went into creating a traditional handmade quilt. She knew the long hours of tedious work, choosing just the right fabric, marking the fabric for cutting, cutting the pieces the most efficient way possible to save fabric, piecing the blocks, struggling to find just the right complimentary sashing to set off the blocks; the uncomfortable job of measuring, marking and cutting the long pieces; ironing to insure its smoothness when finished; putting it all together as a quilt top; marking out the quilting pattern, laying out the backing, batting and quilt top; the frustration of working with the large pieces of each of the three layers when trying to keep them straight while laying them out for final assembly; basting the sandwich together then mounting it on a quilting frame or hoop; and quilting together the three layers stitch by tiny stitch, back, neck and arms tired, stiff, and aching from hours of work bent over the task.

Camille loved that no matter how tedious, tiresome or uncomfortable any of this was in the process of creating and making the quilt, absolutely none of that showed when the quilt was finished and laid over someone or on a bed, couch, chair or even on the grass for a picnic. It was so worth every single discomfort of the quilter, big or small. The quilt always just looked, quite simply, beautiful. It just felt comfortable. It gave whoever was under it, delight for the eye and comfort for body and soul. The quilter's journey of untold hours of getting to this point just all melted away. All a quilter saw, all anyone saw, was a beautiful, comfy cozy quilt.

Who wouldn't love a quilt?

Camille knew all of this from having made well over thirty handmade quilts herself, beginning at age 11 or 12, and all of it made her appreciate the quilts even more and what went into making them.

She knew that washing them would rid them of the dirt, oil and grime they picked up along the way, sometimes, years in the making of the quilt, but it would not wash away the energy that the quilter had sewn in. Nothing would. That good energy was a big part of what made the quilt such a comfort.

Washing this quilt would be a pleasure, thought Camille. It was sure to clean up well and be a welcome addition to her newly renovated guest room and home.

CHAPTER 3

amille lifted the freshly washed and dried quilt from the dryer and carefully shook it out and folded it. She knew there would be quilting purists who would be appalled at her machine washing and drying the quilt. But she believed in making quilts that could be truly lived with, and that included getting dirty and being able to be washed. Besides, after quilting for years, she also knew that she knew enough to gauge when it was permissible to do so with her quilt finds. Her new find looked great and smelled wonderfully clean. She took the warm quilt up to the guest room, removed the one now on the bed and replaced it with her incredible new find.

It had just the desired effect. It made the room look even cozier, homier, more welcoming and more comfortable. "Comfy-cozy" thought Camille. The most important thing that a guest room should be, in her mind. No matter how much someone may like being away from home visiting loved ones, friends or family, it wasn't home.

They weren't in their own bed. They weren't in their own familiar surroundings. So, for her, it was absolutely essential that any guest room in her home be comfortable, cozy, more welcoming and more comfortable than a hotel room, or just a nice looking room in someone's home. Making people feel comfortable was her love language, according to Gary Chapman's book of the same name, and this quilt fit perfectly into that in this spacious, bright, newly renovated guest room to do just that.

As she smoothed out the quilt and tucked and pulled here and there to perfection, she was surprised to see that there was an opening in the quilt's border trim.

"Wait! Is that a tear?!" Camille exclaimed. "In my new quilt?!! (Well, new to me)...How did I miss that?!! Is *that* really why Charlie was smiling?! And to think he gave me that cock and bull story about it being called The Wandering Quilt and why! Darn it! Is that why he knocked off $25 and didn't complain about the low price? Well, I guess the joke is on me after all. Here I was thinking I got a great deal, and it turns out, the darn quilt is torn!"

Upon closer inspection, Camille realized that what she saw wasn't a tear, but instead a small opening along the border's trim. That made sense, since she would likely have seen a tear. "Oh! OK. It's not torn," she thought. "It's just a few missing stitches that I can easily repair with a bit of whipstitching. Whew! I'm so glad. Sorry, Charlie, for accusing you of trying to cheat me! This isn't so bad after all. I just missed it when I was examining the quilt in the store, I'm sure. My fault!"

Camille went into her sewing room, gathered a needle and thread to match the border trim, and returned to the quilt. She stitched the lost stitches in no time. "Great! Just like new. Well, maybe not new... after all it *is* a used quilt. But it's in great condition and with the missing stitches replaced, it looks just fine!" And with that, Camille straightened up and lightly dusted the perfect room, closed the door, and went on her way. "Lots to do!" she whispered to herself as she quickly descended the stairs and got on with the business of getting things back in order after their vacation.

CHAPTER 4

"Hi!!! Come in! Come in! It's so good to see you!! I'm so glad to see you!!" Camille said as she gave her mother a warm, welcoming, body hug embrace. Tristan, Leslie and Luke all converged in unison, hugging poor, beleaguered Naomi, who loved every second of it. "Grandma! Grandma! Hi, Grandma!" Leslie and Luke screamed at the top of their voices as they jumped up and down holding onto Naomi to get a hug. Tristan waited for the fracas to die down and swooped in and gave Naomi a warm hug, lifting her short, light body off the floor. "Whooo! Tristan! Put me down! I'm too heavy for you!" tiny Naomi cried in her high, reedy little voice. Tristan did, but not before giving her another warm hug for good measure.

"Let me take your bags upstairs, Millie," said Tristan, grabbing them and setting off. Millie was Tristan's own private pet name for his mother-in-law. He'd adopted it after seeing conversations online in which posters (usually angry) wrote about some problem they had with their "MIL." It took him a minute to figure out what the letters stood for, but it was clear from the context that they were talking about their mothers-in-law, and not in a good way.

But Tristan never had a minute of trouble with Naomi. She had accepted him from the start, first as Camille's boyfriend, then fianceé, then husband, and finally, as the father of her grandchildren. She was always warm, loving, supportive, non-judgmental, calm, and she did not interfere with Camille and Tristan in any way, either as a couple or as parents.

He used the term "Millie" affectionately because he loved the fact that she was his mother-in-law and his name for her was a constant reminder of her exalted status in his mind. A fact that he very much appreciated, given what he heard from many of his friends about their problematic mothers-in-law.

Although Tristan took on the task of taking Naomi and her luggage up to the guest room, it was the entire family that clambered noisily up the stairs right along with them. "I hope you didn't need a bit of rest," Camille said, laughing. They all joined in.

With her luggage, Naomi may have looked like she had come from out of town, but the truth is, she had not. She and her other two daughters and their spouses lived in town but were all staying at Camille and Tristan's for their annual holiday celebration. Camille and Tristan had finished a major renovation and everyone wanted to help them celebrate their new digs and to enjoy being together 24/7 for their favorite family holiday gathering.

"It looks like that's not in the cards, Mama. We've all missed you and couldn't wait for Christmas to come so you would be here with us for a while rather than just visiting, and now, here you are! So, of course, here we are too! Right here with you! Apparently, we're not letting you out of our sight!" she laughed.

"Yaaaay!!!!' yelled Luke and Leslie.

Tristan placed the luggage near the foot of the bed and stood up. He bent down a bit again, and peered at the quilt near the foot of the bed, slightly narrowing his eyes.

"What's going on, Tristan? What are you looking at so hard?" Camille asked.

Tristan stood back up and said, "I was looking to see if this was what it seemed like. I think there are a few stitches missing from the trim on the border of this quilt we got in South Carolina this summer when we were on vacation. If that's the case, I knew you'd want to know because I know how much you love this quilt and I just didn't want the opening to get any bigger. It looks small enough that you'd be able to quickly fix it."

Camille looked startled.

The place that Tristan was looking at was the very place that she had repaired when she put the quilt on the bed after returning home from vacation and washing it.

With preparing for the start of the kids' school opening soon after their vacation, then both herself and the kids getting back into the swing of a new school year and the kids' extracurricular activities, and them visiting family for Thanksgiving, she had not been in the guest room until she gave it a good going over yesterday just before her Mom came to visit. She didn't understand why, but the area Camille had repaired when she first saw the opening in the quilt when first placing it on the bed, had been open again.

Tristan, Luke and Leslie had no reason to come into this room, and Camille was sure they had not. No one else had been upstairs in her home. No one had been in the room since she put the new quilt on the bed when she got back from vacation months ago, until yesterday when she came in to tidy up the room in anticipation of her mother coming to visit. When she ran the dust mop under the bed near the very place that Tristan was looking, she had seen the quilt opening.

Although she could not figure out why, the same space had been open, so she had once again repaired it. She could swear that there was now an opening where she had repaired it just yesterday. She could be wrong, although she didn't think she was, but she could swear it was the same place. She couldn't understand how she had missed it if it was in a different place, or how it could have come back open after she had repaired it in the same place. She had dutifully darned the opening, but could not understand how it could have happened.

"Oh, no worries!" Naomi said brightly. I can repair it in a jiffy!!"

"But, Mom," Camille said hesitantly, staring at the opening, "*repairing* it isn't the problem. I can do that, although I know how incredible a quilter you are. It's a simple issue, and I know that you know I can handle it as well. The problem is that I am *sure* I repaired it *already*.

"*Twice*!

"I saw it after I washed and dried it after I came home with it this summer and put it on the bed. I fixed it then. When I came into the guest room to tidy it up for you yesterday, I saw it again and once again repaired it. Now, seeing it in the same place for the third time? That is more than …. I don't even know what.

"Coincidence? It's not that! I didn't see it in the shop when I bought it. It is entirely possible that I missed it. But I didn't miss it when I brought it home, washed and dried it and put it on the bed and saw it. I fixed it then. It wasn't a 'coincidence' that I saw it when I tidied up the room for you just yesterday and saw it again and fixed it. And it isn't a 'coincidence' that we're seeing it now. It's *not* a coincidence.

"It's just plain *weird*!"

When Camille stopped to take a breath, she realized everyone was staring at her, and she realized that she had gotten much more exercised about this than she had intended. In fact, it wasn't intended at all. It was a complete, utter and total surprise and it rattled her. She didn't understand what was going on. Her husband had not done this. Her children had not done this. Her mother had not done this. No one else had been upstairs in her house. She didn't understand.

Camille simply didn't understand.

"Well," Naomi said gently, "We can certainly repair it once again and not give it another thought."

Her mother's cool, calming voice brought Camille's blood pressure back down to normal, as it usually did, and the rest of the family looked relieved. Naomi had such a calm, warm, confident, reassuring demeanor, presence and spirit, that it couldn't help but have that impact on anyone around her in any situation she was in.

Camille had seen it work time and time again, from cops who stopped the car they were in, totally ready to dole out an expensive ticket for nonsense without a second thought, who ended up sending them on their way with a smile, wave and sincere admonition to be safe because they worried about them, without so much as a written warning in sight, to intense heated sports altercations between players on her sister's teams, where the upset players walked away with their arms around each other's shoulders, once again the best of teammates.

It was like the old "Christmas Carol" movies where the supremely jolly, capacious Ghost of Christmas Present, waved his magic Horn of Plenty at quarreling neighbors, only to have them immediately stop fighting and instead embrace each other and go off for a drink at the local pub.

That was Naomi. She spoke calmly, warmly and reasonably, sprinkling her fairy dust of positivity over all and sundry, and suddenly everything was OK; everything looked better; things didn't seem so intense; people couldn't remember why they were even making such a big deal out of what had gone on only moments before.

"OK. Well this time, you fix it, Mom. Maybe you can work your magic and it will stay," said Camille.

To everyone's total surprise, Naomi opened her purse, pulled out a tiny sewing kit, chose a perfect matching color thread, threaded the needle, bent down over the opening and began to whipstitch the opening closed. So Naomi. Always prepared.

Just as Naomi put in the last stitch, the doorbell chimed. Everyone jumped, not realizing how much they had all been focused on Camille's story about the mysterious opening and Naomi's repair of it. Leslie and Luke tore down the hallway, then the stairs, screaming at the top of their lungs. Naomi and Camille looked at each other and both said at the same time, "The sisters!"

Naomi gave the repaired spot a gentle pat, replaced her sewing kit and she and Camille filed out of the spacious, sunny room and down the stairs, though more calmly than the excited screaming children.

By the time they reached the landing, Tristan had opened the door, and true to their prediction, in had filed the remaining two sisters, Dreah and Tess, and Dreah's identical twin boys, Aaron and Shawn, age 7, now in the midst of a whirlwind of arms and legs and kisses and hugs all round. "Auntie Dreah! Auntie Tess!! We missed you!" Leslie and Luke yelled. "Grandma! Auntie Camille! Uncle Tristan! We missed you!" yelled Shawn and Aaron. "Yaaaay!!! Now we're all here and our Christmas celebration can begin!!!!!!!!!" they screamed as they jumped up and down with excitement.

CHAPTER 5

*N*aomi and Camille quickly bridged the space between the two of them and the sisters and kids and gave warm hugs, high fives and kisses all round. They had almost missed Tess's girlfriend, Renée, and Dreah's husband, Brian, who were bringing up the rear, and so brought them into the whirlwind. Smiles were as wide as Halloween pumpkins, laughter was loud and hearty and everyone felt the feeling of wholeness now that the entire family was together for the holidays.

Camille and Tristan knew it was a lot to ask for them to leave their homes and all be together for the holiday gathering and experience her and Tristan's newly renovated home, but everyone was more than happy to do it. They loved the idea of being together for the holiday and not having to worry about driving under the influence, getting up and dressed, going back and forth to visit each other, etc. And they knew that any friends any of them wanted to include as a part of their own holiday plans were absolutely welcome.

Almost to the second, all three sisters broke away from the group and did the usual ritual they'd done with each every time they had met up with each other ever since they were kids, dancing, bumping hips, crossing over high fives and ending up with a 3-way hug.

As usual, the orange tabby, HeavenSent, and black fluffy longhair cat Love, both with huge ridiculously flamboyant tails, tried to get in on the act, weaving in and out of the sisters and rubbing their bodies on the sisters' legs as they meowed their welcome, knowing the cat-loving family meant more love and rubs for them.

Renée, deaf, but who read lips, clapped to get everyone's attention. As everyone focused on her, she signed in American Sign Language. "Merry Christmas!" and signaled for them to mimic her movements. Everyone did it, practiced it a few times, then signed it in unison. They wiggled their fingers as the sign for clapping, and they all laughed a hearty laugh.

"Are the kids going to live through this?" Brian laughed "They are so excited that I don't know if they are going to make it. I thought Aaron and Shawn were excited on the drive over, but this is a whole new level and now they have their two cousins and family added to the mix. Anybody got anything to calm this crew down?" he laughed. "Or us?" he laughed even harder and he and Tristan did a knowing high five.

"It's Christmas! And it's family! And it's gathering to have a great time making lifetime memories," Naomi said, looking over the gathered group so full of joy and energy, anticipating the holiday with great gusto. "Don't forget to make sure you turn to Renée so she can read your lips." Everyone gave a thumbs up. Renée signed a big thank you.

"I don't want to go anywhere or know anyone who doesn't want to be full of joy and excitement at Christmas, with our family gathering for it, especially kids!" said Tess, eyes rolling and hands on hips, with her usual down-to-earth, totally funny framing of events that was always right on target. She was their family fun spirit.

"It's true!" said Dreah. "Fun and family is what it's all about! Especially at Christmas! We didn't do all of this to get here for anything less! We are just as excited as the kids are; only, as 'grown ups' we just handle it better. No, I won't even make that qualitative judgment about it. I won't say we handle it better. I'll just say that we handle it *differently*," she laughed. Everyone joined in.

"Yes," said Camille, "We're *all* excited! There are plenty of goodies in the kitchen! I know my family! I know how you are when you arrive! We've got food, we've got drink, and we've got fun, all in the kitchen!" she laughed. "Go ahead and get your drink on, Tess. The champagne is right in the fridge, nice and cold for you. I know my sister!" she laughed. Tess headed straight for the fridge, thanking her sister who knew her well.

"Camille! The fireplace turned out *great*! Look at that great roaring fire!" Dreah said as they passed by the family room on the way to the kitchen.

"Thank you, Tristan!" Dreah continued. "I know you worked that out! I love how it's in the family room, but it serves the family room as well as the kitchen and the dining room and makes it work for all three. That is very clever. I hate it when I'm in the kitchen or dining room and have to miss out on the fireplace while I'm getting things together for a gathering. This is *great*. I know you are so glad that you and Tristan finally finished up the renovation. And by the looks of it, it was so worth it to wait until you could get what you really, really want. I'm so impressed!" Dreah said as she drifted into the spacious kitchen along with the rest of the family. "Look at that gorgeous sunroom! Awesome, Girl!!"

"Four seasons, too!" replied Camille. "Cool in the summer, warm in the winter, with a heated floor. Don't you just love those floor to ceiling windows? I can't believe that I fell in love with it when I saw it on our Cotswold tour in England, then came back and saw it set up as big as day in Sam's Club, of all places! It was just meant to be, for us to have it. And it's such a great reminder of England, my spiritual home," laughed Camille. Everyone laughed, knowing that she was a great lover of English murder mysteries.

"It really is beautiful. I love the sort of garden-y furniture you chose for it!" signed Renée. "It's absolutely perfect for that room. The room is so inviting! Bright, comfortable, but still cozy. The plants bring out the white tile and window trim so well."

"Give the credit to Tristan and the kids! You know how much I hate picking out stuff like that. I don't know how we managed to do a big renovation, given my feelings. But Tristan is great. He is awesome at it and loves doing it. Thank goodness! Talk about Yin and Yang!" Camille laughed. "He completes me!" she said dramatically, putting the back of her hand to her forehead and throwing her head back, teasing the group because everyone knew she hated that sort of dramatic female clinginess. She believed everyone was whole and significant others should simply be a wonderful addition to your life, not a part you couldn't function without. As much as she loved Tristan, and Lord knows she loved that sweet man and would be devastated to be without him, she knew she could do it if she had to. She wouldn't collapse as she had seen friends and acquaintances do.

When everyone was well fed and fully satisfied, the kids scampered outside to play. After taking care of the dishes, Tristan and Brian were drawn into the family room like a magnet, watching football, with an eye on the kids playing just outside the large family room window. Camille went upstairs to help Naomi unpack. Dreah, Tess and Renée went to do the same in their guest rooms.

As Renée passed by Naomi's room at the top of the stairs, she noticed a slight uneasy feeling. She couldn't quite tell why, but it did not feel OK. She had eaten a good meal, but not so much that it made her feel uncomfortable. All the great food was familiar enough that it wasn't likely to have made her feel ill. She noted the feeling, but continued on to her room with Tess.

"Girls! Come see Camille's newest quilt!" Naomi called out a few moments later. Dreah, Tess and Renée found their way into Naomi's guest room as Naomi pointed to the bed as Camille looked on. "Look at this," said Naomi. "Camille found this one while she was on vacation with her family this summer as they passed through South Carolina. Isn't it beautiful?! And in such good condition! She got it for a steal, although it was the shop owner that named the price for her," Naomi told them. "We never want to take advantage of anyone, do we? Especially for something like a quilt. We want only good vibes. We don't want any bad karma coming back and slapping us in the face. Just do the right thing. Camille did, and here is this lovely quilt that she got for a song, considering the beautiful work in it."

Renée, who loved the beautiful quilt, found it more and more difficult to ignore the queasiness in her stomach and the nauseous feeling that had intensified when she walked into the room. "Weird," she thought. Tess looked over at her and saw her looking rather green around the gills. Alarmed, Tess signed, "Renée! Are you OK? You look like you're sick! What's wrong?!"

Embarrassed that anyone had even noticed, Renée wondered to herself, "What the heck is this about?" Interjecting a bit of humor into the situation that clearly was making her nervous about her beloved, Tess said, "Well, one thing we know for sure: You're not pregnant——at least not by me!"

Tess laughed. The rest of them joined in and even Renée felt a moment of warm mirth. But, it was momentary. She immediately went back to feeling queasy.

Naomi asked the women in the room to pick up the four corners of the quilt so that they could better see the complete quilt all at once. As they did so, and the entire quilt came into view, they all oooed and ahhhhed at its beauty, delicacy, intricacy and the extraordinary handwork. White muslin background blocks, with a quarter-circle curved dramatic purple, white and gold paisley piece at each corner sewn onto a central piece made to fit the curves. On this were appliquéd green leaves and flowers which had appliquéd into their middle, contrasting yellow circles forming the middle of the flowers. The quilt blocks were set on the diagonal, with a white muslin block in between. Incredibly intricate feathered heart and feathered circle shapes were quilted in purple thread in the plain white muslin squares, bringing them to life. Hearts were liberally used throughout as the quilting itself.

The border of the quilt was scalloped, with the green, yellow, and purple fabrics from the quilt, used to create what looked like pizza pie slices interspersed with the muslin upside down pizza slices between each colored fabric. Each of the pizza slices around the edge of the quilt creating the scalloped border was quilted with hearts. The scalloped edges of the border were finished off with a delicate, tiny bias edge of white fabric hand sewn onto the border,. The overall effect was dramatic and wonderful.

Dreah stood holding the left bottom corner of the quilt. As they all stood admiring it, Dreah looked more closely at the part of the quilt she was holding in her hand. She saw a rather small opening in the border. She was not sure anyone had noticed the opening. But she knew her sister well enough to know that Camille would never want there to be an unrepaired opening in her quilt.

Being the quilter and quilt collector her sister was, Dreah knew that Camille would not allow such a thing to happen. She would want to repair it as quickly as possible not only make to sure it was at its best, but also so that it would not grow any larger. She knew Camille truly believed that "a stitch in time saves nine."

"Ummmm....Camille, I think there's something here you might need to take care of," Dreah said.

Camille, whose curious face filled with concern, came around to the edge Dreah was holding near the foot of the bed and stared in disbelief. Eyes wide, mouth opening and closing like a fish, Camille looked up from the quilt and over at her mother. Naomi, staring at her daughter's face from the opposite end of the quilt, knew immediately what she must be seeing.

The opening Naomi had stitched back together just a little while earlier, had not only reopened, but the opening appeared to be larger than when she sewed it back together, Camille saw. Renée felt a strong wave of nausea. Dreah, Renée and Tess stared. They stared at the opening, then from Naomi's face to Camille's face, confused.

"What is it?" Tess said, looking at Camille for answers. "It's just a tiny opening in an old quilt. What's got you looking so upset? Why are you and Mama acting like this is such a big deal? I'm confused."

Camille did not answer immediately. She was too busy staring.

"OK, Y'all are scaring me," Tess said. "What?! What's going on?!"

She threw down her corner of the quilt like it was a hot coal and jumped back. "Y'all are scaring me!" she nearly shouted, looking around the bed at the other women almost frantically.

"I'm beginning to think there may be something to be scared about," said Camille slowly.

"When I bought the quilt in South Carolina, the store owner, Charlie, told me that it had a name. He said it was called The Wandering Quilt. He said that he had owned the store for 30 years, and the quilt had come back to him several times over the years for various reasons. When I pressed him about it, he said that even before he owned the store, he had heard rumors, which he considered to be just talk around town, that people brought the quilt back because they were uncomfortable with it for some reason.

"Charlie didn't really name what the discomfort was, but now that I think about what he said, it seems like what he was really talking about was some sort of bad juju or something. Some sort of negative energy connected to the quilt."

They all stared at Camille. They all seemed to realize at the same time that they were not even breathing, and slowly let out the big breath they had been holding.

Renée fainted.

CHAPTER 6

ach corner of the quilt was dropped by its holder and the
quilt fell rather haphazardly back into place on the bed as the
women all rushed to Renée's side. "Give her air," Naomi said
calmly, as she reached under Renée's head and cradled it.

"Let's put her on the bed in our bedroom," said a clearly worried Tess,
holding Renée's hand and rubbing it rather vigorously.

Each of the sisters was glad for Renée's lithe build, light weight, and
habit of running daily. It was easy enough to carry her to Tess and Renée's
guest room.

"Call Tristan!" Dreah exclaimed as they laid her on the bed. "He's a
doctor. He'll know what to do!"

"Are you serious, Dreah? Did you forget I'm a doctor too? Just because
I retired this year doesn't mean I've forgotten forty-five years worth of
medicine. She has just fainted, honey. She'll be fine. Bring a glass of water,"
Naomi said calmly.

"Sorry, Mama. I'm just discombobulated about her fainting," Dreah
said warily.

"Are you sure, Mama?" Tess said tentatively, her voice filled with a level
of concern and caring that bordered on panic.

"I'm sure, Tess. She was perfectly fine before this, right? She hasn't
been sick?"

"No, she's been fine. Right up to the time when she started looking a
little green around the gills," Tess said.

"Then, I'm sure she has just fainted and will come around soon," Naomi said calmly. "But I do wonder what caused it." They could hear the concern in her voice even though it was the calm, steady voice of an authoritative doctor used to dealing with such things.

The sisters all knew how much Naomi's calm, professional demeanor had meant to so many people who were sick, and their families as well. She was cool, calm, in command and totally level-headed in a crisis. She was never the least bit rattled by the chaos surrounding her. Naomi was exactly who you would want dealing with an emergency.

Just as Naomi said the word 'it,' Renée stirred, her legs moved, and her eyes fluttered open.

"Wha…what happened? Why are you all looking at me? Why are you looking down at me?!" Renée said, panic rising in her voice. "Oh, my God, what am I doing on the bed?! I'm not even in the same room!" Renée started up from her prone position, but Naomi put a hand out and gently stopped her.

"Hold on, Renée" Naomi said softly, making sure she fully faced Renée so Renée could read her lips "Just hold on a minute. You fainted. You'll be fine; but you need to take it slow," said Naomi.

Renée stared at her in disbelief. Fainted? She fainted?! She had never once fainted in her life! How embarrassing!! The only thing that made it less so was that she was with people that she loved and trusted and who she knew cared deeply for her.

"OK, let's see if you can sit up OK, but do it *slowly*," said Naomi.

Renée cautiously sat up and looked around. She felt okay. She felt like she could breathe for the first time in a while. Pretty much since coming upstairs. She did not feel as nauseous as she had in Naomi's room.

Camille handed her the glass of water she had run to get for her, and Renée sipped it slowly.

"What happened?" Tess signed to her. Renée handed the water back to Camille.

"I…I….I'm not really sure. I don't know. I've been feeling uneasy and queasy ever since I got up here, sort of, but I can't figure out why. Then, when I went into Naomi's room and got nearer to the quilt, it just seemed to get worse and….well….I guess I just fainted," Renée signed. Tess interpreted for the family.

They all stared at Renée. Renée only saw faces of concern and care surrounding her.

"Well, are you feeling OK now? Are you going to be OK? Do you feel like you need a doctor?--Another doctor? Or can we have some fun now?" said Tess, half seriously, half-jokingly. It was no wonder why she was everyone's favorite party starter and life of the party.

"I don't get the whole 'doctor' thing," Naomi said ponderously. "'Does she need a *doctor*? *Another* doctor?' To hear you all, you'd never know that your mother standing right here is a doctor and has been for all of your lives. I don't get it. Did you all suddenly have mass amnesia? I'm not stuffy about being recognized as a doctor, but to listen to you all, you don't even know that I *am* one!"

"We are just rattled, Mama," said Tess. "No one was expecting Renée to faint! We know you're a doctor, but we were here for our famous annual family holiday family gathering and this is so unexpected. In this context, we just think of you as Mama, not Mama the trailblazing, world famous doctor!"

"Well, you had me worried there for a moment. I wasn't sure if you'd forgotten. I love Renée. I would never let anything happen to her," Naomi said.

"Yes, Mama." Tess sighed heavily, coming as close to rolling her eyes as she dared. Her mother did not abide disrespect from her daughters, regardless of age. Thankfully, it was extremely rare to nonexistent, and only happened when they were greatly distressed. In fact, the only two times Tess could remember were during the high-stress occasions of the weddings of her sisters. "We know you're a doctor. And I didn't mean any disrespect when I asked Renée if she needed another doctor. We just think of you as Mama. Not Mama the doctor who is known around the world for her innovative medical skills and inventions. You're just Mama to us. *Now* can we have some fun?!"

"Sure! I feel fine! Let's get this party started!" Renée signed, laughing, and everyone broke into relieved laughter, knowing exactly what the sign language for 'party' meant.

CHAPTER 7

And party they did. The wine flowed, the hot chocolate was delicious, the snacks were tasty treats, and the kids, so tired they could hardly stand, were eventually packed off to bed grumpily complaining that they were not sleepy. The only thing that soothed them off to sleep in their dead tired, but excited, state was the reading of a selection from the Thornton children's extensive Christmas book collection lovingly saved from their parents' childhoods and added to each year since Leslie and Luke were born. That Christmas story, and a reminder that tomorrow they would have a full day of fun with the family once again, did the trick of sending all little ones off to dreamland.

After a few glasses of wine, the women broached the subject of what had happened upstairs in Naomi's guest room and the quilt and its story.

"That's some weird stuff!" Tristan said when he heard that the quilt was open once again. "I saw Millie take out her needle and thread to make the repair before I went downstairs to open the door. I'm sure she did it well. Thinking it is open again is crazy. Brian and I were watching the kids while they were playing outside, so we know it wasn't them. Why would they go into the room and pick at a quilt anyway? Especially in the very same place that it had been repaired earlier in the day. In fact, the twins, Aaron and Shawn, weren't even here and didn't even know about it. The kids were so busy having fun, they wouldn't be the least bit interested in it anyway."

"Well, weird is right. So, y'all do your manly duty and listen up for anything that goes bump in the night," Tess said, only half joking.

"Oh, don't worry about us. Nothing is getting in here to mess with our women and children," Brian laughed. "Even though I own 67 guns, purely for hunting and didn't bring even one to this Christmas family gathering, you'd better believe that both Tristan and I are fully prepared to kick the ass of anyone who even remotely thinks they can get over on us. You are in good hands, ladies. Not to worry. Sleep soundly, knowing we are on the job and you are weeelllll protected," he said confidently, even triumphantly. Every single one of the family gathered around the table laughed loud and long. And with that, they retired to beds covered in beautiful and bountiful handmade quilts, fully prepared to rest well... or whatever...for a full eventful day of family fun starting in the morning.

CHAPTER 8

"I promise you, I sewed the opening back up before I went to bed last night. We'd forgotten all about it in the rush to help Renée when she fainted. But when I went back upstairs to go to bed, I repaired it once again. When I woke up this morning, not only was the place on the quilt open again, but all night long, I kept pulling the quilt up on me and it kept creeping down. I'm not easily rattled, and at 71, and being a doctor for the past 45 years, I've seen a lot. But this is just plain weird," the usually unshakeable Naomi said in a low shaky voice.

Not one mouth around the table was closed. They were all hanging open. Every single pair of eyes was as big as saucers. The only saving grace was that Leslie, Luke, Shawn and Aaron had not awakened yet, so the adults did not have to worry about the children being scared out of their wits with the report that Naomi was providing after what had been a supremely comfortable, fun, then restful –and fun–night for the rest of them.

"I don't know how you lasted all night," Tess said. "I would have run screaming down the hall, waking up all of you! I wouldn't care!"

"What the hell?!" Brian breathed. He was fuming at the thought that something was disturbing the women in the house and the mother-in-law he adored, and it didn't seem like there was anything he could do. It didn't sound like strength or even one of his guns, if he'd brought one, would help this situation.

"What can we *do*?" asked Dreah, to no one in particular. "Camille, do you want to send the quilt back to the store?"

Camille looked disturbed and pensive. "No, I really don't want to do that," she said pensively. "Not only is it a beautiful quilt, but I don't believe in that nonsense. What? Like it's a haunted quilt or something? That's silly! It's beautiful! I want to keep it. But I just don't understand what is happening. Four times it was repaired. *Four!* There *must* be an explanation."

"It's five now, because I repaired it again this morning," added Naomi.

"Well....," Renée sighed and slowly and hesitantly signed to Tess.

"Well, what, Renée?" Tristan asked levelly.

"Well, I have a friend who lives here in town and happens to be here because the weather canceled her travel plans. She might be able to help," Tess interpreted to them as Renée hesitantly signed the statement.

"Help? Help how?" Brian asked. "We don't even know what in the world this is. If we don't know what it is, how can she help us deal with it?"

"Well," Renée signed, slowly and even more hesitantly, "she's a medium."

Everyone stopped what they were doing and stared at Renée as if she had just sprouted wings before their very eyes.

"Did you interpret what she said correctly, Tess? Did she say 'medium'? As in 'I see dead people' medium?" asked Brian. He made sure his face was turned to Renée so that she could read his lips.

"I know it sounds crazy!" she signed. "I have no idea what's going on either. But it couldn't hurt and it might help," Renée signed solemnly.

"Renée's mother told me that ever since she was a little girl, she could feel presences," said Tess. "We'd call them spirits, or ghosts, I guess. She said Renée could feel them even as a kid. Maybe that's what's going on and why Renée felt so odd yesterday, especially in the room with the quilt last night."

Renée looked at her, startled. She had not put that thought together in her mind yet, even with all the pieces pointing in that direction, and even though she had made the suggestion about the medium. She loved this house and these people. Everyone and everything was so comfortable. The people are so loving. The rooms are so welcoming, cozy and livable; the quilt so beautiful and such a wonderful centerpiece for Naomi's newly renovated guest room; and she loved the loving family so, and had such fun with them that she never attached anything negative to any of it. But the more she thought about what Tess said, the more sense it made.

"Tess is right," she signed heavily. "I have felt spirits ever since I was a little girl, but I had never really put the pieces together with what I was feeling here because I love it here so much. I love the quilt so much. I love you all so much. But the more I think about it, the more sense it makes to have my friend, Tabitha, come over for a visit. She works with her husband, Paul. They don't do anything weird. They just have a sensitivity to these things and can usually feel if something is going on. I can feel presences, but it's not like it is a formal thing for me. I don't do anything but feel them. I can't talk to them or hear them or see them or interact with them or anything. They can. I think we should give them a call."

Everyone stared at Renée.

They simply stared.

CHAPTER 9

"I promise you that we don't do anything weird when we come into a space. We don't have electronic equipment, technology, divining rods or anything even close," Paul laughed. "That's not how we work."

"We just come in and basically take a look around and see what we can pick up," said Paul openly, and half-jokingly. He stood there in the entrance hall looking casual and handsome, with a warm, open smile. His wife, Tabitha, a few feet from him, was hugging her friend Renée, with whom she had communicated, but had not seen in a while.

"Well, we're glad to hear it, because we really aren't believers in this sort of thing," Brian said, eying Paul warily.

Paul laughed. "Well, that's not the first time we had ever heard *that* one!" he said heartily. "But it doesn't take believing in anything in order for us to do what we need to do and tell you our impressions," he said mildly.

"Well, let's get started, shall we?!" said Tabitha brightly. "Now, you all can stay here if you want, or you can come with us. But, you really won't see much of anything. We're only going to be taking a walk through the house and making mental observations about what, if anything, we pick up."

Camille, Tristan, Naomi, Dreah, Brian, Tess and Renée all looked at each other inquiringly. Did they want to go with them? If all the couple was going to do was to just look around, there really didn't seem to be much point. But it was an intriguing idea.

"Well, do you need us to show you around?" Camille asked. "Do you need us to show you what the issue is, why it is we called you in?"

"Actually, if you don't mind, we'd prefer that you didn't tell us anything. We can chat after we've taken a look, but we'd rather not have any preconceived notions. Renée didn't tell us anything when she called and asked us to come over, other than she wondered if we might be able to stop by the house she was visiting and take a look. That's all we know.

"Luckily for Renée, our Christmas travel plans were canceled because of the weather where we were headed and we are still in town. If you tell us something, it might interfere with our own ideas and thoughts about what we pick up because we'd be looking for something without even meaning to. We'd rather have it be fresh and untainted.

"We think it helps you too. We think people feel more like they might be able to trust what we tell them after we take a look if they know we don't know anything that could skew the findings. Does that make sense to you? Are you OK with that?" Tabitha asked.

"Well, yes," Camille and Tristan said at the same time, looking around at the others for assent. They all nodded their heads in agreement.

"Yeah. That makes sense," Brian said. I can come closer to believing what you say if I don't feel like we fed you something that gives you the information you needed to find on your own." Dreah glanced at her husband with a look that clearly said, 'Seriously, Brian? Did you need to go there?'

Brian put his arm around her shoulder. She put hers around his waist and he drew her close. She deeply appreciated his fierce love for his family and his willingness to do whatever he could to keep them safe. "Yes, that sounds just fine," he said.

"Well, then, we'll get started. Just point us in the right direction, and we'll take it from there. If you don't mind, we'll just wander all around all over the place. If there is somewhere you don't want us to go, just let us know," said Paul.

"No. There's nowhere you can't go," Camille said quickly. "You're free to take a look wherever you want. We'll just be here waiting for you when you finish. Take all the time you need."

With that, the couple walked off in the direction of the kitchen. The family meandered into the family room and took up space around the inviting fireplace, all ablaze. They could see the kids romping freely outside in the yard and were relieved to not have them here asking questions and being "scared to death of ghosts." The adults had been careful not to allow them to hear any of their conversations, and the kids had suspected nothing being amiss. Snow that had fallen the night before had them squealing in delight as they threw snowballs, and slid around on the snow saucer.

"Ah, the bliss of childhood," thought Camille as she stared out at them. She worried they'd want to come in if it got too cold. She did not want them to come in while Tabitha and Paul were still wandering around. That would look too suspicious and strange and they'd ask questions. "Well," she thought, "if they got too cold, they could always come in and watch a movie in the new theater. I'll make them hot chocolate after being out in the cold and they will be totally distracted."

"Anybody want a glass of wine or a beer, or anything else?" Camille asked. "I do!" she heard six times over. She went out to the kitchen, followed by Tristan. They returned with trays laden with something that would please every taste. The family welcomed the two back just a little too eagerly, belying the fact that the five of them were anxious over the visiting mediums wandering around the house and what they might find.

CHAPTER 10

"Finished already?" Naomi, who was standing by the fireplace, asked as she was the first to spy the couple returning to the family gathered in the family room.

"Yes. We think we've seen all we need to see," replied Tabitha.

"Can we get you a drink, water, coffee, tea, or anything?" Camille asked.

"No, thanks. We're fine. We never eat or drink when we're working. We find that it can interfere with our ability to concentrate and maintain focus," said Tabitha quickly.

"We visited every floor, every room, top to bottom, and we think we have what we need. If we can, we'd like to have you come with us to the room where we both had a particularly strong feeling."

"Sure," they all said in unison, looking around at each other, both out of curiosity as well as apprehension, not knowing what that meant. They slowly rose from their seats and turned toward Tabitha and Paul. It was clear that everyone was wondering if the room the couple wanted to take them to was the guest room with the quilt. If it wasn't, they were in big trouble because they wouldn't know where to go from there. But if it was, they were in trouble then too. Time to see.

Before joining the group, Tristan looked out the window to make sure the children were settled enough at play for the adults to go upstairs for a few moments. Seeing that they were totally involved in snow frolics and looking like they'd be fine, he joined the others.

Tabitha and Paul led the group out into the hall and up the stairs. Camille couldn't believe that out of the entire house Tabitha and Paul inspected, the couple was leading them upstairs.

Everyone's question as to the room they were being taken to was soon answered.

Tabitha and Paul led them right into Naomi's spacious, sunny guest room and waited until everyone had filed inside.

Tabitha spoke first.

"Paul and I don't really talk to each other when we are viewing a space. We are not even always together during an inspection. Each of us has different things we are attuned to and sense and we address them in different ways. I feel energy. Paul sees and hears things most people cannot and he can interact with it. We don't talk to each other while we are inspecting a space because we want to leave each other free to experience whatever it is that may be there without it being impacted in any way by what the other is experiencing.

"We do not speak to each other until we are both finished. We then tell each other what it is we experienced and we go from there. Sometimes Paul sees or hears things I do not. Sometimes I sense things that he does not. Most often, we end up experiencing activity in the same place and with similar conclusions. We just do it in different ways.

"After inspecting your home, Paul and I spoke with each other and we both felt a presence as soon as we entered your home. It did not feel malevolent or like it wanted to do harm. In fact, it felt sad and morose more than anything else. Almost like it was lamenting something, feeling guilty about something. Paul even heard weeping. The energy feels like that of an adult, rather than, say, a child or a teenager.

"It could be anything from a lost love the presence shut out of its life while living, to an abortion that seemed the right choice at the time but they ended up regretting, even a lost friendship or family relationship that was not repaired before the person died and the spirit regretted his or her pettiness in allowing that to happen, or someone the presence hurt but now sees it was wrong to do so. It could be anything. But that is what Paul and I I sensed. A spirit lamenting something.

"That feels quite different than, say, a panicked presence that doesn't know where it is because it does not recognize that it has died and doesn't understand what it is going through, or even a happy presence that wishes to stay where it has experienced so much joy. No, this presence, for both Paul and I, felt like it was a lamentation.

"So, we both felt a presence when we entered the home. However, as we traversed the house, the place where both of us felt it the strongest was in this beautiful, comfortable, room. The room was so comfortable, cozy and beautiful that we were both taken aback at what we felt. We, of all people, should know that the presence of a spirit is not limited to dimly lit or sad looking or scary places. But, it just took us both by surprise that we would feel the presence so strongly here in this beautiful room.

"For both of us, it felt even stronger as we got closer to the bed. That was a surprise too, because, as it turned out, we both only came closer to that space because the quilt was so beautiful that each of us, separately on our own, wanted to get a closer look.

"But, as we came closer, we could feel the presence grow stronger and stronger. It wasn't as if it was threatening us. Not at all. It didn't feel dark or evil or anything like that. For both of us, it was more like it wanted us to know something. Rather like there was unfinished business that they did not get to take care of and they wanted to have someone be aware of it.

"Of course, we have no idea what it is.

"At first we both thought the stronger feeling near the bed may mean that someone had died in the bed and did not want to let go of life or was in great pain or distress or something there. That's what is usually going on when you feel strong feelings near a bed. But neither of us got the impression that that is what was going on. It just didn't seem to be what was involved. Again, we don't know what it is but it did not seem like it was that.

"We felt nothing of any kind anywhere else in the house. Nothing. Unless you count the joyous energy that seems to permeate every inch of the home. Energy that we can feel comes from a family that loves each other deeply and enjoys tremendously being together, having the children enjoy themselves and the season. Other than that, there was nothing except the presence we felt in this room."

"So, let me get this straight," said Brian, crisply, sharply, with laser focus. "Are we talking about dead people here? Are you talking about feeling ghosts or spirits in this house? Is that what this is? Is that what we're talking about? I'm just trying to be clear. Especially since I don't believe in ghosts, but you seem so sincere."

"Yes, that's what we're talking about. The presence of the lingering spirit of someone who has most likely died," said Tabitha.

"We are not just our physical bodies," she continued. "We are spiritual creatures as well. When we die, even though our physical body has ceased to live, sometimes the spiritual part of us lingers on here for some reason. Like I said before, it may be confusion about the fact that they are dead, or it may be that they don't feel ready to leave yet, or even that they fear what is next.

"Or, and I think this is the case here, it can be that there is some sort of unfinished business that the spirit feels it needs to do before it can pass on. It weighed on them so heavily in life, and it was unfinished when they died, so even in death they want to see if there is anything they can do to have the matter taken care of.

"For instance, someone may have died without their family or friends knowing about money they had stashed away somewhere, and they try to make contact with someone by whatever means they can, to let them know. What the person living may experience, is, say, a drawer continually opening without anyone touching it.

"When they go to investigate the desk and how this could happen, they discover the money stuffed in the back in a secret compartment no one knew about. We worked on a case like that. Of course, the family was glad to get the money, as it was a significant amount. But it came from the strange phenomenon of the drawer opening without anyone touching it. It was the spirit trying to get them to find the unknown money stash.

"But those are the sort of things that happen. And spirits don't have a sense of time like we do. They could have been around for an hour, a day, a month or a hundred years. Time doesn't mean the same thing to them that it does to us because spirits are eternal."

Paul picked up Tabitha's thought. "So, whether you believe in ghosts or spirits or life after death, or whatever, these things happen and they can have significant consequences. Like finding such a substantial amount of money after the loved one died because the spirit showed them where it was."

Brian simply stared at Paul, with Brian looking like a cross between being duly chastened when faced with the realities Paul and Tabitha shared, and scared witless at the idea of a ghost he could not see disturbing their peace and, potentially, threatening his family.

"So, like we said, we felt something really significant in this room. Is this why you called us here? Did something happen here? Did you experience something? Do you know if there is, or was, something going on in this room or with this bed that would have been a basis for you calling us in?" Tabitha said, looking around at each of them.

They, in turn, looked at each other, then Tabitha, then Paul.

Brian was the first to speak.

"Hold on a minute. I want to make sure I understand what you're saying here. Are you telling us that something is here? In this room? Seriously? Do you mean like a ghost or something? Because, again, I don't believe in all that stuff. None of us do." He quickly looked over at Renée and revised his statement.

"Well, not quite none of us. Tess told us that Renée has been able to feel the presence of spirits or something ever since she was a little girl. No disrespect to Renée, but I don't believe in that spirit stuff and I don't think the rest of us do either. Except Renée, like I said," he ended, looking Tabitha and Paul straight in the eye.

Camille cleared her throat nervously, gave a little cough, and opened her mouth to speak, but nothing came out. She re-grouped and started to begin again.

Before she could do so, Naomi said to Tabitha and Paul, "Well, since Camille bought the quilt and has had the most experience with it, I think it would be best for you two if Camille tells you what she knows in answer to your question about why you were called here and whether something is going on with the bed." Naomi gave Camille an encouraging look and nodded her head toward Tabitha and Paul as if to tell Camille to go ahead and tell them what she knew about the quilt. Camille looked at Tristan and could feel his belief in her, his support of her.

Telling her family members what had been going on with this weirdness involving the quilt was one thing. They knew her, they loved her, and they trusted her. But telling complete strangers, even ones that were quite lovely friends of a friend, was quite another. Staring at Tristan, and although feeling suddenly silly and as if she had overreacted to the whole quilt thing, Camille nevertheless hesitantly began to share with Tabitha and Paul what had taken place.

But the more Camille took in the supportive vibe Tristan silently communicated to her, and the more she told Tabitha and Paul of the experience with the quilt, the more she realized that she was not overreacting. Even Tabitha and Paul expressed surprise when she told them the story Charlie had told her when she bought the quilt, then after she brought it home, that the quilt had been mended several times, and several times the opening had returned; how Renée had felt a growing discomfort, especially after going upstairs and even more when she entered Naomi's guest room, and fainted when they had all held up the quilt; and how the quilt kept coming off of Naomi in the night, unlike any cover Naomi had used in her entire life.

When Camille was finished speaking, Tabitha and Paul stared at her as if unable to speak, as if they didn't know quite what to say, as if they had never heard of such a thing before, even with all the years of experience between them. They looked at each other uncomfortably and didn't say a word for a moment.

Finally, Tabitha said, "I must be honest with you, Camille. I have never heard anything quite like this in my life. Like Renée, I have been able to feel the presence of spirits for my entire life, but I have never seen or heard of anything quite like this. So, it is not the bed that is the issue, it is the quilt?"

"Yes, it is the quilt. Nothing was going on until the quilt came into the house," Camille said quickly.

"Is it possible for whatever you say you feel—-spirits, ghosts, presences or whatever— to be attached to something like a quilt?" Dreah asked. "To be attached to a thing rather than a place?"

"Oh, yes!" Tabitha quickly answered animatedly. "Spirits attach to wherever or whatever was significant to them or that they think may help with some issue they had in life or want people to know about after death.

"Just because I haven't seen an issue with a quilt before doesn't mean it isn't possible or that it doesn't exist! It's just that I, personally, have never seen it, nor, I think, has Paul. I don't think we were quite prepared for that to be the source of what we were sensing.

"Like I told you, we only each, separately, and without consulting each other, came closer to the quilt in order to be able to examine it closer up because it was so beautiful. Your now telling us it is the quilt that is presenting the issue is a surprise. But it is totally consistent with what it is we felt.

"We just thought it would be the bed, because often people experience illness or death in a bed, so it is not unusual for their spirit to linger there. It doesn't make your issue any more or less likely or important because it is the quilt. We are just surprised because we've never experienced that before. And we didn't sense death or illness involving the bed, but that feeling of wanting something to be known.

"When you think about it, actually, it makes perfect sense. When we think of quilts, we think of comfort and cozy. We don't usually think of stress. But, when you think about it, if someone was in distress, because quilts make us think of being comfortable and cozy, it makes sense that someone in distress would snuggle up under one. Or even that we would put one on someone who was ill or in distress in the bed and they died with it on them."

The seven pairs of eyes around the room stared at Tabitha and Paul soberly. It was really difficult to take in what was being said. They were all rational, intelligent human beings and professionals. Doctors, lawyers, professors, athletes. It was a stretch to embrace what was being said.

What Tabitha said made perfect sense as she was saying it, but who in the world thought of such things in real life, or when they looked at a beautiful quilt? You just thought about the quilt pattern, the fabric, the stitching, the beauty of it, the comfort of it. You didn't really think about the history of it, what the quilt had experienced in its journey from creation, or how it got to the place where you were holding it in your hands. Thinking about that put a whole new spin on things for someone like Camille who both made and collected quilts.

She knew quilts had their own journeys and stories, but she never really thought past that fact to the specifics because there was no way to know. When she thought about it, knowing her own quilts she made by hand and how they were a part of her life while being made and after just like the ones her mother made that they all still had, she realized she should have thought about it, been aware of it. Of all people, she should have thought about it since she lived it with every stitch she took and every quilt she purchased for her collection.

But she hadn't.

"So, since you now think the quilt is the issue, is there any way you can figure out what's going on, or how to fix it, or whatever it is that you do?" Tess asked anxiously. "We have four children in the house. And of course, us seven adults. Is this something that could hurt us? I don't know about the rest of you, but this is creeping me the hell out. I don't want to be murdered in my sleep by a quilt ghost!"

Everyone's eyes grew wider as they nervously laughed. It was clear that Tess had voiced what had been floating around in the back of their heads as they tried to remain rational and calm in the face of this weirdness none of them ever expected or had even thought about in their lives.

Tabitha and Paul's eyes did not grow wider. Their eyes showed amusement—something the rest of those gathered in the room couldn't understand since they were practically shaking in their boots with what Tabitha and Paul had told them about the reality of spirits and the idea Tess had voiced that they were all thinking.

"No! No! You won't be killed in your sleep by a quilt ghost!" Tabitha giggled. "Not only do we not feel anything anywhere else in the house, but from what you've told us, the only activity has been around the quilt itself, and even that, as we told you at the beginning, has not felt malevolent. It feels more sad than anything else. Morose, forlorn, remorseful. So, nothing wants to hurt you. It is more likely that it wants your attention and your help.

"As for helping you out, or fixing this situation, there are things we can do, but because we don't know the source of the discomfort the spirit is feeling that makes it want to communicate something to us, we can't say for sure what it is that will make it feel ready to move on. The best thing we can do right now is to let the spirit know that we know it is there.

"That is huge. Especially since it apparently has tried to communicate to the other quilt owners and it didn't work because they just became afraid and got rid of the quilt. We will also let the spirit know that we are willing to do what we can to help the spirit to do what it needs to do to find peace, if we can."

"You… I mean, we…. can *do* that?!" Dreah breathed, wide-eyed at the revelation. "The law covers a lot, and I'm known as a fierce legal advocate in a courtroom, but this is beyond anything I ever imagined in real life. Seeing it in a movie or TV show is one thing. Having a medium—something I'm not even sure I believed existed before this—standing in my sister's home and telling us that spirits actually exist and that we can communicate with them, is quite another. Give me a crazy court case any day." All the family members chuckled nervously, totally endorsing what Dreah said.

"Sure you can communicate with them!" Paul said heartily. "Spirits are all around us all the time, whether we realize it or not. They generally either want to help us and they do so in ways we don't realize, or they want us to help them, in which case they try to communicate with us in some way, like what is going on with the quilt. They really love helping us.

"It just so happens that I am more sensitive to their presence and have the ability to communicate with them. Actually, we all have the capacity to do it, but most people don't want to out of fear, or they simply aren't interested. I've always been more sensitive to their presence, just like Tabitha and Renée, but I can also hear and see them, so my job is really to help them when I can, if they need help to sort out issues that are keeping them here, so they can move on."

Brian glared at Paul like he was the proverbial carnival hawkster or snake oil seller.

Paul didn't react. He was used to it. It was the norm for him for people not to believe in what he could do or was able to sense.

"Did you see a ghost here? Here in this house?" asked Brian, clearly disturbed, his voice tight and rising.

"No. I did not see a ghost. I could not tell you if it is male or female. It takes a lot of energy for spirits to manifest so that they can be seen. Spirits will only allow themselves to be seen or heard if it is necessary for what it is they want to have happen. Both Tabitha and I felt the presence of a spirit, and we both felt the same energy from it. The sadness, the regret, the need for help. I did not see the spirit, but I heard it. I heard weeping. Not screaming, crying, weeping and wailing or anything dramatic like that, but more like when someone quietly weeps when they are sad or upset.

"Because the spirit was crying and this is a quilt, it may well be a female," Paul said. "My experience has been that women tend to cry more frequently than men, and tend to quilt more than men–at least in our country. I've actually seen quite beautiful quilts being made by males as they sit in the marketplaces selling them in Egypt. But the crying may not have to do with making the quilt but something that happened involving the quilt, and that could mean a male or female.

"But the truth is, we really can't be sure. We don't know if the attachment is to the quilt because the spirit made the quilt—which would most likely be a female, though not necessarily—or because it has some special significance to the spirit. And, again, not only female spirits cry. I've heard male spirits cry as well.

"What I hear from spirits isn't the way we usually hear sound. Ordinarily, when we hear someone crying, we would usually be able to tell if it is a male or female. It is not the same with hearing spirits cry. You can't always tell. There's just no way to tell here whether it is a male for female, and I did not see the spirit. I sensed it.

"Knowing the gender of the spirit usually really doesn't matter anyway, except in terms of trying to figure out who it is for purposes of figuring out what it is the spirit may want from us or need us to do.

"Our spirits are who we are inside, not outside; our spirits are not our physical bodies. In most societies, what we think of as gender is a social construct rather than an actual thing. Spirits aren't restricted by the idea of if they are female they must do this or that, or if they're male they have to do this or that. It is totally irrelevant. Our spirits are about what is inside, not the outward appearance. How we act, how we go through the world, how we treat people, how we handle situations, and so on.

"There is no gender designation on, say, kindness or compassion or love. Anyone can do it. But societal acculturation tends to tell us, for instance, that women are more compassionate or kinder, or more loving than men. Or that men don't have the same emotions. That isn't so. That idea, and the acts that arise from it, comes from societal conditioning and acculturation, not innate capacity.

"Spirits don't deal with such boxes. So, whether this spirit is male or female only helps us with the issue of figuring out who it is and, therefore, what this may be about. Since it is not materializing, apparently, we don't need to see it, or to know its gender, except to figure out the issue. That is, since I can't see it, it must not need to manifest in order for you to figure out the issue."

Brian looked somewhat relieved, although he wasn't sure that it made much difference whether or not you could see a spirit if it was clear to someone who deals with these things–or whatever– that it was present. Or, as may be the case here, the spirit is actually doing something like taking out quilt stitches. "Listen to me!" Brian thought. "I'm acting like this crap is real!" He drew his attention back to the group.

"So, exactly what is it we need to do in order to figure out what we need to do for this spirit to be okay, Paul and Tabitha?" Tristan asked in a low, steady, soft voice.

CHAPTER 11

Everyone's eyes turned to stare at Tabitha and Paul.

"Well," said Tabitha, I was thinking about what Camille said about the space that keeps opening up in the quilt border trim. It seems to me that since the stitches are being pulled out each time the quilt is repaired, we may want to start there. I have no idea what it means, but since it keeps happening, maybe the spirit is trying to get your attention."

"Well, it certainly did *that*," said Camille emphatically. There were murmurs of agreement all around.

Tabitha moved to the place where Camille had noted the stitch issue. She picked up the border of the quilt to take a closer look. When she did, they could all clearly see the open space. The space in the border was open. The stitches had come undone yet again after Naomi had stitched the spot back up this morning when she discovered it open after her night of wrestling with the creeping quilt. Naomi and Camille, at the same time, looked at the space and nearly exclaimed, "It's open again! But it's bigger!"

This startled Tabitha, who was holding on to the border, and she quickly dropped it.

"What?! What do you mean?" Tabitha asked, her voice sounding tight.

Both Naomi and Camille began to speak excitedly at the same time. That was unusual for Naomi, who was normally cool, calm, and collected.

Finally, Tabitha said, "OK, only one person tell me what you're talking about."

Naomi nodded to Camille to let her know Camille should speak. Camille excitedly said, "The space is larger than it was! We have repaired the quilt like five times and each time it was always about the same size. But this time it's larger!"

Tabitha picked up the open border trim edge once again. "Maybe it's larger for a reason," she said slowly. She brought it closer to her face, and stared, startled. "You all didn't tell me that there was writing on the inside."

CHAPTER 12

"What?!" Everyone exclaimed at once, practically jumping back, away from the quilt.

"Writing?!! What writing?! We've repaired this border five times and not *once* did we see writing there!" Camille practically shouted.

"I second that!" Naomi said. "I repaired it three times myself! I saw no writing! What are you talking about, Tabitha?!"

"What the hell is going on here?" shouted Brian, adding to the building chaos.

Tristan, standing close behind Camille, brought his arms around to her chest and drew her close to him, her back touching his chest, to steady and calm her. He could feel her back trembling against his chest, feel her labored, shallow breathing. Camille put her hands on his arms and could immediately feel his calming presence. Tristan, literally, had her back. She was upset, but she would be fine. Tristan was right there with her. His calming, unwaveringly supportive presence always had the odd impact on Camille of both calming her because of his presence, yet reminding her of how strong she was in her own right.

"I feel like backing away slowly," said Tess, holding tightly to Renée's hand and noting that Renée had been eerily quiet the entire time they had been in the room. In fact, throughout this whole visit of Tabitha and Paul's.

Brian glared, looking extremely apprehensive at the idea of something he couldn't see or touch doing something so upsetting to his family that he loved so much and desperately wanted to protect. He would do anything for them. Even now, he took care of his aged pain-in-the-patootie elderly aunt nearly every day because, for Brian, that's just what you did for people you loved and cared about. That's what you did for your family. Dreah stood by him, holding his hand and his arm. More like holding him back, she thought. She could feel his nervous energy; he was tight as a drum. She could feel his consternation. His concern. His apprehension. His—dare she say it?---fear?

Dreah knew that Brian took no prisoners when it came to his family. Neither did Tristan. But Brian tended to wear his heart on his sleeve a bit more about it. Maybe it was the difference between an emergency room doctor who had to remain cool and calm, and a courtroom lawyer who had to rather fiercely advocate, Dreah thought. She understood, since she too, was a courtroom litigator.

Tristan and Camille just looked like a mixture of being startled, apprehensive and borderline afraid, but standing resolute.

Naomi stared serenely as if taking it all in and waiting for understanding. She looked like whatever the issue, she would be fine; all would be well. They would be fine. Dreah figured that must be her decades as a doctor, having seen things others would never likely see—even though that didn't cover this.

"Well, I know it all sounds weird, but it may well be that the writing was there before but was not being shown to you because what the spirit needed in order to be helped was not yet here for it to be able to do what it needed to do."

All seven pairs of eyes stared at Tabitha, speechless, clueless.

"What in the world does that mean?" Brian said, lips tight, glaring.

"Well, let's think about this," Tabitha said, the picture of reason—if there could be such a thing with a subject matter as strange as this. "Renée could feel the presence but whatever she was feeling made her feel ill and she fainted. At first she did not even connect that what she was feeling could be a presence. So the presence likely knew Renée was not a good candidate to try to communicate its message.

"Bringing Paul and me in was a different matter. We were sensitive enough to feel the spirit's presence, and also strong enough to deal with it. The spirit knew it could do what it needed to do. That is, to communicate to us the message or whatever it was they needed taken care of.

"It appears that what they needed to do was to show us something. They kept opening the border trim to get your attention, but since none of you is sensitive to spirits except Renée who kept getting sick, they knew that you would not be good candidates to show you what it is they needed to show. But, I think they kept opening the quilt for you because they sensed that while you couldn't feel their presence, you were someone they believed would be open to their plight once you knew.

"Paul and I, on the other hand, are able to feel its presence and strong enough to do so without any ill effects like Renée had, so it could go ahead and use us to do the rest of the job of getting across whatever it is they wanted you to see.

"That might even be why they led Renée to call us to come over. Since she became ill, they sensed that she could sense them, but when she fainted, they knew she couldn't handle it, so they had her invite someone over who could."

"Are you saying that they planted an idea in Renée's head to call you and Paul? That they can use mind control over us?" Brian said, growing ever more tense.

"Remember that we told you that spirits interact with us all the time?" asked Tabitha. "Most of us don't recognize it at all for what it is. Keep in mind that we also told you that spirits are all around us and they are often here to help us. But they generally do so in ways that we don't even recognize.

"One of those ways is to give us an idea that would be helpful to us. Have you ever had something just pop into your head that ended up being a really good idea that works out really well for you but it wasn't something you felt like you thought up on your own? It may well have been a spirit that put the idea there. They can't *make* you do anything you don't want to do, and they cannot interfere with your life. But they can try to help you and one of the ways they do that is through putting helpful information and thoughts into your head. You can do with it what you will.

"Often we ignore such thoughts. Just as often we realize we should not have. When we use the idea, we tend to just think we came up with the idea on our own, even though we don't know where it came from. But the truth is, we may have had help," said Tabitha sincerely and warmly—the latter an oddity not lost on anyone, given the circumstances.

Brian looked at her as if he didn't believe a word she said or, that if it was true, it was problematic.

"So what do you think they want us to see?" inquired Tristan evenly.

"Well, I think we need to take a look at the writing," said Paul. "The writing that did not make itself known to you before, but is doing so now that you have brought someone here that may be able to help get their message across."

Tabitha picked up the problematic quilt border and took a look at the opening in the trim again. "Show me where the usual spot was that kept coming open," she said to Camille.

Because the actual border was scallops formed by the upright and reverse pie slices, the bias quilt trim around it was tiny. No more than half an inch. The open spot was not obvious and did not detract from the quilt; but knowing what could happen if it was left unattended, any quilt maker, quilt lover, or quilt collector would certainly want it mended. It was not the least bit of a big deal to do so. But when it was mended, it should have stayed.

After all, Camille had quilts that were still in fine shape even though she had made them when she was a teenager. The same went for the ones she made for Luke and Leslie when they were born and then toddlers. They had undergone washing after washing after washing with the stitches still intact. But these same types of stitches on her new quilt did not hold. Without even being washed, they came undone. It made no sense.

That should not be. That was, in Camille's view, knowing what she knew from sewing and making quilts, impossible.

Camille and Naomi agreed that the open space had been about a one-inch opening exactly where Tabitha was now holding the border. Only now it was open about three inches. Tabitha, slowly and carefully untucked the tiny folded binding around the scalloped border. Tabitha looked closely at the faint letters written on it. In fading permanent ink she saw:

"E.T. I lied. I'm sorry. C.B."

The room was deathly quiet. You could hear the proverbial pin drop. It was as if no one was even breathing.

Tabitha stared at the faint, but clear inscription. Then finally, after what seemed like minutes, but she knew it could have only been a few seconds, she raised her eyes and read it out loud to those who she knew were waiting with bated breath to hear it.

After she read it to them, Brian gave a low whistle, followed by an unmistakable "what-the-hell-is-this?" look that no one missed. In fact, they each pretty much had some version of the same look on their own face. All anyone could do was stare at the binding in Tabitha's hand. Even though her hands trembled so much that the cell phone camera flashed the message for her to stop moving, Camille had the presence of mind to take a photo of the inscription. She was trembling so much that the first photo was simply a blur. She trashed it. In the second photo, the inscription was faint, but absolutely clear. Camille gulped hard.

Finally, Tabitha broke the silence.

"I think this is what the spirit has been trying to communicate all this time. It kept unraveling the repair stitches you made in order to get your attention. It has been patient, but communicating whenever it could. It was on an infrequently used guest bedroom bed, so there was little opportunity to communicate. But whenever it could, it did. With you, Camille, twice before Naomi came. That is, when you washed and dried it and put it on the bed, then again when you came into the room to tidy it up for your Mom before her Christmas visit.

"Then, Naomi, it came loose the day you arrived and you repaired it, then the same night it had come open when you showed the quilt to the women and repaired it again when you went up to bed. By then, you'd repaired it twice but it stepped up its game by pulling the cover off you in the night and opening up the space once again. Three times you had to repair it. All of it was to get your family's attention. My guess is that it sensed that it was finally with people who would be able to help it do what it needs to do.

"Renée, it could have been that your feeling ill, fainting in this room, or even your failure to connect your illness with a presence was the spirit's effort to get you to call us to come in to help. It could even be that that is why our travel plans did not work out. The things that can be gathered in furtherance of a spirit's plans can be far-reaching."

They all stared. Tess's look clearly said, "WTH?!" — or worse. Holding Renée's hand, she looked like she was ready to run screaming down the stairs and out the door.

Brian's look said he didn't know whether to be relieved that they finally figured out something about this weirdness, or to be afraid that a spirit was capable of, among other things, being persistent enough to get their attention, make someone ill, change weather and plant ideas in people's heads. He couldn't even believe he was thinking about a spirit as if it was a real thing. Dreah held his hand, as much to draw comfort from him and his determination to protect his family, as to soothe him and remind him that she loved him for it.

Tristan, ever the even more reasonable, level-headed persona in the group that drew people to him by his very presence, his charisma, looked at Paul and Tabitha as if what they said had value.

Looking at Tristan's countenance, Naomi was reminded of seeing lions in Kenya when the family was on safari near the Masai Mara. So very different from seeing them in captivity at a zoo or circus. A true alpha male is quiet, known to all the others for his unquestioned position in the group not because of his might or his roar, or constant busy-ness, but for his countenance. His mere presence commands respect. He's usually pretty still, never has to raise his voice for control. In fact, it's a sign of weakness to the others in a group if he does so, because it lets them know that he is not in control. His very countenance, the fact that he is self-contained, self-possessed, not prancing around drawing attention to himself to convince others he is in control, tells you who he is. His countenance is never, ever overbearing, prideful or overconfident. It doesn't need to be. Naomi had seen Tristan have that impact in a room many times over the years.

She was glad he was Camille's partner in life. She knew they would always take care of each other, give each other what they needed. She knew that Tristan's countenance, while all his own, was also greatly enhanced by what he received from Camille. They were a great pair.

"So what do we need to do now that we've seen this?" asked Tristan, slowly, looking from Tabitha to Paul.

CHAPTER 13

"Well, I think the first thing you may need to do is to try to track the quilt's journey," said Paul.

"'Quilt's journey'?" inquired Tristan.

"Yes, you have the quilt now, but you have to figure out how it got to you, who it is you need to contact so that you can figure out who E.T. and C.B. are. That means going back and trying to figure that out. All you really know, Camille, is that you got it from the store you purchased it from, right?"

"Yes. But the owner, Charlie, told me it was called the Wandering Quilt because people kept giving it back to the store for various reasons. He said that the people who owned it while he had the store for the past thirty years were local but that he thought it was made in Mississippi. Maybe the Delta."

"Can you call Charlie and see if he knows the name of the people who he was talking about, Camille?" Tabitha asked.

"If you mean the people who bought it from him then brought it back, I'm pretty sure I can," said Camille thoughtfully. "It's been several months since I was there, but I'm pretty sure I have the card of the thrift store I bought it from around here somewhere. I usually save them in case something goes wrong with my purchase in some way. He may remember me since he told me that story about the quilt being named The Wandering Quilt.

"But I don't even know whether or not that story was true. But even if it wasn't, he may remember that he told that yarn to this silly midwestern tourist who came through last summer just because tourists expect people in the south to be full of ghost stories and other such shenanigans. I'll look and see if I have the card. I usually keep them in a special box in my sewing room."

"Okay," said Naomi. "You go look for the card to see if you can call Charlie, and I'll look online and see if there is a quilt-dating service anywhere nearby. Quilting guilds usually have someone who can date quilts to within a reasonable time of their creation, by looking at the type and styles of fabrics used, the pattern, etc. If we get a ballpark figure of when the quilt was made, or even when or where the materials were made, we may be able to get closer to who owned it," Naomi said, heading off to find her cell phone.

"Alright, folks. It looks like you have everything under control now, so we'll be taking our leave," said Tabitha brightly. "I don't know that I would be able to be that bright and cheerful if I could feel dead people all the time," thought Dreah warily.

"Are you sure you need to go already?" Renée asked hesitantly through Tess.

"Well, there's nothing left for us to do, really," said Paul, looking directly at Renée so she could read his lips. "We've established a pretty solid case that the issues you have been having with the quilt have come from a spirit trying to get your attention in order for you to see what was written in the quilt border trim. Now it's your job, if you want it, to figure out who the initials belong to so that you can see if you can figure out what the message is about. Who are E.T. and C.B. and what did C.B. do to E.T. that C.B. is apologizing for? What did C.B. lie about? What did it have to do with E.T.? Where are they? What happened? Those are things that you all are going to have to work on yourselves, if you choose to."

"Well, is the thing you say was messing with the quilt still here?" Tess and Brian asked at virtually the same time in virtually the same way.

"Are we safe?" asked Brian, cutting to the chase even as he realized that his question meant he believed to some extent what he had denied all this time. Everyone looked at him. It was strange Brian would be asking that question since "he didn't believe in this ghost nonsense" they all thought. But to a person, they all certainly understood.

Brian looked sheepish at first, as if it was silly of him to ask the question, given the looks he was getting. That sheepish look quickly turned to a look of near defiance and bravado, as he lifted his chin and moved his broad, strong, shoulders back as if to straighten his spine and prepare for a confrontation if necessary. Even a loving one.

"I believe you're perfectly safe," said Paul, unwilling to feed into or exacerbate what he knew to be Brian's anxiety about his family's safety. "Like I said, Brian, there was never a feeling of malevolence attached to this entity. It is more sad than mad. Based on my years of experience I am positive it just wanted to get your attention so that, by the looks of the message in the quilt, you could help get a message to someone.

"Now that we have seen the message, I don't think it will bother anyone anymore. It won't likely do anything else weird. Of course, you can always try it out by mending the quilt once more and seeing if the stitches stay put. But, I don't see why they wouldn't stay put. We've seen what the spirit needed us to see.

"The spirit wanted to bring your attention to the message in the quilt and you have now seen that message. It can't really do anything else. It doesn't need to do anything else. If it opened up the stitches again, what would be the point? It has already had you read the message. Opening up the stitches again is unlikely to reveal yet another message. The message we saw looked complete.

"The only thing left to do is find out what it means. But the spirit continuing to open up the stitches isn't likely to make you do that. It's not helpful. Besides, you've already begun to try to figure it out. It would know that. Harming you is not only something it does not want to do to you, but it would be counterproductive for the spirit. If you are hurt, you are less likely to be able to find out what the message means and do whatever it is that needs to be done. If it does open up again, it would likely only be to remind you to track down what it is in need of. That is, the reason it keeps opening, which, I believe, is to have you notify someone of something."

"That makes sense," Brian reluctantly agreed, relaxing a bit. Dreah looked at him with love and appreciation.

"Think about it," said Tabitha. "If Charlie actually was telling the truth and everyone who had the quilt brought it back to his shop, those were clearly not people who were willing to do what needed to be done for the spirit. But you did not take the quilt back to the shop. You called in a medium. So, the spirit already knows that you are willing to help. Why would it hurt you?"

"So, you think we're safe and that there will be no more ghostly shenanigans?" Dreah asked hopefully.

"I don't want to have to go home and miss being together with my family for our annual holiday gathering and miss all the fun we have together in order for Renée and me to feel safe," Tess said, warily. "But I will if I need to. I don't want Renée to be sick. This was supposed to be a very special time for us. We were planning to announce our engagement while everyone was here together for the holiday.

"But if we don't feel safe staying here, or Renée is sick from staying here, we can't do it. I wanted our engagement announcement to be memorable, but not because we were being chased by some damn ghosts, and not even Ghost of Christmas Present bringing all sorts of goodies."

Everyone laughed at her joke, then immediately realized what Tess had just said.

"What?!! You and Renée are getting married?!" Dreah squealed. "AWESOME!!!!!" Dreah hugged Tess and Renée tightly and planted kisses on both cheeks.

"Congratulations!" Tristan and Brian said, and gave Tess and Renée hearty hugs.

"What's all the fuss about? What did I miss? Clearly it was not only something, but something big! Tabitha and Paul, what in the world did you say while I was gone?" asked Naomi, who was coming into the family room from the kitchen just as Camille was returning from her sewing room after searching for the store's card with Charlie's number.

"It's *good* fuss! GREAT fuss!" Dreah nearly shouted. "Wait till you hear! Tell them Tess and Renée!"

"Well, Renée and I were planning on announcing our engagement while the family is all together during this holiday family gathering, but I'm trying to nail down whether it's even safe to stay here with this quilt spirit crap, or whatever it is, going on, or whether we should go home."

"What?! My last Baby Girl is getting *married*?!! Niiiice!!! Congratulations!!!!" exclaimed Naomi.

"*Really,* Tess?!" squealed Camille. "I'm so happy for you both! It's about time, Girl! You sure waited long enough for the right one to come along!"

"She *is* the right one, and *yesssss*, we really are getting married in the spring! She said yes!" Tess stated definitively, holding Renée's hand and twirling her around as if they were dancing.

"Congratulations to you both!" said Tabitha and Paul.

"What?! The spring?! We can't get things together that fast, Tess!" Naomi, Dreah and Camille all shouted some version of that sentiment at the same time.

"Not to worry," said Tess, "We've already pretty much worked it all out. We have plenty of time for the type of event we want it to be," she said

"Uh-oh!" Naomi looked concerned, while Dreah and Camille rolled their eyes and looked deadpan at Tess.

"Mama, Dreah, Camille, Renée and I are grown-ass women and we know what we want," said Tess. "We appreciate the sentiment, and offers to help, but we know that if we let you handle it it will be a bunch of frou-frou, formal, sedate stuff like Camille and Dreah's weddings, and we would hate it. So, the only way we'll let you help is if you *totally* honor our wishes and help in the ways that we want you to. If you don't want to do that, it's fine. No hard feelings. But this is our day and we want it to be what we want it to be, what is meaningful to us."

Renée looked at Tess admiringly with a look no one missed that also said she seconded that emotion.

"Fine! Well! We will certainly have to have a toast to this in a minute. But right now, let's get back to what brought this up," Naomi said smoothly and warmly. "It seems to me that the issue of whether you should go back home rather than stay here with the family for our awesome holiday gathering has been addressed.

"Renée is no longer sick since this spirit has apparently contacted us about what it wants. Tabitha and Paul both seem absolutely certain that there is no feeling of harm coming from the spirit, and it has done what it needed to do. I am the one who slept under the creeping Wandering Quilt last night and I'm still here to tell the story. If the spirit wanted to harm me, it certainly could have done so in my sleeping state. Instead, it just kept pulling the quilt down off me and taking loose the stitches, apparently to get my attention, and it worked.

"Now that we know what it wants, I don't think we have to worry about being harmed any more. Those are my four grandchildren and you are my three daughters and their significant others, I wouldn't want to leave you in harm's way for anything. And, I'm willing to spend the night under the quilt again, to boot. How's that for trusting that everything is OK now?" Naomi finished calmly.

As usual, Naomi did the magic she does, and everyone was calmer.

"I found the card from the store where I bought the quilt," Camille offered. "I'll give Charlie a call."

"OK. Well, I guess we don't need to go home, then," Tess said. Renée gave a relieved smile.

Brian was coming down from looking like men look when they have run into a spider web. They were fine with fighting a bear they could see, but let them run into a spider web they couldn't, and they turned into little kids looking like they were fighting an invisible monster. He looked leery, but seemed settled on the fact that his family was safe.

"Well, Tabitha and Paul, I guess you're right. I guess everything is OK and we will be safe while we try to track down this quilt's journey, as you call it," Tristan said cordially. So, I guess you really can leave us now. We'll be OK. We will call you if anything comes up. Meanwhile, we have some family celebrating to do. Appears that in addition to a wonderful family holiday together, we have an upcoming wedding to celebrate! How much do we owe you?" Tristan asked, reaching into his back pocket for his wallet as he led them to the door.

"Oh, for heaven's sake! Renée is my *friend!* You don't owe us *a thing!*" Tabitha said cheerily. "Just let us know if we can do anything else *at all* to help. And have a happy holiday!"

Everyone cheered them out the door with their thanks and holiday greetings and with that, they were gone.

And out came the champagne and a little blue box with a ring in it.

CHAPTER 14

"I can't believe how fast the holidays whizzed by!" Camille mumbled to herself as she emptied the dryer. "But what fun!!" she thought. "I LOVED having my family around for the holidays, especially to help us celebrate finishing our renovations! Having family in a house always makes it feel more like a home. It was such fun watching the kids enjoy having their family around. She loved it when her and Tristan's kids were able to get together with their cousins. She'd grown up with close cousins and wanted the same for her children. All the sisters did. And, of course, she loved being with her zany sisters and her supremely calm mother. Brian was always lots of fun. He'd been a real hoot. And now they could add Renée to their tribe! Boy, would they have stories to tell about this year's gathering for years to come!

It never ceased to amaze Camille how her mother could be in the midst of a whirlwind of activity, but still remain as calm as if she was in the eye of a storm. Although the activity still went on crazily around her, her mother's very presence seemed to have a calming effect on that activity, so that it was a calm, joyous craziness rather than chaos. Hard to describe, but you couldn't help but feel it in her presence. Naomi was a quiet force to be reckoned with, but in such a calm way.

Tess and Renée's engagement was an joyous added bonus! She couldn't wait for the spring wedding when all their extended family and friends would be able to get together at something other than a funeral. She was sure that with Tess in charge of the event, it would no doubt be a memorable one.

"Oh! Speaking of presence," Camille said aloud, although still to herself, "That reminds me that I need to put in a call to Charlie about the quilt."

Once things with the quilt calmed down and Naomi was able to sleep in the guest room under the quilt without it creeping down, and the stitches stayed where they belonged just like Tabitha and Paul thought they would, it was easy to forget about the quilt drama in all the joy and activities around the holiday celebration with her family.

Christmas was a blast. New Years was a blast. The week in between was a blast. A whirlwind of activity that included awesome time spent watching the kids and their unending delight and wonder, being in front of the fireplace (and S'mores!), Christmas cookie baking, cooking their favorite dishes, snowball fights, Midnight Service, carol singing, Christmas movie bingeing, gift wrapping, hiding surprises, joyous unwrappings, and then Dreah's birthday just after New Year's. She was so glad everyone stayed to celebrate it. Being able to have her family all together for it made it so special for Dreah.

But in the midst of all the holiday excitement and because things had calmed down with the quilt, everyone forgot all about the drama they'd had for the first two days of the holiday celebration. After Tabitha and Paul's visit, the stitches stayed put and Naomi slept under the quilt with no problem at all. In fact, she said it was the best sleep she'd had in ages. She felt wonderfully rested, calm and when she slid into the covers at night, she felt comfortable, safe and protected, like it formed a cocoon of safety and goodness around her.

So, Camille had forgotten to begin the search for the quilt's journey by contacting Charlie. She knew she needed to do it in order to keep the stitches from coming loose again in an effort to remind her there was work to be done. She promised herself she would do so as soon as she finished folding this load of clothes. And she was good on her promise.

"Maypole Sundry Thrift Store, here, Charlie speakin'," the southern accented voice on the other end of the line rang out.

"Hi, Charlie! My name is Camille Thornton. I'm going to ask you to stretch your brain for a moment, if I can. I came into your charming thrift store this past July and I bought a quilt."

"I'm sorry, Mam. We don't 'low no returns after 30 days," Charlie said as if he was striving to sound officious.

"No, no, Charlie! I'm not trying to return it! I just want to ask you something about it."

"Oh, Mam, I wouldn't know nothin' 'bout no quilt I sold somebody six months ago."

"I think you're probably right for most quilts, Charlie. But this one was a little different. While you were wrapping it for me, you told me that it was called The Wandering Quilt. You said that it had been returned to your store so many times in the thirty years you owned the store that you began calling it The Wandering Quilt. You told me it had been returned by locals, but that you thought it was made in Mississippi, in the Delta. You told me the town talk was that people returned it because it just didn't feel like they thought a quilt should feel. Do you recall the conversation, Charlie?"

"Welllll... Ms.... Camille, you say?"

"Yes, Charlie, Camille. Camille Thornton."

"Well, Ms. Camille, it sounds to me like I was just runnin' my mouth off more'n I shoulda' done that day, huh?" he said with a chuckle. "I told you that? And I told you the town talk? I don't generally do that. Things must have been mighty slow 'roun' here for me to do all that jawin' with a customer and tell her things I shouldn't ought to say. You can't keep good business that way. I shouldn't have done that," Charlie said rather forlornly. "But I can't take the quilt back now."

"No, Charlie! I didn't take it that way! I didn't feel like you were talking out of school, like you were saying something you shouldn't have said. Not at all! And I don't want you to take the quilt back. It's a beautiful quilt. I want to keep it. I just want to ask you about who had the quilt before you sold it to me.

"You told me people brought it back to you, and that they were locals. Can you tell me the name of anyone that had the quilt before me? I don't want to give the quilt back. I want to keep it. But I am trying to figure out the quilt's journey to me, so to speak."

Camille was speaking so earnestly that she felt like she was begging Charlie for scraps of information.

"'Journey' to you, Mam?" Charlie said. "That sounds kinda strange. It's a quilt. You either like it or you don't. It either fits your bed or it don't. It either fits in with your colors or it don't. I don't know nothin' 'bout no journey. 'Ceptin', of course, I hear tell it come from Mississippi from the start, if I 'members correctly.

"Well, Mam. I don't know 'bout tellin' you 'bout who brought it back in here to the sto,' even if I did 'member it. I don't think I could tell you even if I knowed. Ain't I hear'd tell of some sort of law or something protectin' what peoples do and say from being tol'?"

"Um…Charlie, I think you're thinking of attorney-client privilege, or even priest-penitent privilege. I don't know of any sort of store owner and customer privilege protected by law. It would be fine for you to tell me. I don't want anything from the folks who bought the quilt from you and returned it, except to ask them what they know about the quilt. I promise," Camille said in her most sincere voice.

"Are you sure they ain't no, what you call it? Oh, yeah, that there 'privilege' what I'd be breakin' iffen I told you somebody who brought the quilt back? I wouldn't get in no trouble? Nobody ever asked me anythin' like that before."

"No, Charlie. You would be doing nothing at all wrong by telling me anyone you know who owned the quilt before and brought it back to you because they decided they didn't want it anymore."

"Welllllll….." Charlie said hesitantly.

"Yes, Charlie?" Camille said expectantly, silently urging him on, urging him to spill it.

"Well, Ms. Camille, you seem like a nice lady and not one who would hurt somebody. So I guess I'll tell you what I 'members. Gracie Poohks brought it back last. And before her, it were Carmody Sellers. Jenniffer Jones and Anne Alexis did too.

"They all said it didn't 'feel' right. I didn't even have no idea what in tarnation that even meant. I even let 'em bring it back after the thirty-days return policy because ever' single one of 'em pitched a fit and said they would say terrible things about my store if I didn't take it back.

"I even let it stay in the storage closet for years at a time, sometimes, because I was a'feared to put it back out. It were a beautiful quilt, to me, but they acted like it had cooties or somethin.' I knowed it didn't 'cause I always wash my soft goods 'afore I put 'em out on the floor for sale, even if they look clean. I don't sell just anythin'.

"You may think I'm just a small hick sto' in some backwater town in South Carolina, but I am particular about what I sell, and I don't sell no mess. I sell clean goods. I don't mind takin' 'em back iffen somethin' is wrong with 'em that the customer or me missed when they buyed it. I am a honest business man and I have been doing business in this town, in this sto' for the past thutty years. Axe anybody. I don't try to just cheat tourists when they come through here 'cause I know they won't likely be back this way, just to make a buck. I don't believe in that.

"I'm a honest business man; and even if the tourist goes back to Ohio or somethin', I want 'em to think back to my little thrift sto' and what they bought here and think well of it. You never know when they may tell someone who's a comin' this way to look me up. Yep, I am honest. So that quilt was clean of cooties. Nothin' was wrong with it. Absolutely nothin'. But those womens brought it back and I took to calling it The Wanderin' Quilt."

"I believe you're an honest business owner, Charlie, and wouldn't want to cheat anyone. Thank you, Charlie! That's great! Providing me with all those names is great. Anyone else you can think of? Do you have addresses for these people? Are they still in town as far as you know? You said they were local people."

"Well, far as I know, they all still somewheres 'round here. You sort of don't come to a town like this and leave, 'cause the only reason you're here in the first place is because of your kinfolk," Charlie said.

"Do you remember the first person who gave it to you, Charlie?"

CHAPTER 15

amille decided to take a wild chance that the person who first brought the quilt to Charlie might still be around and able to give her some information about the quilt. Her thinking was that the buyers who had brought back the quilt after the first one probably didn't know much about the origins of the quilt since they just happened to wander in and buy it from Charlie's thrift store because it was so beautiful. Perhaps if she could find the first person who ever brought it to him in the first place, she might be closer to figuring out where it came from.

"You said there had been talk about the quilt even before you took over the store thirty years ago. Do you know who the talk was about or what was said?" Camille inquired.

There seemed to be no one on the phone line. Camille waited, listening, thinking maybe Charlie was just thinking hard trying to remember the answer to Camille's question. Finally, she heard his voice.

"Well, Ms. Camille….I don't like to gossip or tell tales out of school. And, o'course, my memory ain't what it used to be…….I'm not even sure I can 'member that exactly. But, like I said, you seem like a nice enough lady. I 'members you now. You had on that purty blue dress jes' like that TV Mama used to wear back in the '50s or '60s. I couldn't figure where you even got a dress like that from. But, I liked it. I knowed you was a nice lady when I saw that dress. I'm pretty sure that you wouldn't be takin' all this time to call me and axe about the quilt if you wanted to do somethin' bad with what I told you.

"So, I'll tell you. It were Ms. Sarah what first done brung the quilt to the sto'. I didn't own the sto' at the time. Hank Friggers did. When he got sick, I took over the sto' 'cause I was working here and Hank trusted me. I did a good job and Hank didn't want the sto' to die, and it sure woulda' done, sick as Hank was. By the time Hank passed over to Glory a few years later, I done real good not letting the sto' go down, so he'd let me have the sto' on good terms and I run it ever since.

"Ms. Sarah brung the quilt to Hank a while 'afore he got sick. It were sold to Gracie Poohks. Gracie didn' have it no more'n six or seven weeks 'fore she brung it back with some wild story about it not 'feeling' right. What do that even mean? Well, I hear'd her a tellin' this yarn to Hank and I didn't pay her no mind. I figured she was just short of cash and figured she didn't really need that pretty quilt as much as she needed the money, so she brung it back to Hank for a refund.

"Hank didn't really mind. He didn't pay no mind to the yarn she spun 'bout it, 'cause that were crazy; but he knew that as purty as that quilt was, he'd be able to sell it agin' with no trouble. She hadn't done no harm to the quilt while she had it, so he let her give it back to him. And he was right. That quilt sold to somebody else in no time. But, 'afore it sold, we heard tell of peoples talking 'bout that quilt. Gracie Poohks had done gone 'round town tellin' folks that quilt was weird. Nobody knowed what a weird quilt was, so they didn't believe her. How could a quilt be 'weird'? They's just beautiful covers, that's all. They's just comfortable, that's all. But in a small town, where nothin' ever happens and they's nothin' to talk about, the story got 'round.

"Now, Carmody Sellers, who bought it next, likely didn't hear 'bout it because she lives on the outside of town and don't come in much. When she did, she bought that purty quilt. But, twarn't no time at all 'afore Carmody Sellers was back in here asking for her money back. I never knew if she finally hear'd tell of the Gracie Poohks story or she had somethin' going on herself, but I just give her her money back. By then, Hank had passed on to the Great Beyond and I was a' runnin' the sto'. Well, I don't set no store by stupid soundin' trash like Gracie Poohks and Carmody Sellers' stories. Excuse my harsh words, Ms. Camille, but sometimes that the only words that'll do. But I thought I'd better give that quilt a rest for a while. So, I set it in the storage room. I warn't gonna give it away. It were too purty. I knew it would sell. But I figured I'd better let things cool off for a bit since there had been two silly stories 'bout it.

"I forgot all 'bout it were back there 'cause I was always a' puttin' stuff in the storage room and it just sorta disappeared from my eyeballs. I'm glad I had put it in one of those big zippered plastic storage bags, 'cause it stayed just B-U-tiful. Not a speck of dust or nothin'. I brought it back out years later when I found it and put it back out for sale.

"Jenniffer Jones had moved into town long after the stories made their rounds, so she didn't know nothin' 'bout the quilt when she walked in, saw it, and brought that beautiful thing right then and there. She said it put her in mind of the quilts her Mama used to make, she did. Talked 'bout her Mama makin' one sorta like it. She said she called it her Ancestor Quilt what she made to honor her slave ancestors, especially her great-great Grandma, Dinah who she found in the 1900 Census.

"Jenniffer said her Mama told her the 1900 Census said Dinah was 85 years old and living' in a sharecroppers' shack in North Carolina with her son and his wife, the wife's Mama and sister. Both sisters had a passel of children— five each. All in that little bitty shack. So, Jenniffer's Mama was so glad to see her great-great Grandma Dinah in the Census from 110 years before, that she said she truly understood how important the Census was; and she swore that iffen she ever got the chance, she would work the Census herself.

"She did work it. She worked the 2010 Census. As she sat at the table in the public library where she handed out Census forms to peoples who passed by. While she did it, she worked on hand piecin' that quilt for Dinah. She finally gave up the Census job to let someone who really needed a job have it. Jenniffer said her Mama was really a professor at a big university and was only doin' the Census job on the side to keep her promise she made when she found Dinah in the Census, so she felt guilty 'bout having the job when the news reported that peoples needed Census jobs. She finished piecing the top, but then life took over and she stopped a' workin' on it.

"Five years later, in 2015, Jenniffer's Mama realized it was the 200th anniversary of Dinah's birth, accordin' to the Census; and she vowed to finish the quilt that year, and she did. But not 'afore the lamp over the quilt stand burned a hole straight through all the layers of the quilt, and

Jenniffer's Mama was so upset that she had to leave it for a while and come back to it. She fixed it up so purty that Jenniffer said you cain't even tell it was ever burned.

"She said her Mama had purple in it for royalty for her ancestors, and yellow flowers with green leaves for the cotton her Ancestors picked, and hearts all around it in the quiltin'.

"She said that The Wanderin' Quilt was right purty and put her in mind so much of her Mama's quilt, that she bought it right off. But a few weeks later, she brought it back too. She didn't really say why, but she looked so upset that I went ahead and gave her her money back and didn't ask her a thing. I figured that if she brought it back after telling me that long story 'bout how much it reminded her of her Mama's quilt, somethin' must be really bad, so I just let her give it right back to me. I didn't have the heart to let it go no further.

"Since that poor purty quilt kept going from person to person, I just started calling it The Wanderin' Quilt. But I put it away again for years.

"Finally, Anne Alexis saw it in the storage room when she was workin' here one Christmas when I needed help with all the Christmas rush customers. I didn't tell her why it was in there. When she brung it out and saw it, she just plum fell in love with it and wanted to buy it right then and there. I let her, but since she worked here, I gave her a little discount. It wasn't too long 'afore she brought it back too. She wouldn't say why. She just said she had just washed it 'afore bringin' it in. So she came in, folded it up real nice to fit real nice in that zipper bag and put it back in the storage room. She didn't even ask for her money back. I don't know what happened. Didn't look like she wanted to talk 'bout it, so I didn't axe her. But that were sorta scary. So bad she didn't even axe for her money back? It musta been pretty bad, whatever it was.

"But, the next time I put it out years later, you came along on your way through town, saw it, fell in love with it and bought it. I remember you axin' me iffen that was the best I could do for the price and I knocked a little off. I didn't think you knew 'bout the weirdness in its history and were asking for that reason, but just in case, I took some money off for you so's you'd still buy it. And that's all I know."

Camille, on the other end of the line, was speechless. She, literally, didn't know what to say. Charlie had been such a wealth of information in ways that he did not even realize. Not only did Camille now know more of the history of the quilt than she ever thought she would, but she also knew who it was who had first brought the quilt there to South Carolina. If she could speak with that person, she might well be able to get even more of the history of the quilt, and closer to what the inscription meant.

"Charlie. I can't believe what a fount of information you are. You have given me so much more than I had ever dared to hope for. I appreciate it so much. I just have to ask you one more thing. Do you have any sort of contact information for any of the people who brought the quilt back?"

"Well, Mam, I thank you for that. I 'preciate it, I do. My folks always told me that people don't have to be nice to you, so when they do be nice, thank 'em. And I thank you. T'warn't nothin'. This is a small town and not much goes on. This is just stuff what happened and that I happened to know. I'm right glad you think it might help you. And I can give you some of that contact information you was wantin.'"

And Charlie proceeded to do just that.

CHAPTER 16

amille could not believe her luck. Never in her wildest dreams did she think that Charlie would be such a rich source of information. But he was. It was incredible. Not only the names of every previous owner of the quilt that he knew, but even contact information as well!!! "Awesome!!" thought Camille, gleefully. She had to admit that she was pretty shocked that such a little out of the way place kept such great records. "Can't judge a book by its cover," Camille reminded herself.

Via email, Camille began reaching out to the buyers Charlie gave her information for. Charlie didn't feel comfortable giving out anything but their email addresses because that seemed less intrusive. He still wasn't totally comfortable telling Camille about the buyers, and this seemed a good compromise. Thank heaven for technology, Camille thought.

Businesses now requested things like email addresses for sending store receipts electronically; and to Camille's surprise, this was true even in this little out of the way thrift store. Technology. Gotta love it. Camille was thankful because it gave her what she needed from Charlie. That, in turn, allowed her to reach out to the buyers without seeming to sandbag them by calling them on the phone out of the blue. With email, they could choose to think about whether they wanted to reply and when.

Except, of course, Sarah. That transaction had been long before the omnipresence of computers in store purchases, so Charlie did not have Sarah's email, only her phone number. After some convincing, Charlie gave the phone number to Camille. Despite all of her rhetoric about not being intrusive, some things just required her to be what others might consider to be pushy. Now that she had the information, she wanted to deal with this immediately.

Camille dialed the number, having no idea if it was even still a working number. That was shortly made clear when the phone number connected and began to ring. The number rang five times. Finally, a voicemail message came on. "You have reached the number for Sarah Marsden. I am not available right now, so just leave a message and I'll get back to you when I can." Frustrated, Camille left her name and phone number and asked Sarah to please give her a call.

Camille glanced at her watch and jumped up when she saw the time. "Lord! Where did the day go?!" she wondered frantically. She grabbed her keys from the heart-shaped key dish on the table in the entrance hall; shoved her cell phone with her ID, credit cards and money in her pocket; and ran out the door.

"Mama! Mama! What *took* you so long?! You're usually the first one in the car rider line!" said Leslie in a stern, but worried voice as soon as she and Luke clambered into the car through the open door held by the car rider duty teacher whom Camille did not notice waving at her, and wrestled their way into their seatbelts. All the activity raised Camille from the reverie she had drifted into as she sat creeping slowly along in the car rider line and thought about her call with Charlie as she waited for school to let out and her kids to get into the car. Time had gotten away from her when she'd called and chatted with him. While she was usually the first in the car rider line, today she was at least number twenty-five.

Being first every day created a sense of normalcy and predictability and trust for her children that was totally and directly related to what was in their world, but it meant Camille arriving at their school at least forty-five minutes ahead of school dismissal. Camille didn't mind a bit because it gave her forty-five minutes to do all sorts of things on her cell phone and computer, as well as go inside and help out however she could on some days. When she sat in her car, it was great, concentrated, undisturbed work time.

Yet again, Camille was eternally thankful for the flexibility of her schedule that being a professor gave her. What a great career she had chosen for her life's work. Not only did it allow her to do what she wanted to do professionally, but it gave her the flexibility she needed for her family. She was not only tenured, but she had enough time on the job and gravitas from being around so long, involved in so much, and being such a highly regarded academician, to be able to pretty much choose her class schedule.

That came in really handy when the kids were born and all four of their lives later began to heat up with school and activities added to work, parenting, civic activities and extended family. This was especially helpful since Tristan's schedule as an emergency room surgeon was rarely predictable. While he was planning to take care of this by going into a practice rather than working at a hospital, right now, her flexibility was crucial and she loved that she had it.

"Sorry, Crew! Mama was talking on the phone with someone about an issue she needs to deal with and time got away from her! But, I'm here now and off we go! Everybody all buckled up snug and tight?"

"Yeeeeeeeeessssss!" came the chorus from the backseat.

"Let me see you pull them tight for Mama." They did so and all seemed as it should be, so off they went.

"What're we having for dinner, Crew?" Camille asked Luke and Leslie. The kids loved to not only help with meal preparation, but help plan their menus as well. If truth was to be told, it was often more trouble than it was help; but Camille understood how important this was to them feeling like they were capable human beings who could do things, and it was great, great family bonding time. Some of her fondest memories were of helping her Mom, and at times, Dad, prepare meals in the kitchen when they were growing up. The feeling she got from that is something that she and Tristan definitely wanted to pass on to their children.

"How about Butter Garlic Shrimp Spaghetti!" yelled Luke.

"Oh! That's a great suggestion, Lukie!"–her pet name for her son– "and really quick!" said Camille. "I like it! We won't use very much butter," she giggled. She tried to be really intentional with their nutrition, but sometimes it was dicey. Trying to do the right thing most of the time, and moderation, were key. "Who's making the salad to go with it?!" she laughed.

"Well, if we put asparagus or broccoli in the spaghetti, do we have to have a salad?" asked Leslie.

"Well, I'm not sure I really care where your veggies come from, as long as you get them, Leslie Pooh," calling her daughter by her pet name left over from her love of A.A. Milne's *Winnie the Pooh* when she was a tot. "We have both asparagus and broccoli, so we can do that. If we throw them in with the spaghetti, it would save us some time. Great idea, Leslie Pooh!" Camille said.

"Well, if Leslie had the idea, does that mean that she gets to choose whether it's broccoli or asparagus? I want it to be broccoli," Luke sort of whined.

"Not if the way the person asks is like a whiney-puss," laughed Camille.

"Whiney-puss! Whiney-puss!" teased Leslie.

"No teasing, Leslie. Let's give Luke productive feedback instead. What productive feedback can you give your brother to help make him better, Leslie?" Camille inquired.

"Stop whining, Luke! Nobody likes a whiner!" Leslie intoned.

"Well, can we be a little bit more positive with our feedback, Leslie? Luke, when you ask for something, just ask for it in your normal voice. Don't whine. Not only does it make you sound like a baby instead of the big boy you are, but also, you are awesome and we want you to sound like it," Camille said. "Whining sound anything but awesome."

"Oh....allllright," said Luke, sulkily.

"No sulking," Camille was about to say, when she looked in the rearview mirror and saw that Luke had brightened up already and was back to his normal happy self.

"OK, so we're having Butter Garlic Shrimp Spaghetti, but not with a lot of butter, with Broccoli for dinner, and we'll have our protein, carbs and veggies all together, right, Crew?" Camille asked.

"Yesssss!!" Luke and Leslie said in unison, louder than was comfortable for Camille. But the joy of being released from school, being reunited with their Mama, planning a great dinner, looking forward to being at home and seeing their Dad, had all combined to create this joy, so Camille did not mind a bit. She was not about to rain on that parade merely to save her eardrums. She just smiled a smile that came from a joyful heart.

CHAPTER 17

Camille loved that man. Tristan had done the dinner dishes while she finished looking over the children's homework; and by the time they were both done and the kids in their rooms for a bit of free time before story- and bedtime, he had put out a glass of Camille's favorite Prosecco for each of them in the family room on the table in front of the welcoming fire. There they sat, and for the first time since Camille had spoken to Charlie, she was able to talk about the phone call and what it had meant.

"Wow! That's great information, isn't it?" Tristan asked her.

"Yes! It is incredible! I never expected to get that much information! I haven't been able to speak with the first person who brought in the quilt to the store yet, but I've put in a call to her and left a message. I just hope she returns my call," Camille said hopefully.

"That's pretty amazing. You bought that quilt months ago in a little place we just randomly stopped by in South Carolina and we could be close to actually tracking down a good deal of the quilt's journey. I'm not sure I really believed it could be done. It was all so random, not even in the same state. It was just a random store we stopped in. I just didn't know if it would be possible. But, here we are," Tristan said. "I'm so proud of you, Camille," he said, as he placed his arm around her shoulder and pulled her in for a snuggle.

"Thank you, Tristan. Well, I really only made a couple of phone calls so far; but it does look promising, doesn't it? For some reason I feel good about the prospect of Sarah returning my call. I'm putting it out into the Universe, and I hope the Universe supports me and that she returns my call and that she has information we can use."

The Prosecco did its job and warmed both of their insides enough to relax the events of their respective days in their heads, make them snuggle up on the couch and smooch a bit until Leslie called down that she and Luke had washed their faces and brushed their teeth and were ready for their bedtime story and prayers.

Even though they knew that call was coming, and those chores of story and prayers had to be lovingly done, Camille and Tristan didn't mind. They both knew it meant that finishing up those nightly tuck-ins was also the prelude to more delicious, uninterrupted, intimacy between them.

CHAPTER 18

"Darn it!" Camille said under her breath as she closed out her call. "Why won't she call me back?" She had just left her third message for Sarah in as many days, and she didn't understand why Sarah wasn't returning her call. It's not like anything awful had happened and Camille was a reporter hounding her or something. Even if Charlie had called Sarah and told her that Camille would be calling, that was not a reason for Sarah to avoid returning her call. Even if Sarah didn't want to talk to her, which Camille couldn't imagine since it was just about a quilt, for Pete's sake, she could at least call her back and tell her so. But as much as Camille had kept her phone in her hands as much as possible so as not to miss Sarah's call, there had been no call to miss.

Sarah had even left her phone on—not on silent as she *always* did—-in class. Because research showed that students having a cell phone on their desk in class was distracting even when it wasn't turned on, Camille had a strict no-phone policy in her classrooms. Although her students found it incomprehensible since cell phones were such a part of their lives, leaving them off for the 75 minutes of class was not a burden, even though the students thought of it as one. Just as they thought her strict attendance policy was a burden. But, students didn't have to take her course if they didn't want to.

Camille taught elective courses, not required courses. Not only were her classes always full, with very few students dropping them during the drop/add period, but she also always had a waiting list of students wanting to get in. Not a semester went by when she wasn't deluged with emails and office visits from students giving her all sorts of reasons why they were begging her to let them into her classes that were already full. Her favorite reason remained that the students wanted to get in because they had heard that Camille taught students how to think critically.

But Camille stuck to her guns and kept her classes at a size she could manage that would most benefit the students. She, not her research assistant, needed to be the one to read her students' essays, daily journals, and research papers—20 assignments in all—during the semester, so keeping the numbers reasonable made sense. But the heavy course assignment load, the strict attendance policy, and the banning of cell phones did not keep students from lining up to take her courses.

Given how strict she was with her rules, it would hardly look good for Camille to break her own rules that students had consequences for breaking. So, she used the same rule for herself that she used for her students. If they told her they needed to have their phone on in class for a good reason, like a family emergency unfolding or a potential employer's call or some such, they only needed to let her know before class. She then allowed him or her to go out and take the call.

So, at the beginning of class, she warned the students that her phone was on because she was waiting for a very important call; and if it came through, she would step out into the hall and take it and be right back. She would not be on the call long.

But the phone did not ring.

Camille decided to give it one more try before giving up. On the drive home, she dialed the number one last time. To her utter surprise, someone picked up. An older woman's voice came through the other end of the line. Camille was stunned.

"Hello?" the voice said.

Camille was so taken aback that she couldn't even find her voice. Her mind went temporarily blank.

"Hello? Who is this?" the woman said impatiently, clearly annoyed at the silence on the other end of the line.

"H…hel….hello? Is this Sarah? Sarah Marsden?"

"Yes. That's who you were calling, isn't it? You're the one who called me. Don't you know who you called? Who is this, please?"

"Oh, my Gosh, Ms. Marsden! I've been trying to reach you for *days*! I am so glad I finally *got* you!" Camille exclaimed, a bit more eagerly than she intended.

"I don't recognize your voice, so I don't know you, so I can't imagine why you would be calling me for days and be so eager to speak with me," Sarah said, rather coldly. Sarah's voice had the high tremor that the voices of the elderly often had, but it also sounded strong and resolute.

Camille was driving, but once she heard Sarah come on the line and actually speak to her, she clicked on her turn signal and carefully pulled over to the side of the road so that she could fully focus on the conversation she'd been waiting for so anxiously. She also needed to get something to write with in case there was a need. She couldn't believe how unprepared she was for this, considering she'd been wanting it so desperately. Camille gave silent thanks that she was on a little traveled road that had a wide shoulder, little traffic and a strong phone signal.

Finally, frantically finding her voice, organizing her thoughts and considering herself ready to launch into the conversation she had been waiting to have, Camille said anxiously, "Oh! I'm sorry! I didn't even introduce myself! I was just so glad to finally reach you! My name is Camille Thornton. I am a law professor." Camille immediately wondered why she said that since it was irrelevant to the quilt inquiry and it might scare Sarah away to think she was talking to a lawyer. She felt so discombobulated.

"I got your name and phone number from Charlie Racker who owns the Maypole Sundry Thrift Shop in your town.

"I know who Charlie is. What's going on? Why would he give you my number?"

"Well, last summer my family and….that is, my husband, Dr. Tristan Thornton and our two children, Leslie, a 9-year-old girl, and Luke, our 6-year-old boy…" —Camille felt like she was babbling but couldn't seem to stop herself—"came through your town while we were on vacation. We stopped by Charlie's thrift store," Camille rushed. "I saw this beautiful quilt….I am a quilter and I also collect quilts….and I ended up buying it. I—"

Before Camille could finish, Sarah interrupted her.

"Oh, so you bought The Wandering Quilt, did you?" Sarah asked flatly.

Camille was surprised at the question, or even that Sarah knew it was called The Wandering Quilt.

"W....w....well, yes, as a matter of fact, I did. I'm not sure I thought you knew it was called The Wandering Quilt. I think I'm pretty surprised at that. And that you so quickly knew what I was talking about."

"Camille," Sarah said wearily, "I can't imagine that you don't realize that in a small town with that sort of talk going around there's no way I would *not* hear about it somehow, even though I sold that quilt to Harry decades ago."

"Um...I guess that makes sense. You're right. Yes, I live in a pretty small town, and I know how people talk. Did you hear the talk about what happened with the people who bought the quilt? Did you ever talk to them about it?"

"Well, I can't say that I've talked to them directly. You know how small towns are. You know who people are but you don't necessarily actually know the people. And as time went on and it was bought by people who hadn't lived in this town when I came, but came in later, I knew them even less. It's not like me originally taking the quilt to the Thrift Shop and them buying it and taking it back as well bonded us or something.

"Frankly, I think that what the buyers experienced was probably so weird that it wasn't something anyone wanted to talk about. I certainly didn't want to talk about my own experience with the quilt and why I took it to Harry at the thrift store. It wasn't the same anyway. From what I've heard about what the other buyers experienced, people would think they were crazy. But, yes, I know pretty much what it is they say about the quilt," Sarah said wearily.

"Can you tell me what you know? Charlie told me his version of the returns of the quilts, but I don't know if you know anything more, and I'm trying to find out all I can."

"Why?" Sarah said warily, suspicion dripping from her voice.

"Well....." Camille hesitated. She could hardly ask this perfect stranger, whom she called up out of the blue, to tell her all sorts of personal information and Camille then not share with her any reason why Camille wanted to know or what Camille's own experience with the quilt had been. If Camille wanted to get information about the quilt from Sarah, she couldn't be totally closed about what had happened with her own situation. She had to be willing to give Sarah something. She didn't want to tell her all of it at this point, but she would say what she thought she could get away with.

"I bought the quilt and it didn't really feel comfortable like all my other quilts do. I make quilts and I collect quilts from all over; so when a quilt feels different, I notice it. I never had a quilt feel this way before."

"What do you mean when you say it 'felt different,'" Sarah asked skeptically.

"Well, I guess I mean pretty much the same thing that the other quilt owners meant when they said it. What it is you heard. It just seems like there is an energy to the quilt that is not like what a quilt ordinarily feels like. Ordinarily we look to quilts to not only provide warmth, but also to make us feel sort of comfy cozy, secure. I'm not sure I feel this with this quilt. Did the quilt make you feel that way?"

"Comfy cozy, you mean, or *not* comfy cozy? Secure? Actually, I couldn't tell you. I never used it. I wasn't exactly in a 'comfy cozy or secure situation," Sarah said flatly.

"You didn't feel the same thing the other people who bought the quilt felt?"

"Well, from what I hear, they said pretty much the same thing you did. It was a beautiful quilt, but it didn't feel right. 'Comfy cozy' was not used to characterize how they felt about the quilt.

"I, on the other hand, *needed* to feel comfy cozy, secure, but that was the *last* thing I was feeling. I don't know why I'm even telling this to someone who called me out of the blue and who I don't even know, who doesn't even live here. But I guess those are the very reasons it doesn't matter. You don't live around here. You don't know me or the people here. You won't be likely to gossip about what I'm telling you.

"I took that quilt into the Maypole Sundry Thrift Store and sold it, but it wasn't really mine. I mean, it was mine; I didn't steal it or anything. But that quilt came from my husband's family. We lived in Mississippi, in the Delta, and we got married really young. The marriage wasn't really right from the start, so it was only a matter of days after we were married that my husband, Clyde, hit me for the first time.

"The bacon I cooked him for breakfast wasn't crisp enough. The next time it was because the grits weren't soft enough. Then it was that his shirt wasn't ironed the way he wanted it. It really didn't matter what I did, how I cooked, ironed, or what was going on. If he felt like it, he just beat the hell out of me.

"I was young and had seen wives and girlfriends beat up all my life, so it didn't seem to me to be that big of a deal. I actually took it for thirty years. People knew and all they'd say is, 'That tiny little thing sure can take a lickin'!' It was just what that place was like. They didn't know I knew what they were saying; but thirty years is a long time, and my situation was pretty well known, not that I ever discussed it with anyone, mind you."

"Thirty years?!" Camille breathed, not even realizing she had said it out loud. She couldn't imagine Tristan hitting her even once. Not even close. It was simply unimaginable that that loving husband of hers would ever be able to do such a thing. They were each other's best friend and still such close, intimate lovers after years of courtship and marriage that Camille simply couldn't even form the thought in her head.

Camille had heard that women often kept domestic violence a secret, and she could certainly understand why; but she didn't think she even knew a woman who had been hit by her significant other. She knew she could be wrong. She knew domestic violence existed, of course, but it simply wasn't a part of her immediate known world. She didn't even know how to respond.

"What happened after thirty years? He stopped? What made him stop?"

"He didn't stop. He died," Sarah said without any emotion. "He was in an accident at work. Cut his head clean off."

Camille gave an audible gasp. She wasn't expecting that.

"I won't lie and say I was sorry to see him go. He was a violent, selfish, mean, ornery sonofabitch who beat the crap out of me just as easily as he'd look at me. I may have been stupid for staying, but I did. I thought marriage was for life. I thought the way I was living was all there was. The best thing I can say about that man is that we did not have any children. I don't know why. I don't know if it was him. I don't know if it was me. I was so scared to bring a kid into that hellified existence that I didn't even care. I was just glad."

"Sarah, I am *so* sorry that happened to you," Camille said sadly. "I really, really appreciate you telling me something so personal." Camille was close to tears just listening to Sarah's story even though she didn't even know her. She couldn't imagine living what Sarah had described. "That could not have been easy."

"Well, it wasn't your fault, but thank you anyway for the sentiment. When that man died, I gathered up his shit and got rid of it so fast that he wasn't even in the ground yet. That quilt came from his family. I never once used it from the time we got it.

"Clyde's family hated me and I hated them. I'm surprised his aunt even gave him the quilt. But she made beautiful quilts and he got married, so she gave it to him. Us, I guess I should say, since I was the bride." Sarah gave a harsh sardonic laugh. "But, that quilt always stayed in a closet. I never once used it.

"Of course, Clyde didn't give a crap about a quilt. He never once used it. The only reason I took it with me when I came here to be with the part of my family I'm closest to, who had moved here after we were married, was because I had to wrap something in it to protect it for the move. I did not want a single, solitary reminder of being with that bastard or being a part of that family.

"Once I got here and unpacked, I washed that sucker and took it to Harry's thrift store to see if he was willing to take it off my hands. It hadn't even really been used and was a nice looking quilt. All it ever did was sit in a closet, then protect something in the move. I just didn't want to have anything to do with it. I didn't even want to look at it, no less have it on me. I didn't want any reminders. Harry owned the store then. Charlie took it over later after Harry got sick and then died.

"I never denied that it was a beautiful quilt. It was. But I just didn't want any reminders of Clyde and I didn't want any reminders of his family who hated me because even though my skin tone and my hair are the same color as theirs, I'm African American and they're white. So they hated that Clyde married me.

"But the quilt was in good shape, so there was no reason for Harry not to buy it. It was new, essentially. It had never really been used. So, Harry bought it over thirty years ago, and the rest is history. I never felt a thing from that quilt because I never used it for comfort or coziness or security. That's not what it represented to me. To me it represented Clyde and his hateful family. To me the gift of that quilt for our wedding present was totally wasted on us. I'm sorry his aunt wasted her time on it. The only thing I used it for was to wrap something in when I moved here, but that was it. I never once put it on me. Why in the world would I?

"Actually, after I started hearing things about the quilt, and it was happening with more than one buyer, I wondered if what had been happening with Clyde and me had somehow seeped into the quilt and given it that feeling everyone who bought it seemed to have. I don't believe in stuff like that, but I couldn't think of any other reason that a beautiful quilt like that would feel weird to people. Especially once I realized they were not talking about the feel of the fabric, but instead some sort of feeling they got from the quilt," Sarah said, increasingly slowly, as if she was running out of steam.

"I have never told any of this to anybody. Not one word of it. I mean, people back in the Delta knew Clyde hit me because that's just the way it was in that place. It was kinda hard to hide it too, since he beat me all the time and I was always walking around with a busted lip, black eye, bruised arms, or handfuls of hair pulled out.

"But I never talked about it. And I certainly never told anyone about it after I came here. And I never talked about that damn quilt because there was nothing to say. It was from Clyde's aunt and she was part of Clyde's family and I didn't want anything to do with him or them, so there was nothing to say. But now that I've said this to you, I'll never speak about it again. I feel sort of better getting it out, but now, I'm done."

And with that, she hung up.

CHAPTER 19

"Oh, my gosh," exclaimed Camille. "Hello? Hello? No! Sarah! Sarah! Sarah are you there?! Hello?! Sarah! Don't hang up! Hello?! I need to know something! *Please* don't go!"

But Sarah had done precisely that.

Camille knew she was doing a useless act yelling into the phone. But she couldn't believe that Sarah had hung up and Camille had no idea of the name of the aunt who had made the quilt. And Sarah said she would never talk about this again.

Camille frantically redialed Sarah's number. No answer. She tried it three more times. No answer. She finally texted Sarah asking for the aunt's name. No response.

Camille was bereft. So close, but yet so far.

Before she started up the car again Camille three-wayed her sisters, Dreah and Tess on her cell phone. She was so relieved when they both picked up and were available.

"Hi, Sibs. I'm so glad you were both available. I am so *totally* bummed. I just need to hear your voices," Camille said. For years, "Sibs" had been their nickname for their collective of the three siblings. Sometimes it was Sisters, other times it was Sibs. This time it was the latter.

"Why, Camille?! Do we need to take off our earrings and get ready to kick somebody's ass?" said Tess in a half serious, half teasing voice.

They all erupted into laughter, Camille, in spite of how frustrated she was feeling. She could always count on Tess for a laugh.

"What's going on, Sister?" said Dreah soothingly. Of the three of them, in some ways, Dreah was the most like their mother, Naomi. All of them had parts of Naomi, but sometimes it was Dreah that was most like her. Right now, like their Mama, Dreah could always be counted on to bring Camille back down to a more comfortable place.

Plus, Camille knew that for each of the three of them, just even calling the sister "Sister," always gave them a sense of comfort. They were not in this—whatever "this" was–alone. Despite having a close, warm, wonderful family, they knew that the world could be a big, cold, cruel place. It was nice to know there was someone who *always* had your back. Their Mama did, of course, but that was different. Their Dad, Cameron, did, but he was no longer among the living. But Camille knew that her mother wasn't about to take off her earrings to settle a situation like her sisters would do.

From the time they were little girls running around in the neighborhood, you could always count on Tess to take off those earrings and whip someone's butt first, and ask questions about who was right and who was wrong later. She was 100% all-in when it came to her sisters. One of them might have done something stupid to create a situation that Tess ended up fighting in, but she'd never let the other person know that. She'd just later give what-for to the sister who had done something dumb to "necessitate" the fight.

And, of course, it went without saying that Naomi and Cameron were never to know. They still laughed at some of the shenanigans they managed to get away with without their parents knowing, especially in a town where so many people knew their family and neighbors all lived by the "It takes a village" edict. The neighbors were free to discipline children other than their own since parents couldn't be everywhere at once. Everyone operated by the same set of values, so the privilege of helping lovingly raise someone else's child was never abused. It's just how they operated.

Now that Camille thought about it, their Mom and Dad probably knew a lot more than they let on, but never mentioned it to them. Camille had no doubt they would have stepped in if they had viewed their daughters' actions as anything other than the normal hijinks of childhood. In retrospect, while it seemed daring at the time, childhood hijinks really was all they engaged in. No doubt it was monitored from afar by not only their own parents, but other watchful, caring parents in their neighborhood, ready to step in if need be.

"It's just the quilt," Camille said sadly, bringing her thoughts back to the reason why she called.

"Oh, *hell* no! Is that damn quilt being ghostie again," Tess nearly shouted. "I thought we took care of that at Christmas and laid it to rest! No pun intended if it's really ghosts involved," she laughed. Her sisters giggled.

"Well, not exactly. I mean, no, it's not acting weird again," said Camille. "That part is OK. It's been fine ever since Tabitha and Paul came over and figured out what was going on. But, remember that after we saw the inscription, Tabitha and Paul told us that we needed to figure out who the initials represented and what the inscription meant? The quilt acted normal after that and we got so caught up in the fun we were having during the holiday celebration, that I forgot all about the rest. So a few days ago I finally called Charlie, the guy who owned the thrift shop where I bought the quilt."

"Was he able to help? Was he able to provide you with any helpful information?" Dreah asked.

"Yes! He was a storehouse of information! He was incredibly helpful. He told me all he knew. He went all the way back to before he owned the store. He worked at the shop for the former owner. The man who owned it got sick and Charlie ended up taking over the shop during that time and bought it just before the man died."

"Well, that's nice," said Tess, sounding bored. "But did he tell you anything useful?'" she asked. "Anything that would help you find out who made the quilt or what the inscription means?"

"As a matter of fact, he did!" Camille said excitedly, feeling better now that she was remembering just how much information Charlie had given her.

"He told me the name of the original owner who brought it in before he even owned the store, when he just worked there, as well as the names of all the buyers that bought it over the years and led to him calling it "The Wandering Quilt." He gave me the email address for all the other buyers, but the first one was before computers got so omnipresent, so he had to give me her phone number rather than her email. Well, I mean, he didn't *have* to give it to me, but I persuaded him to.

"I called her several times, but there was no answer. I kept leaving messages but it went on for days. She finally picked up after I decided I would try giving her a call one last time. I couldn't figure out why she wouldn't talk to me since it was really not a big deal. It's not like I wanted anything from her other than simple information. She had sold the quilt to the thrift store over thirty years ago and it wasn't a big deal. Or, at least it didn't seem to me like it should be such a big deal. I didn't know if Charlie had called to give her a heads up that I was going to call or what, but it didn't make sense that she wouldn't take my call.

"At any rate, she finally spoke with me when I called the final time. I just spoke with her before I called you, as a matter of fact. It turns out the quilt came from her white husband's aunt, but his white family hated her because she was Black, and her husband beat her really bad for the thirty years they were together. So, she hated the quilt, never used it and got rid of it as soon as she got there by selling it to Harry at the thrift store."

"Harry? Who's Harry?" Tess said. "I thought Charlie owned the thrift store."

"Harry was the one who owned the store first, who Charlie worked for before Harry got sick and died and Charlie took over the store," said Camille.

"Oh," said Tess. "I sure am glad she left his ass after thirty years of him beating her."

"Actually, she didn't leave him, if you can believe that. He died in an accident at work. An accident that cut his head clean off."

"Ouch!" said Tess. "I don't like to speak ill of the dead since they aren't here to defend themselves, but there's not much to say to defend yourself from violently beating your wife for thirty years. The best I can say is it couldn't have happened to a nicer guy. I'm not even going to ask why she stayed for thirty years."

"Well, what did the woman who gave it to Harry say about it?" asked Dreah.

"Well, she just said pretty much what I just told you. She hated the quilt because it was from the white family of her husband, and they hated her, and her husband always beat her. So she got rid of everything of his before he was even buried and only kept the quilt to wrap something in to protect it when she was moving there. As soon as she got there, she got rid of it. Sold it to Harry for his thrift shop."

"Well, who was the aunt?" asked Tess. "What was her name? Can we track her down?"

"That's why I needed to hear my sisters. I don't know who the aunt is. I don't know her name or where she is or even if she's still living, so I don't know how to track her down. When Sarah—that's the woman who owned the quilt and sold it to Harry, the thrift store owner—when Sarah finished telling me all of this, and she said she had never told anyone before and never would again; she just hung up. I tried calling her back several times, and texted her and she wouldn't respond to either one. I have to think about what to do. But I needed to hear my sisters," said Camille dejectedly.

"Oh! I see," said Dreah. "You're stuck with knowing who owned the quilt and sold it to the shop, but not knowing the name of the person who gave it to her in the first place. That is, you don't know the name of the one who actually made the quilt. That's important since it is most likely the person who the initials are for, so the one most likely to know what this is all about. I doubt if someone else later opened up the quilt trim and put the message in. That wouldn't make sense. Especially since she had it the entire time from when it was made until she sold it to Harry. Well, we should be able to do something to be able to dig into that and find out at least a little bit online. It's hard for someone to have no online footprint at all these days."

"But where do I start if I don't even know her name?" Camille almost whined. So much so that all three of the sisters had a hearty laugh. She thought back to a few days before when she and Leslie called out Luke on the drive home from school for whining. She felt a twinge of guilt for nearly doing what her six-year-old son did.

"I'm sorry, Sibs, but this is so frustrating. I get chunks of great information, but then huge important pieces are missing."

"Well, it shouldn't be hard to find out what Sarah's married last name was," said Tess. "I can't imagine that Charlie doesn't know. How about the other buyers whose names he gave you? Do they know her? Somebody in town must know her name. If you find out her last name, and it's her husband's last name, it may lead you to the aunt's last name if she was from his father's side of the family."

"That makes sense," said Camille and Dreah at the same time.

"But, that's a lot of if's. If I can find out her last name; if Charlie knows; if he doesn't, finding out if one of the other buyers knows, and if they do, if the aunt is from the husband's father's side of the family, and if she did not get married and change her name. It sounds like it's too many ifs having to come together for us to ever really discover it," said Camille, sounding downcast.

"Well, you never know until you try," Dreah said brightly. "Just start with Charlie. As much as you said he knew and told you, I can't imagine that he wouldn't know something that might lead us to Sarah's last name or even her aunt's last name. He may well be willing to call her up and ask her about it. If not, you can ask one of the other buyers if they can find out."

"Sounds like a plan," said Tess neutrally.

"You're right. It's a starting point. I was just so disappointed and frustrated when Sarah hung up on me and wouldn't reply to my text or calls that I lost it. But this makes me feel so much better. Like there really is some way forward after all. Thank you, Sibs! I love you so!"

"That's what we do for each other, Girlfriend," said Tess. "By the way, I almost forgot to tell you Girls that they made me the offensive football coach at the university! They promoted me from assistant! They knew they had a good thing and that I deserved that spot. This is exactly the spot I wanted! It's a dream come true. Sets me up really well for climbing up to the NFL and starting my head coach quest. I can't believe I get paid to have this much fun."

"Oh, my God, Tess!! How could you forget to tell us that?!!" Dreah and Camille screamed.

"That's *awesome!!!!*" Camille screamed. "And you let me sit here prattling on and even whine about this quilt situation and didn't even bother to tell us!"

"Well, I was trying to help a Sistah out," Tess laughed. "It just happened today, just before you called. I haven't even told Renée yet. I was going to do a three-way call to y'all, but you beat me to it, Camille, with your ghostie frustration crap," she giggled.

"Tess, I am so happy for you. You so deserve this," Dreah said excitedly. "Wait till Mama hears! Just wait till Brian and Tristan hear about it! They are gonna *LOVE* this!!!! You know they will be at *every* game!! A huge celebration is in order!"

"Yesssss!!! You know I don't need much of an excuse to party, and this is a big one!" laughed Tess.

"OK, we'll check schedules and make the arrangements and let you know," Dreah said. "I won't tell Mama anything. I'll let you do that. But let me know when you tell her so I can give her a call to begin planning our celebration. If I call her before you tell her, I won't be able to keep such a great big awesome secret," Dreah laughed. "I'm just giving you fair warning! Do *not* forget to let me know you called her!"

"Will do!" Tess said gleefully.

And with that, they rung off.

CHAPTER 20

"Oh, yippee!!!" said Camille excitedly. "One of the buyers finally replied to my email!!!!"

"What did you sell, Mama?" asked Luke, matching Camille's excitement. Camille loved that little boy of her so. He was such a bright little sweetie pie light in the world.

"It wasn't my old bike you said I had outgrown was it?" said Leslie with great gravity. "Because you haven't gotten me a new one yet and I don't want you to get rid of it until I have another one! I can't be without wheels!"

Before they could catch themselves, Camille and Tristan both gave a hearty laugh at the tiny little girl standing before them, hands on hips, looking as if she was a teenager who had lost her car.

"No, Leslie, I did not sell your bike, Sweetie Pie. In fact, Luke, I didn't sell *anything*. Someone else sold something. In fact they sold it several times to several different buyers and I contacted them and I see one of them contacted me back!"

"Why would you want to contact a buyer who bought something that you didn't sell, Mama," said Luke, looking thoroughly confused. Leslie drifted off up to her room, no longer interested in the conversation now that she knew her "wheels" were safe.

Camille looked over at Tristan. He understood totally what she meant and why she was so happy. He knew she wanted to take time to read the email and, if necessary, respond.

"OK, Sport. How about us going outside and throwing around the ball while Mama finishes making dinner for us?" said Tristan to Luke.

Luke jumped up and down excitedly while shouting "Yes! Yes! Yes!"

Camille sent Tristan a look of genuine appreciation, love and thanks. There it was again. That man knew her so well, and always supported her precisely the way she needed it, often without her ever having to say a word. She loved that he was so connected to her that she didn't need to. She loved that it was reciprocal.

With the kitchen empty, and her dinner preparations under control, Camille opened the email from the buyer, Anne Alexis.

Hi, Ms. Thornton. Is it alright to call you Camille? I'm not a formal kind of person. I'll assume it is. So, Charlie told you I bought the quilt then brought it back to him, huh? Leave it to Charlie. Well, I guess it's not exactly a state secret. Yeah, I did. It just didn't seem to feel the way a quilt should feel, so I brought it back. Living out in the middle of the woods by myself is creepy enough as it is, without a beautiful quilt I loved and thought would be comforting, making it creepier. I don't mind living in the woods by myself, mind you, but I'm not up for the kind of creepiness I can't use my gun on.

Camille slowly put down her cell phone she was reading the email on and thought about what Anne Alexis said. "Creepy?" "Creepiness she can't use her gun on?" It sounded like Anne Alexis might have experienced something similar to what happened with the quilt at Camille's house. She decided to see how much Anne Alexis was willing to tell her. She began a reply to Anne Alexis' email.

Hi, Anne Alexis. Calling me Camille rather than Professor or Ms. Thornton is actually what I prefer as well. I am intrigued at what you said about the quilt. Do you mind if we meet via a Zoom call? I'd be perfectly willing to come out to your place in the woods, but I live out of state, not in South Carolina. But I'd love to see your space. Can we have a Zoom chat? Camille pushed 'send.'

She was surprised when her phone pinged almost immediately after sending the reply.

Sure! I don't mind company, virtual or real! We can talk right now. Here's a link.

Camille wondered if Anne Alexis responded so quickly because she was lonely for company out in the woods. But dinner was under control and she had a bit of time before everything was ready, so she clicked on the link and within seconds was looking at Anne Alexis' startlingly beautiful, Earth Mother face. Camille had no idea what she thought Anne Alexis would look like, in fact, she hadn't thought about it at all, but it wasn't this. Her almond, slanted, almost Asian-like eyes, and long, bountiful, clearly lovingly kept dreadlocs, were not what would have come to mind.

"Hi!" Anne Alexis said cheerfully, showing a set of incredibly beautiful, straight white teeth and a dazzling smile.

"Hi, Anne Alexis. Thanks for speaking with me. I really appreciate it!"

"No problem. Living out here in the woods by myself, I pretty much set my own schedule, so I have a lot of flexibility and now seemed as good a time as any. The only real thing that dictates my schedule is sun up, sun down, feeding the chickens and milking my two cows," she giggled. The rest I can do at my leisure. But my chickens make a royal racket if they're not fed, and don't get me started on a cow that's ready to be milked. They let you know it loud and long. 'Moooooooo' is for real," she laughed."

"What in the world are you doing out in the middle of the woods?" Camille knew it was presumptuous of her, but she couldn't help but think that she was not the first one to have asked Anne Alexis this question. She seemed so personable and lively until Camille found it hard to believe she'd seek the solitude of living by herself in the woods.

"Well, after I got my two undergraduate degrees and my Grande Diplome at Le Cordon Bleu in Paris and London, I traveled all over the world for nearly 20 years. My Dad got sick and I came back home to sort of take care of him. Him and my Mom were divorced when I was two, but the two of them were always friendly and he was always a part of my life. He was sick but wouldn't let me do a lot for him, but I did what I could.

"When he died, he left me a nice chunk of change and I decided to buy some land near my Mama, build a home on it, and do sustainability and wellness work to help society and the earth. I managed to get 13 acres of woods for a decent price, had a home built out of two shipping containers (don't think the contractors didn't have a bear of a time getting those things into these woods!) and set up housekeeping. It's just me, my cat Cosmos, my chickens, cows, my garden, my trees, the critters in the woods, my lake, and me. I love it.

"I teach classes in all sorts of things from making soap and oils to mindfulness, spend my time making my place more and more of what I want it to be, and I try to do all of it in a sustainable way. Reduce, Recycle, Reuse, that's me!," she giggled. "My place had actually been given the green light to become a United Nations-funded template for sustainability around the world until COVID brought everything to a screeching halt. Now, I'm re-thinking my plan.

"I do pretty much everything around here by myself. It's so hard to get good —or ANY—reliable help these days. People swear they'll show up and they don't, they swear they see your vision and they don't, they swear they can do what you need and they screw it up. But not before they ask for a date or tell you you have pretty titties. It's awful.

"So, I keep my gun and I'll use it, and I do what I can on my own, including putting the gutters on my roof. I love the internet. You can find out how to do *anything* on that son of a gun. ANYTHING!" she said, laughing. "I also have a job as an online counseling psychologist. That's what I got my master's degree in; Counseling Psychology."

"Wow, Anne Alexis. What a story! You are incredible! How courageous of you!" Camille was genuinely impressed.

"Well, I sort of thought of myself as courageous too, but I think I met my match in that Wandering Quilt. And that's so funny. I've had to deal with foxes messing with my chickens, wild hogs trampling over my land and digging up my shit, people coming onto my property unannounced— and again—I'm not afraid to show them my gun while I'm telling them to turn their ass around and leave because I'm tiny and live alone and you do *NOT* just 'wander' onto this place by mistake. So if I haven't invited you, I assume your intentions are not good. Because I'm tiny and a female, I need to make sure you understand I am not effing around with you.

"But, that quilt? That was another story entirely. That quilt was just plain creepy. I don't have courage for creepy. I have to be able to see what I'm about to get rid of, what's disturbing my peace. With that quilt, I couldn't do that."

"What, exactly do you mean by that, Anne Alexis?"

"Well, the truth is, I never really talked about this to anyone. I live in the woods by myself. I love people, but they can get on my nerves with their bullshit, consumerism, herd mentality, ridiculously vacuous lives, just not living an examined life, you know? I see them around, and I have friends and all, but some things are just sort of too weird to talk about. Plus, talking sort of makes it real. I just wanted to forget that quilt.

"I thought it was just a beautiful quilt I could use to brighten up my space. It sort of reminded me of my life, in a way. The little flowers appliquéd on with so much care, the green leaves appliquéd with each flower, the royal purple. It was just perfect, I thought. It reminded me of my garden. Of the earth, you know? I used it in my spare room because I wanted to preserve it, so I thought it might last longer if it was only used for company rather than as an everyday quilt. I could still see it all the time because the room opens out into the living space I had built between the two containers that has my kitchen and family room spaces," Anne Alexis said.

"But, what happened?" asked Camille.

"Well, if I tell you, you promise you won't laugh?" Anne Alexis said.

"Of course I won't laugh!" said Camille rather forcefully. "After all, you're doing me a favor by even speaking with me!"

"Well, a few times I had folks staying over. Sometimes when people come to visit, they don't feel comfortable to leave out at night because we're in the middle of the woods and there's no street lights or anything and I admit that the long, unpaved road into my place is really pretty scary at night. They're not used to it like I am. I run up and down that road in my Jeep all times of the day or night.

"But they get afraid because it is really dark, so they decide to stay over. Especially if they've had something to drink. I wouldn't trust it either, if I was them and had been drinking. I don't mind them staying over because I have plenty of space, and if I didn't like them, they wouldn't be here in the first place. My bedroom and bathroom are in one container, and the other one has a guest room and a full guest bathroom, so there's plenty of privacy.

"Well, every time someone stayed in the guest room with the beautiful quilt, in the morning they'd come out looking a little the worse for wear, sort of nervous like. They'd say they could swear that the quilt kept creeping off of them in the night. It didn't help matters that since I'm in the middle of the woods, it is really, really dark at night. So to be in complete darkness, not in your own place, and you keep feeling this quilt creeping off of you, must be scary as shit.

"The first time I thought the guest just had too much to drink and was imagining it in a drunken stupor or something. But when it happened a second, then a third time, I washed it and packed that thing up and took it right back to Charlie."

Camille was stunned. She hoped her face didn't show it. But how could it not?

"Wow, Anne Alexis, that is some tale. I don't mean 'tale' as in untrue. I just mean that is some experience you had. I see now why you said it was creepy. Did you ever sleep under the quilt yourself?"

"Are you serious right now? Why in the world would I do that?" Anne Alexis asked Camille, her voice rising as she knitted her brows and rolled her eyes at the computer screen. "I couldn't survive out here in the woods if I took unnecessary chances. I only take calculated risks. My calculation was that that risk was not worth it. I didn't know what the hell was going on with that quilt, but I wasn't taking any chances after three people said the same thing. Of course, I did let that chain saw slip one time and nearly cut my finger off while I was out here working on my land alone, but that's another story," she laughed.

"I don't play when it comes to my life. And if I'm out here in the woods by myself and that thing starts creeping off me in the night, what the hell would I do? At least my guests had me to run to if they chose to do so. I wouldn't have anything or anyone. My trusty gun wouldn't help me. So, no, I did not sleep under that quilt myself. If someone was close enough to me to be here spending the night, they would be someone whose word I would trust. I have older siblings. I know what it's like to not have to experience something for myself in order to see what it's like. You see what happens to your siblings when they try it and you learn your lessons that way. If it didn't work for them, no need to try it for yourself. After having three guests I trust have the same experience, there was no way I was going to try that quilt out for myself. I didn't need to. I believed them. I got the message. It was creepy weird. I do enough on my own in the world doing it my way without trying that out."

"Wow. That is really something," said Camille, blowing out a long sigh.

"Mama, is dinner ready yet? Can we eat now?!" Leslie was suddenly looming large on the Zoom screen next to Camille, demanding to be fed. Camille was taken aback and embarrassed. Leslie knew better than to interrupt her Zoom calls. Or, at least Camille *thought* she did.

Anne Alexis laughed. "OK, I see you gotta go and feed the hungry masses now. I understand that, given my cows and chickens. I'll talk to you later," and her screen went dark.

CHAPTER 21

amille loved the Zoom conversation she had with Anne Alexis, but one thing really disturbed her. She felt like there was unfinished business. She had not asked Anne Alexis if she knew who the aunt was that made the quilt. The good thing was that she felt like she had not been shut out by Anne Alexis the way she had been by Sarah, so she believed she would be able to email her and get a response.

Hi, Anne Alexis! Thank you sooooo much for speaking with me via Zoom just now! What an incredible experience you had! I truly appreciate you sharing it with me. I'm sorry for our abrupt ending, but I had one other thing I wanted to ask you before we finished.

Do you, by any chance, know the name of the person who made the quilt? Or do you know Sarah who originally took the quilt to Charlie's thrift store to sell it? The store didn't belong to Charlie at the time; it belonged to Harry, the man who owned it, but got sick and died and Charlie took it over. Do you, by any chance, know Sarah? Do you know her last name or what her married name was or where she lived before she came there to live years ago? Have you heard anything? Do you know anyone who does or who I could ask?"

Given Anne Alexis's energy, she wasn't surprised to hear back from her staightaway.

No, I don't know the person who made the quilt years before I had it. I know the woman who brought it to the thrift store, Sarah, lives somewhere in town. I have no idea what her name was before she got married. But, I think it's now Marsden. Come to think of it, I don't know if Marsden is her married name or if she went back to her pre-married name, or even whether she ever changed it when she got married. I guess she did. That's what people did back then—or at least, the women in small towns did. I have the feeling she came from a small town rather than a place like New York, even tho I don't know her. I know she's in town, but I don't hear a lot about her. Not only am I out in the woods, but we're pretty far apart in age and don't run in the same circles, if you know what I mean.

As for whether I know anyone you could ask, if it were me, I'd start with Charlie. I only knew one of the other people who bought the quilt. I know Jenniffer. I knew we both bought the quilt, but we never talked about it. I just happen to know who she is because she buys the cheese I make from my cows and sell in town on Tuesdays. Actually, that's how I know Ms. Sarah too, but I can't say as I have really talked to them much. Not personal stuff, you know. Just cheese, the weather, you know.

So, I don't know much that can help you, but it's all I know. Like I said, if I were you, I'd start with Charlie. He pretty much knows everything worth knowing in town.

Camille appreciated Anne Alexis's prompt response, but couldn't help but feel disappointed that Anne Alexis didn't know more. But, Camille guessed she had no choice but to once again go back to Charlie and see if he could come up with a last name for Sarah's aunt by marriage who made the quilt. She hated to bother him again. She didn't want to feel like a pest. But what else could she do? Without something to go on regarding Sarah's last name after she married, hopefully leading to her husband's family's name—which, even then may be a long shot because the aunt may have gotten married again and not had the same name—she was at a loss.

It suddenly occurred to Camille that she had not yet heard back from the other quilt owners that she had contacted by email. Maybe the email addresses Charlie had given her were no longer their email addresses. Or maybe they were busy. Or maybe they didn't deal with email much. Or maybe they hadn't paid their internet carrier bill. "Who knew?" Camille thought in frustration. But for Anne Alexis to be the only one who responded seemed strange. If they didn't want to engage with her—although she didn't know why they wouldn't want to—they could have at least replied and told her that rather than leaving her completely shut out with on explanation as to why.

Camille decided to give it one more try. She followed up her emails with another, last attempt to reach the buyers. She separately sent the same email to each of them.

Hi, (name). I recently sent you an email asking for information about a quilt you bought from Charlie Racker at the Maypole Sundry Thrift Store in your town. I live out of town and purchased the quilt when I came across the quaint little thrift store while my family was on vacation this past summer. Not only am I an avid quilter, but I collect quilts as well. The quilt I bought at Charlie's shop is lovely and I wanted to ask if you know if anyone knows anything about the origins of the quilt. Charlie told me you purchased the quilt and I wondered if you had any idea about who made it. Charlie also told me you brought the quilt back to the store for a refund. If you don't wish to speak to me about the quilt, please just let me know by replying to this email so I will not continue to pester you about it. I just wanted some information. It is not my intention to be a bother. I'm sorry if this comes off that way.

Camille was very surprised when she received a reply shortly after she pushed 'send.' It was from Jenniffer.

Hi, Camille. Sorry I have not replied. I have been busy. I am the art teacher at the elementary school in town, which means I teach every student in the school. I also have two children of my own, so I have very little time for much else.

Yes, I bought the quilt from Charlie. I loved it the moment I saw it because it reminded me so much of a very special quilt that my mother made to commemorate her enslaved ancestors in North Carolina. One of my sister's got the quilt after my Mom passed, so when I saw one so much like it, I bought it from Charlie's thrift shop. But, as it turned out, it did not serve my needs, so I returned it. I heard that the quilt had been around for a while. I'm not sure where, but I'm pretty sure I heard it was made in Mississippi by the aunt of the person who brought it to Charlie's the first time, Sarah, long before I came to town. It's been so long, but if I remember correctly, I think the aunt's name was Carl Barnes or something like that. I thought it was strange that a woman's name would be Carl, but I've gotten used to strange things in the south.

I wouldn't be able to remember who told me if I tried. I seem to remember it as the name because the way it was pronounced reminded me of a "cow barn" and I got a mental image of one, as an artist would do. :-) I could be wrong, of course, but I'm pretty sure that's what I remember.

Good luck. Again, I'm sorry it took so long to get back with you.

Camille didn't realize she was not breathing until she let out a long, low breath after seeing a name. A name! She had a name! She didn't know whether it was accurate or a married name for a single name, but she had a name!

It was a starting point!

CHAPTER 22

"Well, that's better than nothing!" Tristan said after Camille told him about her email exchange with Jenniffer and the name she had learned. She was in his arms, her favorite place to be, and he was helping her mitigate her hesitation about moving forward. He always had a way of making her feel she could do things without making her feel like she was weak for expressing her truths to him. She knew that could be unusual in a man and she valued it greatly.

Besides, just being so close to him always gave her positive vibes, inspiration, courage, strength to make it easier to do what she needed to do. It was all there in her and she used it all of the time to do what she did in the world, but Tristan was like a fuel additive. You needed the fuel (herself), as it was the most important part, but the fuel additive gave things a boost. Tristan, especially being physically close to him, was her fuel additive. And she was his. It never failed. For either of them.

Camille had come down off of her high about Jenniffer providing the name once she realized that Sarah had given the quilt to the thrift store well over thirty years before, and she'd had had it for thirty years by that time since she'd gotten it as a wedding gift and had been married to her abusive husband for thirty years. It was daunting when she realized she was looking for someone–a female at that, who could have changed her name in marriage—that was around somewhere in Mississippi perhaps nearly forty years ago. Mississippi was a big state, so Camille still had her work cut out for her.

"Camille, you act like this is fifty years ago and you don't have technology like we do now. Have you even looked for anything on the internet yet?" Tristan asked mildly, smiling.

"Well, no, I haven't. Not yet," she replied. "I don't feel like I've had enough to even look up."

"Well, you should. Just start there. It doesn't take anything for you to just put the name into a search engine. You may find nothing at all. You may find a million people with that name. But then, you just might find something that leads you somewhere. You're a professor. Research is your wheelhouse. I know that as a law professor you do much more sophisticated research than something like a search engine search, but you know that things are no longer the way they used to be when academics eschewed the use of search engines by students—and academics rarely used them—because they didn't think the results were good enough for academic rigor. I get that.

"But times have changed. Even though there is a lot of crap out there, you aren't looking for political opinions where you're likely to fall down a rabbit hole of wild theories about whether babies are being trafficked in the basement of a pizza parlor that doesn't even have a basement, or whether COVID or climate change is real.

"You're looking for a person. So not only has the internet gotten much more sophisticated and helpful, but your results are much more likely to be useful, even if just to narrow your search.

"Think about it: the first thing I do as a doctor when a patient presents with something I'm unfamiliar with, is to do an internet search. If I can turn to it as a doctor looking for answers about a patient's health or even life, then surely you can at least give it a go to find someone. There's nothing to lose."

"I know, I know, you're absolutely right, Tristan. I think I am just avoiding it because I don't want to be disappointed. I need to get my act together and just do a search for her. If worse comes to worst and I don't find anything, I'm no worse off than I am now. I'll do it."

Camille gave Tristan a delicious teasing kiss that left him–both of them actually—wanting more. She reluctantly left the comfort of his arms, walked over to her open laptop computer on the dining room table and sat down. One of the things she really loved about Tristan was that he had a way of always making her want to do better. Be better. Not because he pontificated about it, or made her feel like a slacker for whatever she was doing, but simply because she watched how he operated in the world. He never let things slip.

Of course, as a doctor, an emergency room surgeon at that, he couldn't afford to. But he'd been the same way as long as she had known him. Many was the time that Camille had taken out stitches in a quilt project she was working on because the "Tristan buzzer" in her head went off and she knew that if it was his project, he would never let such a "less than" stitch remain. So she would take it out and redo it. It didn't matter to Tristan that the thing he was doing would not be seen by anyone but him. His Tristan rule was that if you were going to bother to do something, do it right. Full stop. She had seen it time after time when he was working on making fishing lures either for himself or the kids he taught to fish in the summer fishing camp at which he volunteered each year. The lure would look perfect to her, but Tristan would redo it because he did not feel it was his best effort if it wasn't perfect. It didn't matter that the kids would never know the difference. He did. So it was done over again.

Camille knew Tristan would genuinely love whatever she did, but she valued being better. She really appreciated that he just made her want to be better by being so good himself without in any way putting anyone else down for how they did something. Seeing someone operate like that was bound to rub off. It did. Camille was the better for it. She found herself wondering what it is that she did that rubbed off on him that way. She was sure he'd have a whole list of things if she asked.

Slowly she typed the name of Sarah Marsden into the search engine. After looking for it for a second, she added to the search, the word "Mississippi." Within seconds her screen lit up with a rolling litany of results. Far too many for her taste. Camille rolled her eyes at the screen, then at Tristan, and began to take a closer look. Tristan's comforting smile that still made her knees weak was definitely a much needed boost.

CHAPTER 23

"I can't believe I spent all that time on going through all those Sarah Marsden results and I came up with zilch!" Camille said, frustrated, an hour and a half later.

Tristan just looked at her evenly. "Well, that's one avenue closed—at least in its present state—and you can move on."

"Move on? Move on to what?!" Camille said, with the sound of a cross between frustration, anger and a bit of fear in her voice.

"Camille, you don't have to do this," Tristan said, taking both her hands in his and looking deeply into her eyes—eyes she knew he thought were beautiful and he could get lost in, just as she could his gorgeous ones. "You can send that quilt back at any single moment you want to. Everyone else who bought it did.

"If it's going to cause all this frustration and discomfort for you, why are you doing it? Don't you have enough on your plate with your job, the kids, me, your family, your community work, your hobbies, to keep you busy? Why take on something you don't have to? If you are so frustrated and down about this, I don't think I understand why you are doing it. Why don't you take a break and go spin some wool into yarn or make some beaded earrings or something? You haven't done that in a while."

Camille looked at him, startled. He had a way of getting to the heart of things in such a clear and precise way. Part of her totally understood his statement. Why was she setting herself up for this disappointment? Why was she trying to find a needle in a haystack? If she wanted to do it, why was she feeling so frustrated? No one ever said this would be easy, even from the very beginning. In fact, she never thought it would be.

Tracking down the journey of a quilt she randomly purchased at a random thrift store not even in her own town, or even state? She had no responsibility for this quilt. She'd just come across it in a random thrift store on vacation. It had no sentimental value for her as if she had created it herself for some special reason.

It wasn't as if she'd inherited the quilt from a relative, or even that her mother had made it. The quilt meant nothing to her. Well, not exactly nothing after all she and her family had been through with the quilt. But nothing in the sense of true sentimental value. Its draw lay purely in wanting to track down what they had discovered in the border trim. But she didn't have to do that. She could send it back at any time and dollars to donuts, Charlie, the thrift store owner would give her all her money back. He was used to it coming back. In fact, he'd even named it The Wandering Quilt.

But, it did mean something to Camille. She knew she could send it back at any time. But after what they had gone through with the quilt during the holidays and what they had discovered, Camille had no doubt whatsoever that she was bound to do what she was doing. She couldn't explain it, but she knew something was going on that she needed to track down. She had no real choice. She just wished she was finding out more information.

But she knew Tristan loved her dearly and worried about her feeling so frustrated. Knowing this did not, however, keep her from bubbling over.

"You don't know why I'm doing this?! You don't know why I'm doing this?!" Camille nearly hissed. "How can you say that when you know what we have experienced with that quilt? When you know what we found out, how important this must be to someone?" Camille said.

She was disappointed that Tristan did not realize how important the quilt was to her. How much it had impacted their lives. Even as she had this thought, she knew he did know that. He just loved and cared for her so much and wanted so much to protect her that he wanted to do what he could to lower her frustration.

"I understand that, Camille. Of course I do," Tristan said in a low, steady, intimate voice. "I also know you know that. But it isn't fun to watch you keep being so down and frustrated about everything that you find out—or don't find out. I love you. More than anything. *We* love you. We hate to see you feel so frustrated and disappointed like you've been doing.

"And we miss you." As he said this, he pulled her close and once again held her in his arms. She knew he knew how much it always soothed her. But she also knew he did it because of his deep feelings of love and affection for her and for how holding her made him feel as well. It benefited them both.

Camille loved feeling those arms around her. They always made her feel exactly the way a hug should make you feel. The way you always dreamed that a hug from the love of your life would make you feel. Like you were loved, desired, trusted, not alone, the center of someone's world, that their world was better because you were in it, that you gave them something no one else in the world could give them. She needed that hug. Sometimes she could get so carried away with being productive and being so deep in her research or a project, that she could forget pretty much everything else and needed to be pulled back. She knew this was one of those times.

Camille knew that she had really not been as attentive to Tristan, Leslie or Luke, not to mention her mother and sisters, and extended family as she should be. They may not have noticed but she did. She had been so wrapped up in chasing down this puzzle that she had just sort of been on automatic even when she was present. They had pretty much let her slide with it, her preoccupation, her lack of her usual bright, fun, involved presence.

But, Tristan was right. She needed to back up and gain some perspective. Even if she decided to stick with this search, there was no time limit on it. It wasn't like a new class she had to create by a certain date, a paper she had to write to present at a certain conference on a specified date, a deadline for publication of one of her textbooks. This was a totally voluntary project she undertook in order to try to, of all things, help a spirit. A spirit whose identity she did not know, whose circumstances she was totally unaware of, and whose life was in no way connected to hers.

After all, she reminded herself, her coming into acquisition of the quilt was quite by accident. It could have been bought by anyone. This wasn't her burden to bear. She had to keep that in mind, even as she went about the business of trying to figure out what the issue was behind the inscription they had discovered inside the quilt's trim.

Camille let herself relax into Tristan's embrace and felt the anxiety seemingly lower and drain right out of her toes. Whatever frustration and anxiety was left was totally dissipated by the intimate kiss that Tristan laid on her along with the hug that telegraphed her that they were about to go upstairs and make whatever energy from anxiety and frustration was left be put to a completely different, more productive—not to mention fun– use.

CHAPTER 24

"So, how about going with me to Mississippi to see what I can find out?" said Camille in a drowsy, exhausted voice as she was drifting off to sleep with her head on Tristan's chest after Tristan's passionate kiss and intimate hug had found its incredible conclusion that Camille had not grown tired of after all their years together. "I can go by myself, but I'd like to have you with me."

Camille felt Tristan's chest slowly rise to what seemed his full lung capacity, then fall as he sighed a slow, heavy sigh. "I must be losing my touch," he said. "All of that wasn't enough to take this out of your head? Do I need to up my game? I thought you enjoyed it as much as I did. You sure seemed to," he teased, kissing the top of her head and giving her a warm squeeze.

Camille didn't have to see his face in the dark to know that the corners of his mouth were turned up in that wonderful way she adored when he was teasing her.

"I did! You *know* I did," she said appreciatively. "Letting you know how I'm feeling is *never* an issue between us," she teased suggestively, while running her hands along the length of his body. "In fact, it was so good that it made my mind swirl into fantasyland. Like what if we went to Mississippi and were able to find out something? After all, that's where the quilt was supposed to have been created. Surely someone knows where Sarah came from in Mississippi. We could go see what we can find out. I know it's a big state, I know we don't have a lot to go on. But we could just go see if there is anything we can dig up somehow, some way.

"I don't mean now. I mean in a little while. Say, Spring Break. We usually take that week to go somewhere anyway. Why not Mississippi? You love the blues. Especially serious Mississippi Delta blues. You always say it's like history in song. We could make sure we go see where it came from, where it was created. Surely it's no happenstance that it was created in the Mississippi Delta. Why? Let's go see. Doesn't a famous actor have a blues club there, still? Who was it? I forget. He came from there and when he became famous he went back and started a blues club."

"Morgan Freeman," Tristan said drowsily.

"Yes! Morgan Freeman!" said Camille excited but drowsy. "Well, we've got plenty of time to give it some thought," she said as she drifted off to LalaLand, excited and completely and totally fulfilled and content because of her time and actions with Tristan. So much so that she didn't even hear Tristan say he wondered why her swerve off into fantasyland in the midst of their time under the quilts was about a trip to Mississippi for a quilt investigation.

CHAPTER 25

"I can definitely see why slaves must have felt so helpless and forlorn that their only escape was to sing their lives. Rather like Maya Angelou's "I Know Why the Caged Bird Sings," Camille said. "She said the caged bird sings for freedom because that's all it can do locked up in its cage. Just use its voice. This totally flat landscape stretching for miles and miles—as far as the eye can see, without even so much as a tree on the horizon, must have felt stifling, hopeless to those working there, living there.

"Imagine this space filled with rows and rows and rows of cotton that had to be picked, and the sun is beating down and there was no escape from your situation. This looks like the embodiment of no escape. Of hopelessness. How could you escape when everything was so flat and open and you'd be instantly seen? And you had no transportation? This space goes on for miles and miles. Can you imagine it covered in fluffy white cotton plants ready to be picked? Knowing you had to pick it?

"I saw in a documentary once that slaves were beaten if they did not pick fast enough, so they tried to work as absolutely fast as they could. But the fastest pickers ended up alone way out in front of all the others and began to sing just to take their mind off of what they were doing. They just sang about their day, their lives, their friends, their experiences, limited though they were, their lovers, their owners, anything that crossed their mind. From that eventually came all sorts of things like Blues, Ragtime and Jazz. Just like Maya Angelou's caged bird, singing was all you could do.

"The sharecroppers who eventually headed north in The Great Migration brought their music with them, but changed it up some when they got to the big cities like Memphis, Chicago and New Orleans and that created its own sort of music.

"I love it the way African Americans can always take nothing and create something out of it. Seems like it doesn't matter how little it is, they will work their magic on it and turn it into something. It is amazing how it helped create survival and enjoyment at the same time.

"Whether it was making a delicacy of the discarded guts or body parts of pigs they were only given, like chitterlings or pig feet, or ash cake out of cornmeal, water, and little else, or music totally out of nothing but what was going on in their lives, they made it work. Their bodies grew strong on those pig guts, pig feet or hoe cake and they lived to create the next generations. The music of their lives not only became world famous, but spawned the basis for virtually all the music we know today. It's amazing. So very inspiring."

"Ewwwww…pig guts, pig feet, I don't even know what hoe cake is, but if it's like the first two, *gross*," said Leslie, drawing out the last word dramatically.

"Mama, what's a Great Migation?" asked Luke from the back seat.

"Are we there yet?" groaned Leslie. "We've been driving FOR-EV-ER!"

"Leslie, you aren't a baby anymore. You are old enough to know that it takes hours to drive through states. We want you to have the experience of learning how other places look and what they're like. You don't get that in an airplane. Just be patient. At least we're in our destination state. You two have been great so far. Thank you so, so much. It won't be too much longer," said Tristan, soothingly.

"It's My-GRAY-Shun, Luke, not my-GAY-shun. Migration. Migration is what you call it when people move from one place to another in the same country. They are called migrants. If they come from outside of a country to live in a new country, they are known as immigrants rather than migrants. So, since Black people were moving from the south to the north in the United States, they were migrants. They were leaving where they were in the south to go live in another place in the same country, the north, or west, where they believed they would be treated better".

"Who was treating them bad, Mama? Was somebody being mean to them? Bullying them? You're not supposed to bully people. My teacher says bullying people and being mean to people is being bad and we're not supposed to be bad," said Luke solemnly.

"At one time in this country, Luke, Black people were owned by other people, mostly white people. Some, not all, white people owned Black people. A few Black people owned them too. Black people who belonged to other people were called slaves. The people who owned them were called, among other things, slaveowners. It was not easy to be a slave because it meant a slaveowner could do anything he or she wanted to the person they owned, their slave. A slave couldn't do whatever they wanted to do. They could only do what the slaveowner allowed them to do."

"Leslie makes me do things! Am I her slave, Mama? Am I? I don't want to be Leslie's slave. She can be mean sometimes!"

Tristan and Camille looked at each other and tried hard to muzzle their smiles. It was hard.

"No, Luke. You are not Leslie's slave, Darlin'. Leslie is your big sister and sometimes big sisters or brothers do things to their younger siblings that are not very nice. But they love them and don't really mean it. Also, slavery ended over 150 years ago, so they don't have slaves in our country anymore. It took a war, called the Civil War, to get rid of slavery. The soldiers who were fighting to end slavery won the war, so slavery ended.

"After the war ended, the landowners who used to own slaves were upset because they no longer had slaves to do the work the landowners didn't want to do like grow their crops so they could sell them to make money. The slaves that were now free did not have any money or own anything at all, but they could work.

"So the landowners agreed to have the newly freed slaves work to raise the landowner's crops and receive money by selling the part of the crop that the landowner let them keep for working the land. It was called sharecropping. The landowners would give the workers the seeds, tools and a place to live. The sharecroppers would plant the seeds and grow the crops. When the crops were ready, the owner was supposed to settle up with the workers and give them their fair share of the crops to sell or the money their part was worth.

"The sharecroppers didn't usually have any transportation or money to buy things so the landowners often had stores, called commissaries, where the sharecroppers could get things they might need for their families to live, like flour or coffee.

"Why didn't they just go to the store to get the coffee and flour?" asked Luke.

"Didn't you hear her say they didn't have money or transportation? Even if they could walk to the store, they didn't have any money, silly boy," said Leslie condescendingly.

"Leslie, you really don't need to take that tone with your brother. He's only six. He understands like a six-year-old. You owe him an apology," said Tristan.

"Yes, Daddy. Sorry Luke," said Leslie reluctantly.

"It's okay, Leslie. Mama said sometimes big sisters are mean to their little brothers but they love them and they don't mean it. I love you, Leslie," said Luke, looking over at his sister sincerely.

Camille and Tristan couldn't help but smile as they saw Leslie reach over and take Luke's hand and say, "I love you too, Luke."

"So then what happened, Mama?" asked Luke.

"Well, Luke, unfortunately, after the sharecroppers had worked to grow the crops all year when they went to settle up, the landowners often did not give the sharecroppers anything at all or gave them very little. In fact, sometimes the landowners told them that not only did the sharecroppers not make any money, but that they owed the landowner money for things they had bought at the commissary. That meant that the sharecropper had to stay on the land and continue to work to pay off the money the landowner said the sharecropper owed him.

"Since it had been illegal or punishable for slaves to learn to read or write or do arithmetic during slavery, the sharecroppers often didn't know enough to be able to tell the landowner that they were wrong and that the sharecropper didn't owe them anything. Even if they had known how to read or write or do math and knew the landowner was wrong, the Black sharecroppers were not allowed to disagree with the white landowner, so they just had to take whatever the landowner wanted to give them.

"If the sharecroppers who'd been cheated wanted to leave an unfair landowner and go to another landowner that maybe wasn't as unfair, there were laws that said they couldn't do that unless their landowner agreed to it. Of course, he usually did not agree, so they had to stay and continue to work for him.

"That was *so not fair!*" hissed Leslie. "Mama, are you saying that not only did the sharecroppers not get paid after working all year to raise the crops, but that they *owed* money because the landowner said they *owed* money, so they had to stay there and work for *nothing?* That was like slavery all over again!"

"Yes, Leslie. Exactly. The system lasted for decades. In addition to sharecropping being created after the Civil War ended, the south also came up with something called 'convict leasing.' The Thirteenth Amendment abolishing slavery or 'involuntary servitude' had an exception for criminals. Involuntary servitude could still be used for criminals. Land owners still needed cheap labor to work their land.

"So laws began popping up that allowed Blacks to be arrested for any little thing imaginable, like being in public with no money. These laws were rarely used against whites. When they were arrested, in order to get out of jail, the "criminals" had to post bail. Them and their families rarely had the money for that. Along would come a landowner and pay the bail in exchange for the prisoner working the landowner's land. In fact, sometimes, the land owner told the sheriff they needed a certain amount of men to work the land and the sheriff would just go out and arrest that number of men and let the landowner know they could come get them. Some of these workers were literally worked to death, given little food or clothing, and some were never heard from again. They were treated horribly. It was the birth of the chain gang system states used for getting prisoners to work for pretty much nothing, as well.

"Now you see why so many Black people wanted to leave the south and why it was called The Great Migration," Camille said.

"I sure don't blame them for leaving! I sure would have wanted to leave!" said Leslie, fuming at the unfairness of what she was hearing.

"I'm going to make sure I do my reading and writing and 'rithmetic, now!" said Luke. "I don't want to be dumb and let people make me stay some place! I'm going to make sure to have money from my piggy bank in my pocket too!"

Everyone laughed.

"Yes, Luke, it's very important for you to do your school work and learn all you can, be as smart as you can be," said Tristan. "The sharecroppers weren't dumb. They were just discouraged from having an education because the landowners knew that if they had an education, they would be smart and could read and would learn ideas that would make them know that what was happening was wrong and they wouldn't want to do it anymore. Education is very important, Luke. Always get as much of it as you can."

"I will," Luke said sincerely, as if he understood just how serious it was.

"So then what, Mama?" asked Leslie. Camille and Tristan exchanged surprised glances. It was unusual for Leslie to be so fully engaged in their conversations, especially educational ones.

"Well, Leslie, when the first World War broke out, a lot of the workers had to go into the service to be soldiers or were needed up north in the factories to build things for the war like airplanes and ships, so they began to leave the south.

"The landowners tried to make them stay in the south in all sorts of ways. Sometimes they came and took them off the trains that were headed north. Sometimes they threatened them with guns and dogs to keep them from getting onto the trains, or went to their houses and threatened them about leaving. Sometimes this meant that the workers had to sneak away in order to be able to leave.

"That is crazy, Mama! They wouldn't let them *leave*?! It's a free country! That was illegal! Slavery was over! How could they make them stay?!!!" exclaimed Leslie.

"That's a good question, Leslie. But the country's laws, especially then, were never really applied the same way to Blacks. Blacks were often intimidated, beaten, terrorized, cheated, and many other things in order to make them do what whites wanted to have them do, despite the fact that it was illegal for whites to do it. If the local government officials don't do anything about it, what protection was there for them? Sometimes it was the local law enforcement that was involved in the wrongdoing. Not every white person was involved, but the overall system was widespread in the south.

"But more than six million Black people managed to leave the south and go to the north, the midwest and beyond from the 1910s to the 1970s.

It was the largest peacetime movement of people ever. Black people had a whole different set of problems when they began coming into these new places, many of which are still with us today, but at least they felt a bit more free."

"That is ridiculous that those people were treated that way when the law was supposed to protect them. It makes me so mad. It's so unfair!" pouted Leslie.

"It's all a part of our history, Leslie. It's important for you to know it. I don't want you to get mad about it. I do want you to appreciate the injustice of it. I do want you to know that things weren't always the way they are now. I do want you to know that our country is constantly striving to be better, even though there are setbacks. And I do want you to know how strong the people you come from are to have gone through all they did so you could be here. But there's no use in being angry about the past. Just continue to work to make things better. Understand?" asked Tristan.

"Yes, Sir, Daddy. I will. What sort of problems did the Black people have when they moved north, Mama?" Leslie inquired.

"Well, Leslie, not long after slavey ended, white people did not want to have anything to do with Black people, so they passed laws that separated the races. It was called segregation. They were also known as Jim Crow laws. Jim Crow laws separated Black people and white people in virtually all public spaces like public schools, libraries, hospitals, buses, trains, taxis, theaters, parks, water fountains, bathrooms, swimming pools, stores, funeral homes, prisons, doctor's offices, just everywhere," said Camille.

"'Jim Crow laws'?! That's a funny name for a law, Mama!" Luke guffawed. "Why did they call them Jim Crow laws? Was it because they wanted the Black birds to fly away?" he giggled.

"Clever, Luke," Leslie laughed, joined by Tristan and Camille.

"Actually, Luke, the laws were named after a very silly and mean song and dance routine that was performed by white performers who put burnt cork or some other substance on their face to make them look dark. They made themselves look awful, with big eyes and lips, looking really stupid like their ideas of who Black people were, and pretending to be Black people as they danced and sang around the stage making fun of Black people while white people laughed," Camille said sadly.

"Mama! You're not supposed to make fun of people! No bullying! That makes people feel bad and we're not supposed to do it!" said Luke forcefully. "You're not supposed to say 'stupid' either!"

"They didn't care about Black people or how they felt, Luke," said Leslie, rolling her eyes upwards in exasperation.

"Calm down, Luke. It's OK. I only said 'stupid' because what these people did, either performing the shows or going to the shows and laughing at the awful ways that Black people were portrayed, was so thoughtless, awful and hurtful that it's one of the few times it's OK to say it.

"They don't have Jim Crow laws anymore. They were outlawed in 1965 when the Civil Rights Act of 1964 became effective. In places outside the south, they didn't pass Jim Crow laws at all but they had what is called 'social custom' that did pretty much the same thing Jim Crow laws did. In those places, separating Black people wasn't actually a law, but the effect of social custom was the same. Black people could not live in certain places, go to certain schools, churches, or be in certain organizations because of social custom," Camille said. "People said they did it because it had always been done that way."

"Why did they think it would be so terrible to be near us, Mama?" asked Luke quietly. "What did they think was wrong with us? Did they think we had cooties or something?"

"Baby Boy, there was nothing wrong with us at all. It was all in their heads. They had begun the bad treatment hundreds of years before, Luke. I think that in order to make it okay in their minds to have us be slaves working for them for free, they had to make us seem like we weren't real human beings. Like maybe we were animals or something different than they were.

"I think the fact that we looked so different from them made it easier in their minds to do that. Over the years it just became cast in stone and even today when things are better, there are still a lot of problems with people treating Black people and brown people poorly. But you are intelligent and smart and funny and kind, Luke. You too, Leslie. Don't ever let anyone make you think otherwise. You hear me?"

"Yes, Mama. We won't," said Luke and Leslie.

"What else, Mama?" asked Leslie quietly.

Camille and Tristan both mentally registered the sound in Leslie's voice. It was as if her feelings were hurt. They both understood. They both knew the feeling. They both realized it was part of the unfortunate baggage of being Black in America. They'd love nothing more than to not have to explain these things to their children. They loved this country, faults and all. But not being truthful with their children about its history now would only set them up for a painful fall later. Better to let them learn it, in context while they were right here in the midst of it, and contextualize it for them, than let them remain ignorant. The parents understood that the world would not always treat kindly the two precious offspring they loved so desperately and had nurtured from the womb. They knew that the best thing they could give them to blunt the inevitable was a strong sense of who they were, who they were a part of, how strengthening and resilient that history was, and how much they were loved, cherished and adored. This was not a conversation any parent wanted to have. Unfortunately, it was one that, as Black parents, they had to have. The sooner the better, in age-appropriate doses. It would continue as they matured.

"Well, Leslie and Luke, thankfully, millions of Black people were courageous enough to move out of the south to the rest of the United States, creating The Great Migration. Even though Black people were still treated pretty badly pretty much everywhere they went, deprived of decent jobs, housing and education, one of the things that made them feel better was things that were familiar to them, like their music, food, family, friends and religion.

"So when they moved to these other places during The Great Migration, they brought along their love of the food they knew. Eventually, much like with Italians bringing pizza or the Chinese bringing Chinese food, they opened places to eat that served their delicious southern food like greens, sweet potatoes, fried chicken, potato salad, bar-b-que. They put new twists on it that blended that with where they were now. They brought their music and their instruments, and not only played the music they knew, but also did the same thing by changing it up some because of the music they heard in the places they went. So the music in their new locations was based on what they knew because they brought it with them, but they mixed it with other things in the place they moved to and created something new.

"The music your Dad likes is the kind of music that the people who lived here in the Mississippi Delta invented, played and sang because he considers it to be the pure form of the blues. People's stories of their everyday lives that help us to understand what their lives were like. When the Great Migration took the people to places like Memphis, Chicago, New Orleans, the music changed some, but your Dad considers the Delta blues to be the real deal. Each place has a version of the blues, but it sounds very different from the original. Your Dad likes the original."

"I don't get it," said Leslie. "I can hardly understand the words they're saying and you can't dance to it," she said, exasperated and rolling her eyes.

Tristan and Camille looked at each other and laughed uproariously.

"Well, Leslie Pooh," Tristan said, using his pet name for his daughter, "When people were not allowed to go to school and they were never taught to speak like you were, that is what they can sound like. Delta blues takes some getting used to, it's true. But I've been listening to it for a long time, so I'm more used to it and understand it. I really don't listen to it for dancing. I listen to it to hear the stories they tell about the singers' lives. It helps me to understand better our history where we are now as a country.

"But, I promise you, when these songs were sung and played years ago, people danced to them just fine. They had a great time dancing in little places called juke joints that were usually out in the woods where they could just go and have fun, dance, listen to music, eat, meet people and be with their friends away from the eyes of whites. Sort of like a bar or a nightclub, but not as fancy. And, of course, who wouldn't want to go see people like Robert Johnson, Howlin' Wolf, Blind Lemon Jefferson, Blind Willie McTell, Son House, Charley Patton, Delta Blind Billy?" Tristan said, laughing at the awesome thought of it.

"Huh. Who knew?" said Leslie. "I just thought it sounded like a bunch of no-talking, no dancing noise I couldn't understand and I couldn't figure out why you liked it. I take it those people you named were some of the more famous blues artists back in the day?"

Tristan glanced over at Camille, whose shoulders were shaking with silent laughter when he, too, wanted to laugh, for so many reasons; Leslie's 9-year-old sophistication, them being essentially deemed outdated "old fogies", among other things. He tried to keep his voice steady. "Yes, Leslie, they were famous blues artists."

"Why were so many of the blues people blind, Daddy?" asked Luke.

Once again, Camille and Tristan looked at each other, but this time they couldn't help but laugh out loud.

"Back then, Luke, people called people by names that described them," Tristan said. "It's just what people did back then. It wasn't an insult. If someone was blind, they often learned to play music as a way to earn a living since there were so few jobs Black people were allowed to have and most of those required being able to see because they were farming jobs or manual labor jobs."

"Oh. I'm glad to know that playing the blues didn't make them go blind," Luke said solemnly. Yet another exchange of hidden laughter looks between them, Camille and Tristan stared straight ahead. "What a sweet boy," Camille thought.

"I'm glad we took this trip for spring break," said Tristan. "Seeing this landscape, you're right, Camille, I really do have more of a sense of the desolation and hopelessness that gave birth to the blues. I appreciate it even more now, and I didn't think that was possible," said Tristan, looking at Camille and smiling appreciatively. Both of them knew he was thinking back to his initial reluctance when Camille had first brought up the idea of going to the Mississippi Delta. Tristan smiled remembering their exchange and the occasion of her first bringing it up. Just after a wonderful time under the quilts. "That woman of his," he thought, smiling to himself. "Her and her quilts. But I love every cell in her body."

Tristan was really glad they had come. It was a great opportunity for the kids to learn more about their country, the country they all loved so much. Knowing its true history did not make them love it any less. It just made them understand it more and want to work to make things better.

"Thank you, Sweet Girl. This was a great idea," said Tristan softly to Camille. She squeezed his hand, giving him a loving look of appreciation in return.

"Leslie and Luke, can you imagine having to get up before daylight every morning and get ready and get out to these fields where you'd have to pick cotton until you couldn't see anymore after sunset? Blazing hot? It didn't matter. Sick? It didn't matter. Having a baby? Drop it in the field and keep picking. You're just a little kid? Didn't matter. In fact, if you were a kid going to school, when the cotton was ready to be picked, you had to stop going to school and go to the fields and pick cotton. Period. All that mattered was that the cotton got picked. Period. No questions asked."

"They didn't have to go to school, Daddy?!" Luke said excitedly.

"No, Luke, they didn't have to go to school. But that's not a good thing. It meant not only that they missed school and fell behind in their studies, but also that they had to be out in the fields all day in the blazing sun picking cotton.

"That's what happened to my Granddad, said Camille. After slavery ended, my family was cotton sharecroppers in North Carolina. My Grandad had to leave school when it was time for the cotton to be picked. When they moved north during The Great Migration, my Grandad was academically behind the other kids his age in school because he'd had to keep stopping each year to pick cotton. So he was bigger and older but in a class with younger kids instead of the kids in his age group. He was really embarrassed. But he didn't let it stop him. He kept going to school and eventually got his college degree.

"With my Grandad, who lived in Oklahoma, then Texas" said Tristan, "he wanted to be a teacher. So, he got a college degree, which was not easy for a Black person back then, and was certified to be a teacher. As part of The Great Migration he moved to California, a place where he thought he would be able to have a chance at a better life. Because of his race he couldn't get hired as a teacher, even though he was certified."

"So, what did he do, Daddy? Did he starve because he couldn't buy any food because no one would give him a job?" asked Luke sadly.

"No, Luke. He became a delivery truck driver for Kraft Foods."

"What?!!" exclaimed Leslie. "A delivery truck driver when he had a college degree and teaching credentials?!!"

"Yes, Leslie. That happened to many, many Black people during that time. The truth is, unfortunately, it still happens today, far more than people realize."

"But, that's so *unfair!*" said Leslie.

"You're right, Baby Girl. It is unfair. But, it's the world we live in. The best we can do is everything we can to prepare you for it," said Tristan.

The air was thick with a sober processing of what had just been said. Tristan finally broke their reverie.

"So, to show you how good can come out of a bad situation, Troops," Tristan said, "Like your Mama said, there were pretty serious consequences if the cotton pickers did not pick as much cotton as the overseer, who was the person in charge, thought should be picked. The person who could pick the fastest was often out ahead of everyone else and to pass the time, he just started making up songs about what he knew. That's how the blues started.

"People who picked cotton went to the juke joints on the weekends to have a little fun after working so hard, having such hard lives and often being treated so badly, so disrespectfully all week. Their lives were hard and there seemed to be no hope for anything better, so they got together at the juke joints and lived it up having fun. They liked the blues songs because they could relate to them since the songs were about their lives. Someone was singing what they lived every day and it just grew from there."

"I guess it never really stopped growing did it, Daddy?" Leslie piped up.

"What do you mean, Baby Girl?" Tristan said.

"Well, we learned in music class that that was sort of the way that hip-hop and rap music started. The people just sang about what they knew," said Leslie.

"Well, I guess you're right, Leslie Pooh!" said Tristan. Great connection!

"Both my Great-Granddads moved from where people treated them mean, to find better places to live better, huh?" said Luke.

"Yes, Luke! That's right!" Tristan said. "Another great connection!"

"Yay! Yessss!" Luke said, giving an enthusiastic air fist pump. "It's a great connection! We're famous! We were part of the Great MY-GATION!!"

CHAPTER 26

"Is this it? Are we sure? What a very different, quaint little place!" Camille said as Tristan pulled the car up to a long, low corrugated rusting-iron-roofed building off the main highway that looked like a cross between an old barn on an industrial scale, and a dilapidated, rusted building.

"That's one way to characterize it," murmured Tristan, pulling the car to a stop in what he supposed was the entrance. It was hard to tell. "Hold on a minute," Tristan said as everyone began unbuckling their seat belts and preparing to get out. "Let me go in and check it out first. I'm not sure this is the entrance."

Tristan got out and walked to what looked like a door. He pulled it open. To his surprise, the inside was wide open and looked like it had been, maybe a cotton ginning building that had been renovated and was now a quaint little few-room hotel. Huge cotton sacks like Tristan had seen in photos of cotton picking were hung around, as were old metal soft drink signs and feed, seed, and grain signs from back in the day. Stairs went around the walls and led, Tristan supposed, to the rooms that had been built upstairs around the top inside of the building.

A door near Tristan opened and a man came out dressed in coveralls. "You the folks from the midwest we been expectin'?" he said in a friendly southern drawl. Tristan didn't realize how tense he felt until the man spoke. This was, after all, Mississippi, and he was Black.

"Yes," said Tristan. "My family is out in the car. I thought I'd better check it out first. It doesn't look like any hotel we've ever been in, so I needed to see if we were in the right place."

"Ha ha," he chuckled. "We get that a lot. But you're in the right place, alright. Got your reservation right here. Tristan, Camille, Luke and Leslie, right? Two nights, maybe more?" he said.

"Yes. That's us. Here's my drivers' license and credit card."

"Shucks. We don't need that. I own the place so I get to call the shots. You look like a man I can trust. You already gave it online. It's for sure certain that nobody came in here to pretend they were you, with some little ones. What you gave when you booked online is just fine. Now let me show you the rooms," he said, moving around to the front of the counter Tristan hadn't even noticed because it blended in so well with the surroundings.

"I guess you're wondering what this is. Like you said, it don't look like any hotel you ever stayed in before. The building used to be a ginning mill where you took raw cotton from the field and ginned the seeds out of it and had it bundled into blocks and covered in canvas for shipment. You probably seen something like that in a movie or something. Well, it was real. That's what this place was.

"Then later it was a commissary for the folks who lived on the plantation and needed to buy things. You drove in, so I guess you folks noticed that there's not an awful lot of commerce around here. Just cotton really, except at the junction of Route 49 and 61 on the highway.

"Yes, I noticed," Tristan murmured. The hotelier was clearly on a roll, so Tristan didn't want to interrupt the repartee that he clearly enjoyed imparting to guests. But, the mention of a plantation had definitely registered with Tristan. And not in a good way.

"You know they say that's where the greatest Delta Blues man, Robert Johnson, met the devil, made a pact with him and sold the devil his soul so he could be famous. Of course, I don't know if it was true or just some silly folklore tales people think up because they're stuck out here and don't have nothin' better to do. Or they were jealous of his success. But it's stuck to this day.

"I'm sure it's horse pucky, but people still come from all around to see the junction. And he sure did get famous. Guitar pickers are still trying to figure out how he got the sound to come out of his guitar with just his regular fingers instead of two hands."

"Wow. That's quite a story."

"Well, our family had this building and when there weren't as many people needing the commissary because machines took over a lot of the things they used to do with the cotton, people who worked the cotton moved up north and whatnot. So, of course, we closed it down. But people from all over never stopped being interested in the Junction and coming to see it. Our building was just sitting there unused and there was no hotel where the Junction visitors could stay, so we decided to make it one.

"I did most of the renovation and my wife did most of the decoration, curtains, quilting, and such. We think it looks right homey for visitors," the owner said proudly, slipping his thumbs under his overall straps. Tristan could swear the man stuck out his chest with pride.

"Oh! Your wife quilts?" Tristan said brightly, realizing what the owner had said. "Mine too."

"Oh! Well, she'd probably want to see this, then, he said, picking up a postcard from a stack on the counter. It's just right up the road. As long as you're here and she likes quilts, it's worth a stop-by."

"Thanks," said Tristan, taking the postcard from the owner's outstretched hand.

"Alright. You folks just bring your bags in and take them upstairs to the room at the top of the stairs and the one next to it," he said, pointing up at two doors at the top of the stairs.

"Is there anywhere around to get a bite to eat? You don't serve meals, right? We didn't pass anything on the way in," asked Tristan as he headed to the door.

"No. Cookin' would be too much on us. We just have the few rooms here and that's enough to clean up and stay on top of. There's a place not far away at all. In fact, you may even have heard of it. It's owned by a real famous colored guy who does movies. Freeman. Morgan Freeman. His blues café is just up the road, not far."

"Oh! I'm glad we're close by! I wanted to visit his place. Is it open now or only at night? Is it OK for my children to go or is it only for adults?"

"Oh, shucks, sure it's open and kids are welcome. They'd like pretending that they're performing on the stage, I bet. He has it set up for them to be able to do that."

"Great! Well, thanks—we've been chatting up a storm here and you know my name but I don't know yours," Tristan said, suddenly aware he could not put a name to his thanks.

"Hal. Hal Ikens. My wife's Dora Mae Ikens. Ever'body around here knows us. The Delta's really a pretty small community, really. Just tell 'em Hal Ikens sent you and they'll treat you right."

"Thanks, Hal. I'll go get my family and get us settled in our rooms and go find us something to eat. I'm pretty excited to see Morgan Freeman's Blues café. I love blues, so I'm really looking forward to it.".

"Well, there's not likely to be anyone playing at this time of the day, but you can still see the place and get a bite to eat. If you want to go back at night when it's more of a club than a café, me and the Missus will be happy to keep an eye on the kids for you. That is, unless they're old enough to look after theirselves."

"That's a very kind offer, Hal. We might just do that," said Tristan.

"'Colored?'" thought Tristan incredulously as he opened the door to go out and retrieve his family and luggage. That was a term he hadn't heard in longer than he could remember. "I thought that term pretty much died after the 1964 Civil Rights Act was passed," he thought. Well, he was in Mississippi after all. The Mississippi Delta, at that. The owner seemed friendly enough, but it was a reminder to Tristan of where he was and to not let down his guard. Old habits die hard.

CHAPTER 27

"Oh, my, Tristan! Look at the quilts on the beds! They are gorgeous!!" Camille breathed upon opening the doors to their rooms.

"Oh, I forgot to mention that Hal Ikens, the owner, gave me a postcard that advertises a quilt place and he said it's just right up the road. Not far at all."

"Really?! What an unexpected surprise! I want to make sure we do that!" Camille exclaimed, genuinely delighted. This was more than she bargained for. She came looking for quilt answers, not quilts, but….if the two happened to coincide….well, she didn't mind a bit!

"Yes, but we need to feed the kids first," said Tristan. "We can unpack and explore when we get back. We're all pretty hungry."

"Sure thing! Be ready in a jiffy! I'll check on the kids," Camille said as she headed out to the room next door.

"Tristan, where in the world *are* we?" said Camille, frustration edging her voice. "GPS is doing us no good here. We've been following the directions, but we still don't see it and it is so disorienting to have nothing but flat land in every direction, with no streets, street signs, and just one long road in and out. Hal said that if we got to the correctional facility, we'd have gone too far, but we've been there and turned around three times now. I am so confused. This is frustrating. Thank heaven the kids drifted off to sleep after lunch, so they aren't bugging us about passing by the same thing three times.

"Look, Tristan, I know it doesn't look like much, but it's the only thing we see on this godforsaken lonesome road. Just take that turn. The sign is so low to the ground that you wouldn't even notice it, but maybe it's the Delta's version of a street sign or something or there's someone who can tell us something, if we take the turn. I don't see anything else on this road we can do. I don't see anything in that turn either, but it's a turn, so let's take it," said Camille. "We can always turn around if it doesn't prove fruitful. This is frustrating."

Tristan took the left, drove straight ahead. They were surprised to see a couple of low, unobtrusive buildings that, oddly enough, they would never have been able to see from the road, even on this flat landscape. On the left side of the street was a totally dilapidated building that looked like it had been a clapboard house at one point. Now, however, the roof was totally caved in and the building looked dangerous, like it would fall over at any moment. When Tristan pulled over in front of the building because he could go no further, he and Camille were shocked to see an historic marker outside the driver's side door, in front of the building that looked like a strong wind would do it in.

"What in the world could that historic marker be out here in the middle of nowhere in front of this dilapidated house?" Camille breathed.

"We may as well get out and see," Tristan said, opening his car door.

When they stood in front of the sign, they were both shocked to see that it said that this was the house to which Emmettt Till was brought after he was found in the Tallahatchie River. It had been a funeral home then. This is where Emmettt Till's body had been prepared for shipment back to his mother in Chicago after being heinously murdered by two white men in 1955. The men were tried and acquitted by an all white jury, yet sold the story of what they had done in committing the murder to *Look* magazine mere months later. The murder and its aftermath were worldwide news and re-ignited the Civil Rights movement that resulted in the passage of the Civil Rights Act of 1964.

"What?!!" Tristan and Camille said in unison as they stood there not believing their eyes and turning to look at each other. They had no idea they were in Emmett Till country. They were both speechless. And a bit apprehensive. Tristan thought back to Hal, the hotel owner, calling Morgan Freeman 'colored.' It did not feel good. He had not told Camille about it. Best not to worry her unnecessarily. Tristan's mind went to his brother-in-law, Brian and how he would react in such a place. It brought a smile to his face, even in this serious, totally unexpected, setting.

Camille turned around to see if there was anyone they could talk to. She looked across the narrow street. A nondescript low brick building stood directly across from the funeral home—or what had been the funeral home. In front of the building was a woman standing by a school bus. Camille decided to take a chance.

"Hi!" said Camille. Are you from around here? Can I speak to you for a moment, please? If you don't mind, that is," she asked.

The youngish woman looked up, saw Camille and smiled pleasantly, saying "Of course! Are you lost?"

"Well, I'm not sure if we are or not. We're looking for a quilt place. The hotel owner said it was on this road, but we've been up and down the road three times and we can't seem to find it. We finally decided to turn into this street, even though we didn't see any buildings from the road. But when we pulled up in front of the building across the street, we saw the historical marker saying it was where Emmettt Till was brought when they found him in the river in 1955. I just had no idea we were anywhere near such a thing. Frankly, I'm shocked."

"Oh, yes! That's where you are alright. I'm the high school biology teacher, slash, school bus driver," she laughed. "I've stopped to pick up kids from the plantations."

Camille's eyes widened. "What?! What do you mean 'plantations'?"

The woman looked amused at Camille's reaction. "There are still plantations here in the Mississippi Delta. Cotton is still grown on all this land you see around you, and there are still families who live on the land the cotton is grown on—the plantations. I bet you thought those days were long gone, didn't you? You look like it. You looked shocked," she grinned. "Well, those days are most certainly not gone here. It's sort of a time warp. Of course, most of the work is done by industrial machines now, but they still employ lots of people to help with the cotton. And out here, there's not a lot of choice of employment."

Camille just had to ask. She knew this woman didn't know her from Adam's house cat, but this was such an unexpected event, such a unique opportunity, that she simply could not pass it up. She was too much of an academic with an inquiring mind to stay silent.

"Can I ask you something? And I truly don't mean to sound offensive or insulting. I know you don't know me enough to know I'm not mean or just plain clueless. I promise you, I'm not. In fact, I'm a law professor. But, can I ask you: why is it that people stay here? Why are you here? Black people, I mean, given the history of the place and what you describe. I can see it if someone didn't know there was another world out there, but you've obviously been to college, you're educated, and yet here you are. Can I ask your name, if you don't mind? I truly hope I'm not offending you!"

"No! Not at all! Sereta. Sereta Wilkerson. I'm here for the same reason so many of these people are here. I'm here because it's home. It's not all I have ever known as it is with most of them, but it is where my heart is. There is no substitute for home, family, familiarity, even when home has been as oppressive as the Mississippi Delta has. I worked cotton growing up. I know what it feels like. But I work to get my students to see beyond the Delta, to know there are choices.

"Oh, like many before them, people from the Delta have taken off for places like Memphis, New Orleans, or Chicago. But often they come back home. Little beats family, home, even when it leaves much to be desired. Also, you may not have noticed as you were going down the highway because you were busy looking for the quilt place, but there are buildings now named for Emmett Till. There's even an Emmett Till museum just down the road. People haven't forgotten what happened here. These folks are resilient. You have to be in order to live here. But generation after generation have stayed here no matter what was dished out to them."

"Well, Sereta, I have to tell you, this is so much more than we bargained for when we went looking for the quilt place. You have given us such an insightful lesson," Camille said. Tristan nodded in agreement, adding, "Absolutely."

"Oh, that reminds me! I think this is the place you're looking for! It's the Community Center. The Tutwiler Quilters meet here, along with people from the community. They quilt here and have quilts and other items for sale."

"What?!! Are you serious?! This is the place we were looking for?! I would never have known it if you hadn't told me! This was meant to be! It wasn't clear from the postcard that advertised it didn't say whether it was a quilt store, a quilt shop, or what," she said as she held out to Sereta the hotel's postcard advertising the quilt place.

"Yes, that's this place," said Sereta, looking at the postcard.

"Now, I see why it wasn't clear what it was. It's a community center that sells quilts the Tutwiler Quilters and people in the community make. Awesome! Thank you! I can't wait to see them! Thank you so much for taking the time to speak with us, Sereta. We really appreciate it. What an incredible lesson you've given us. It's not biology, but it sure is important for us! You really *are* a teacher!" Camille laughed.

"You are so welcome. And thank you for your very kind words. I appreciate them," Sereta said as she stepped back up onto the school bus.

Tristan and Camille checked on the sleeping kids, but did not want to awaken them since they did not know what was inside the building, or even if it was open right now. The hours were not on the postcard. They made sure the windows were down a tad to allow for air circulation. They were pretty sure that the kids would be safe in this spot that did not have traffic and the building was so close and obviously not a large one they would get lost in. Tristan opened the door to the low brick building, allowed Camille to walk in and followed in behind her. They found themselves in an open space with fabrics, posters, quilted items including potholders, table runners, and, of course, and much to Camille's delight, quilts and women who were doing all stages of quilting.

"Oh, my," Camille breathed. "Quilting in the Mississippi Delta. I am in absolute heaven." Tristan squeezed her hand, knowing her delight.

As they came in, a rather officious-looking woman stood up from her quilting project and quickly strode across the room toward Tristan and Camille. She smiled and held out her hand.

"Well, hey there! I'm Gertrude Hudson. Y'all come to see the quiltin'?"

"Yes," said Camille, taking her offered hand enthusiastically. "I'm Camille and this is my husband, Tristan. When Tristan checked into the hotel not far from here, Hal, the owner, gave him a postcard for this place and we thought we'd stop by. I'm an avid quilter and quilt collector. Tristan told me Hal said that his wife Dora Mae quilted as well."

"Oh, I'm so delighted that Hal did that! Oh, yes, we know Hal and his wife, Dora Mae, quite well. Dora Mae is an avid quilter and comes to the center often to enjoy the company of other quilters as they all work on their projects."

"We saw her beautiful work on the quilts on our beds today!"

"Well come in, come in, do look around all you want. We have quilters here who have been quiltin' since long before we had a nice place to do it. They got together in their homes and made not only their own quilts, but helped with the quilts of others. There's probably not a quilt in this county and the surrounding ones that hasn't been touched by our hands in some way. We have quilters going way way back."

"She talkin' 'bout me, I reckon," came a strong, steady voice from the corner closest to the door. Seated behind a lap quilting frame was a stark, white-haired older woman who sat ramrod straight in her chair as she quilted. Camille was envious. In her mind she could see her own self slumped over her quilting. Or at least it would seem that way compared to this much older woman's posture. She made a vow to herself to try to do better.

"Talitha Goodhue's the name. I was born in 'de year of our Lord nineteen-hunnert and forty-one. I be eighty-two on my next birf'day, May 19. I was borned on 'de Goodhue Plantation and I still live d'ere today. I seen a lot in all 'dose years an' if it warn't for quiltin', I think I might have done lost my mind. I say 'Quiltin' keep me sane.'"

"Oh, Ms. Talitha, you're fine," laughed Gertrude heartily.

Ms. Talitha gave Gertrude a withering, annoyed look that said Ms. Talitha was old enough to know perfectly well what she was talking about.

"Ms. Talitha, I can't believe it! That is exactly the same thing *I* say!!" exclaimed Camille, as much to inform as to ward off apparent nascent ill feelings between Gertrude and Ms. Talitha. It was pretty clear this wasn't new. Camille glanced over at Tristan knowingly. He returned her look. He had posted himself by the nearby door so that he could keep an eye on their sleeping children.

"Yep, I seen a mighty heap o' things in 'dis here life, but I just keeps a quiltin' right th'ough it. Many womens has come and many womens has gone, but I'm still here a' quiltin'. I kin 'member nigh 'bout ever quilt I or anybody else ever made. And that's a lot o' quilts. But 'dey becomes a part o' you, you know? You spend so much time wit' 'em, you be so close to 'em. You just knows 'em. Like your own chil'lun. I don't forgets any quilt I laid my hand to, and I been a' quiltin' since I were knee high to a grasshopper."

A look passed between Tristan and Camille. Tristan knew exactly what Camille was thinking. He excused himself and quickly went to the car, made sure the kids were okay, quietly took The Wandering Quilt out of the trunk and went back into the building.

Camille looked relieved when Tristan returned with the quilt. It warmed her heart to know that he knew her so well and supported her so completely. She did the same for him.

"Ms. Talitha, we actually came into the Community Center almost totally by accident. During Spring Break, my husband, children" —-at the mention of the word 'children' Camille looked at Tristan in a panic at the thought that they'd forgotten about them being asleep in the car. Tristan knew exactly what her face was about and nodded his head and indicated that they were fine. Drawing herself back into the conversation, Camille continued. "Well anyway, we decided to take a trip to try to track down the maker of this quilt. We are pretty sure it was made in the Delta, but we don't know who made it or even where in the Delta it was made. We weren't exactly sure where to go, but we came across your quilting Community Center through Hal giving us a postcard advertising it."

"'Ho-tel Hal'?" Ms. Talitha chuckled.

"Yes Mam," Camilled giggled. "We searched for the quilt place but couldn't find it and turned into what was, I guess, a street, and ended up right here and the teacher/bus driver told us this was the quilt place we were looking for. So here we are. We have no reason to connect you with this quilt, but can we please show it to you to see if you know anything about it or have seen it before or know who made it?"

"Sho', Chile'. Ain't gon' hurt nothin' for me to take a look at what you got. Where did you get it from?" inquired Ms. Talitha.

"We bought it last summer on the way through South Carolina while on vacation. We took the children on a road trip to see parts of the country they hadn't seen before." Tristan handed one side of the quilt to Camille as she chatted and they unfolded the quilt and shook it out for Ms. Talitha to be able to fully see. They looked over at Ms. Talitha to see if the quilt looked at all familiar to her.

That's when they saw the look of pure unadulterated terror on Ms. Talitha's face. Ms. Talitha looked like a cross between nervous and scared to death. Her hands that had been working on her quilting as she talked, were suddenly fluttering like little bird wings.

CHAPTER 28

"Ms. Talitha! Are you OK?" Gertrude and Camille said at the same time.

"Water! Water! Someone get some water!" said Gertrude through tight lips, clearly trying to stay calm in the midst of this totally unexpected turn of events.

One of the quilters quickly appeared with a glass of water. Ms. Talitha eagerly grasped the offered glass and gulped it as if she was on fire. Within minutes, she began to resume her composure.

Tristan stood at alert. Although he looked completely calm, he was totally focused on looking for signs that only a doctor would quickly recognize as serious distress needing his intervention as a medical professional. At Ms. Talitha's age, that was a distinct possibility. As an emergency room surgeon, he was used to seeing the full range of possible signs and he would move in and deal with it if it was called for. But Ms. Talitha seemed to be rallying.

"Ummm.......Ms. Talitha? I take it you know this quilt?" asked Camille after Ms. Talitha had downed the water, gathered herself and regained her composure.

Ms. Talitha straightened her spine, looked straight at Camille, and said, "Oh, yes, Mam. I knows 'dis here quilt. I was jes' a young thing when it were made. I was 14 year-old. I helped make it. I say 'dat quiltin' keep me sane. But I think 'dat what *she* tried to do. But, it were hard to do. To stay sane, I mean. All the quiltin' in 'de world warn't gon' erase from her mind what she done."

"What do you mean, Ms. Talitha?" asked Tristan gently, in a low and soothing voice. "Who are you talking about?"

Ms. Talitha's face clearly looked like she was fighting several emotions. She seemed fearful, like she was going to say something she shouldn't make known. At the same time, she looked defiant, courageous and strong, as if she knew that what she shouldn't say should be said and she was going to do it. Seconds passed while they stared at Ms. Talitha, waiting for her response. At last, she spoke.

"'Dat boy what were visitin' from up norf ain't nevah do to her what she said in court 'dat shoulda got him kilt' like 'dat. It were awful. Horr'ble. It scairt' me to deaf' when it happen 'cause he was 'zackly 'de same age as me. 'Dat part of why it struck me so hard. He were my age. Jes' a young thing. He jes' didn't do nothin' so awful 'dat he shoulda' died at all and surely not like 'dat. Made all us chil'lun so scairt 'cause we all knowed 'dat if 'dem mens came in to his great-uncle, Rev. Mose Wright's house in 'de middle o' 'de night and took-ed 'dat boy right out and warn't nothin' his own uncle Mose Wright, a preacher, and respected person 'roun here, could do, 'den warn't *none* of us chil'lun safe. Our mammas and pappas couldn't do *nothin'* if white mens wanted to come right into our house in 'de middle o' 'de night and take us off in 'de night. Awful!

"'De only reason I can think of she lied like 'dat was 'cause her husband and his brother made her do it. It don't make no sense otherwise. She started workin' on 'dat quilt right after it happen, just' afore 'de trial started. We pieced 'de blocks by hand in 'de store when 'dey wasn't no peoples in to buy things. She try to seem okay, but I could see her hands a'shakin' and she keep a'lookin' 'round, scairt' like. I knowed she was nervous. She were not okay. She got more and more nervous as 'de time come for 'de trial.

"Humph! Trial. Even us chil'luns' knowed a trial was a joke. We lived in 'de Mississippi Delta and it were 1955. Colored didn't have no law helpin' 'em. We hear'd our folks and 'dey friends a' talkin'. 'Dey say 'dem white mens warn't nevah gonna send no white man to jail for killin' no colored boy in Mississippi. And 'dey wouldn't let de colored be on 'de jury. Huh! You kiddin' me? Nevah!" she said vehemently, stonily, looking straight ahead, off into the distance, as if the others were not even there. "It just couldn't happen back 'den. 'De white folks wouldn't let it.

"It were a hist'ry-making day when Rev. Mose Wright, stood up in 'dat courtroom an' pointed his finger at 'dem white mens and say 'dey's 'de ones what come and got 'dat po' boy, his own flesh an' blood, out'en his house in 'de middle o' 'de night and he ain't never seed 'dat boy no more till 'dey come get him to go see 'de body what 'dey done pulled outten 'de river three days later. 'Dat po' boy was so messed up till de onliest way Mose Wright could be sho' it were him was by seeing 'dat boy Daddy ring on his finger. 'Dat boy so proud o' 'dat ring. He say he begged his Mama to let him take it wid' him when he came souf' from Chicago and she did. Good thing she did.

"When Rev. Mose Wright did 'dat, 'dat were 'de first time a colored man got up in 'de court and testified against a white man in 'de souf. You couldn't do it or 'dey kill you for sure' Nobody 'roun here nevah seed Mose Wright again. He knew 'dat testifyin' was like signing his deaf' warrant, so he took off for up norf' after he said 'dat in 'de court an' nevah come back here again. Shame 'dat man had to leave his famb'ly, his farm, his church, his friends an' all he ever knowed and loved. A real shame. But 'dat 'de Delta for you.

"I hear'd tell 'de only reason it took 'dem jury mens long as it did to come back and say let 'dem mens go was 'cause dey figured 'dey better drink a Coke-Cola to make it look like 'dey thought it over. Peoples and newspaper folks from out of town was in 'de courtroom, you know," she said the sentence as she leaned forward conspiratorially. She then leaned back and sat straight up and said fiercely, "But, 'dey didn't think it over. Wasn't nothin' to think *about*. 'Dey was nevah gonna convict a white man for killin' no colored boy. Nevah! 'Den 'dey let 'dem mens go, and 'de mens turn right 'round and sol' 'de story of what 'dey done to 'dat po' boy to *Look* mag'zine. 'Dey whole story, 'dey confession, in *Look* mag'zine! Dem mens got *paid* for it! It were like someone got paid for murderin' a 14-year-old boy! Warn't nothin' nobody could do,'dey said, 'cause 'dey had had a trial and 'dey was set free and couldn't be tried again, even 'do 'dey said 'dey done it, right in 'de mag'zine for all to see. Like 'dey was *proud* o' what 'dey done! 'De folks say coudn't nothin' be done to 'dem 'cause it were some kind o' double somethin.'"

"Double jeopardy?" Camille asked gently.

"Yes, Mam. Yes'm, 'dat it. 'Dat what 'dey done say, double jeppidy.

"You can't find *Look* no more 'dese days. I think 'dey musta' stopped puttin' it out a while back. I ain't seed it in years. I wasn't lookin'. But it used to be a big-time mag'zine, even in 'de Delta. Lots o' pictures to look at. Didn't nobody buy it, o'course. We didn't have no money. But 'de barber shop always have a copy and 'dey let us look at it. We didn't believe we could go out to 'dat big 'ol world out 'dere, but we could look at some pictures. Purty pictures too. So we like'ed 'de mag'zine.

"But 'den *Look* ma'azine paid 'dem mens for 'dey story and 'dem men's sat right 'dere and said what-all 'dey done to 'dat po' boy. Do 'dat sound right to you?" Ms. Talitha asked no one in particular. "Ain't none of us looked at *Look* mag'zine since. If 'dey went out o' business, good riddance. Good riddance to bad rubbish. Humph!" she said, huffing, her thin chest heaving, as she angrily turned her head away.

"I say quiltin' keep me sane. But I believe yo' energy go into ever' stitch you makes in a quilt. I nevah works on a quilt when I'm angry or scairt' or mad 'cause I believe 'de quilt will pick it up and pass it on to 'dose 'dat lays under it, jes' like 'de good feelin's you put into it do. Peoples can feel it when 'dey use 'de quilt. It make you feel good and warm and com'fable knowing somebody took 'de time to make it. I nevah felt good 'bout 'dis here quilt. I lived on my Marster' plantation and was just a chile' Marster loaned out to Ms. Carolyn to help her with 'dis here quilt. White peoples did 'dat to colored peoples in 'dose days. Peoples thought slavery was over a hundred years before, but 'dat weren't so in 'de Delta. Colored peoples was still treated like 'dey was slaves.

"Ever'body knowed I was good wif' a needle and thread since I was knee high to a grasshopper, so Marster sent me to help her when she need somebody. I don't know iffen' she paid him somethin' for it. Didn't pay me a red cent. I just done what I was told. Marster tell me to help her, I helps her. 'Dat 'dat. He send me to help her plenty o' times.

"I just felts like Ms. Carolyn was tryin' to quilt her evil doin' away. Ever'body 'round knew 'dat boy didn't do what she said he done, puttin' his hands on her and sayin' 'dose nasty things to her. Whistlin' at her. 'Dey was all kinda stories 'bout it. It just didn't make no sense. I knowed he warn't borned here, but he warn't crazy. An' one day I hear'd her and her mister talkin' 'bout it too. Mr. Roy Bryant. He knowed it didn't happen, but him and his brother wanted to 'keep the niggers 'round here in line,' dey said. 'Dat brother, J.W. Milam, were his name, he was a plantation overseer, you know. He had a rep'tation for keepin' de colereds in line. 'Dey wanted to keep us in line, so Ms. Carolyn said what she said in court on 'dat witness stand. 'Den she wanted to quilt away her lyin' 'bout what 'dat boy done to her 'dat made 'dem jury mens say 'dem mens could go free even tho 'dey kill 'dat po' boy and ever'body knowed it.

"All of 'dat got sewed right into 'dat quilt and 'dey's no way it got out. I don't care where it went or who owned it or how many times 'dey washed it. 'Dat quilt got 'dat woman's bad feelin's inside it 'cause 'dat what she sewed right into it. To tell de truf', I wouldn't be s'prise' if some o' my scairt' feelings got into 'dat quilt too. I don't quilt when I feels bad in my spirit, but I had to do whatever Marster say. I had to help her wit' 'dat quilt. But I was a chile' and I was scairt' 'de whole time. Things was bad 'roun here 'den. I'm sorry iffen' it got into 'de quilt and made it feel bad."

"Ms. Talitha, it's funny you should say that," Camille said slowly. "When I bought this quilt in South Carolina, the store owner told me it is called The Wandering Quilt because people kept bringing it back to him saying it didn't feel right. I decided to try to track down what the issue was and we found on the inside of the quilt trim, an inscription in permanent ink that said "E.T. I lied. I'm sorry. C.B.""

"'Dat were Carolyn Bryant! Had to be! Had to be!" Ms. Talitha said emphatically in a strong, agitated, forceful voice.

"Now that I think about it," said Camille excitedly, "one of the people who bought the quilt and returned it, an elementary school art teacher named Jenniffer Jones, told me that she thought Sarah Marsden's aunt may have been named Carl Barnes. She said it had been a really long time, but she thought that was the name. She said she remembered it because she couldn't remember who told it to her, but the way they pronounced it made her visualize a cow barn. She thought it was strange for a female name, but said she'd gotten used to strange things in the south. I never followed it up after I didn't find a female Carl Barnes anywhere."

"'Dat her! 'Dat her! I *know* 'dat her! She must'a done writ 'dat in 'dere after we was finished wit' 'de quiltin' an' 'de border, an' was sewin' on 'de trim an' she was closin' her part o' 'de trim, 'cause I didn't see it on any part I work-ed on. An' let me tell you, I worked all *over* 'dat quilt from 'de start right up to 'de end. Matter fact, I sewed on a lot o' 'dat border trim myself," said Ms. Talitha. "An' I *sho'* didn't write nothin' in it!" she said, with an emphasis that sounded very much like she was responding to an accusation. One that, of course, had never been made.

"'Den after we finish makin' and quiltin' it after all 'dose months, she give it to 'dat boy an' his colored wife for a weddin' present when 'dey got married-up. She had me run it over to 'em. I didn't want to, 'cause ever'body knowed he was mean an' always beatin' on 'dat poor little colored girl. But, I am mighty glad to say 'dat he warn't to home when I got 'dere. Neither one of 'em was. So, I just left it on 'dey porch. I knowed 'dey got it 'cause 'de colored girl come by to thank Ms. Carolyn while I was 'dere. Ms. Carolyn tried to hurry her off so's nobody would see 'dat colored girl at her door. Ms. Carolyn gived it to 'dem, but was tryin' to almost act like she didn't. I guess wif 'de husband famb'ly givin' her such a hard time 'bout it 'cause 'dey don't like 'dat 'dat boy married 'dat colored girl, Ms. Carolyn sho' didn't want no one else to know she gived it to 'em. Not to a colored girl and not to a man 'dat what married-up wif' a colored girl. It don't matter she look white.

"I hear'd tell 'dat a hist'ry man wrote a book a few year back sayin' Ms. Carolyn tol' him she was lying on 'de court stand, under 'de oath what 'dey swear 'dey's gonna tell 'de court 'de truf' 'bout what done happen. He say she tol' him she lied on 'dat stand 'bout what 'dat little boy done to her. She tol' him she can't 'member 'zackly what happen, but she knowed it warn't what she said on 'dat court stand. She reached out to 'dat hist'ry man after she seed a book he writ 'bout another murder sorta like 'dis one. It were 'de first time in all 'dose years she ever talk a word to anybody 'bout 'dat stuff 'ceptin' her fam'bly.

"Some folks said 'dis warn't no confession 'cause she say she didn' tell 'dat hist'ry man she lied. But what sense do 'dat make? Why 'dat hist'ry man gon' go put somethin' in a book what ain't true? Peoples get dragged up to court for 'dat. Even I know 'dat. He ain't call her! She call him! What sense do it make for him to go an' lie 'bout what she done tol' him? 'Dat hist'ry man ain't make up no lie like 'dat 'bout 'dat woman! 'Dat don't even make no sense!" At this, Ms. Talitha rolled her eyes, sucked in her tongue with a loud smacking sound, turned her head away from the quilt and crossed her frail, bony arms over her chest.

"Dey ain't stopped lying 'bout all 'dat mess even to 'dis day," Ms. Talitha said, sounding totally disgusted.

"I am so sorry you had to go through that, Ms. Talitha," said Tristan, deep sincerity clearly sounding in his voice. "That must have been awful for you as such a young child. I cannot believe that we just happened upon you, Ms. Talitha. This is so incredibly random! What are the chances? All we knew was that the quilt may have been made in the Delta, but we didn't know who made it. We didn't have a name. We didn't have a place. To happen to come in here to see the quilts because of a postcard Hal gave us and to find you here, and even to be parked right in front of the funeral home where Emmettt Till was put into the casket to be sent to Chicago, is just beyond words. This is incredible. You have helped us so much." Tristan's tone was so sincere that everyone could see how much this meant to him and his wife.

"Well, as you can see, suh, don't nothin' much change in the Delta. We got folks here who 'member a lot o' things. 'Dey try to forget 'em so 'dey can live ever'day, but some things you can't forget. What 'dey done to 'dat po' young boy chile' stayed wif' us for a long time. It *still* wif' us. 'Dey may have a school or whatnot named for him 'roun here now, but just look 'roun'. 'Dey's still plantations. Peoples still be scairt' to leave 'cause it's all 'dey knows and 'dey be 'fraid of what's out 'dere, thinkin' it might be worser 'dan 'dis here. 'Dat's mostly due to 'dem being tol' for so long 'dat 'dey's better off stayin' here 'cause 'de white folks wants 'dem to stay on 'de plantations. But, I don't think 'dat's true, 'dat we better off stayin' here," said Ms. Talitha.

"I knowed in my heart why Ms. Carolyn gave 'dat quilt away to 'dat boy what got married-up to 'dat colored girl what look-ed like she was white, but she colored. I'm sho' 'dat's why Ms. Carolyn gave it to 'dem. 'Dat boy family was real mad at Ms. Carolyn for givin' 'dem anythin' when 'dey gots married-up. 'Why for you givin' somethin' to him when he marry a nigger bitch?' his family tol' her. Ms. Carolyn told me 'dat herself. *She* told me *herself* what 'dey say to her, even tho' I warn't no more 'dan a chile'. She was mightly scair't and upset. 'Dey was mad! 'Specially after what Ms. Carolyn husband and his brother done to 'dat boy to send a message to 'de colored folks in 'de Delta, and 'den 'dey nephew go an' marry-up wif' a colored girl—even tho she look-ed white.

"'Dat man, 'dat nephew— Clyde were his name— he beat 'dat po' little girl so bad. All 'de time. Ever'body knowed it. For years. He beat her till de Lawd took him from 'dis here earf', he did. But mean as he was, I don't know if 'de Lawd kep' him. 'De way he act, he must be wif' 'de devil. 'De white folks sure warn't gonna do nothin' 'bout it. It were just' fine with 'dem if a white man beat on his colored woman. 'Dey didn't think 'dey shoulda' got married-up in 'de first place. 'De colored folks *couldn't* do nothin' 'bout 'dat white man beatin' 'dat little colored girl so bad. 'Dis here 'de Mississippi Delta. Colored folks still to 'dis day don't go against white folks. It's a death wish, fo' sho'. I seen it too many times to count. You got to stay in line, even nowadays, or you pays for it.

"I know I ain't 'posed to say 'colored' no more. But I be eighty-two year ol' on my next birf'day. Colored folks names has changed so much in my lifetime 'dat I just plain lost count. I couldn't keep up wif' it. It gone from 'nigger' to 'colored' to 'Negro' to 'Black' to 'African American.' When 'dey kept changing it, I couldn't keep up. I just went back to 'colored.' Now, I'm so old 'dat peoples 'spect me to say old people things. So, I let 'em think what 'dey wants.

"'De colored folks sure did get 'de message to stay in line when 'dem white mens did what 'dey done to 'dat po' boy. But, I think Ms. Carolyn give Clyde and 'dat colored girl 'dat quilt 'cause she felt bad 'bout what she done 'dat done got 'dat boy kilt. So while ever'body else of 'dem white folks hated dat little colored gal and tried to act like 'dat boy didn't marry-up wit' her, Ms. Carolyn gived 'dem prob'ly 'de only present 'dey got from anybody. 'Dat quilt yonder," she said, pointing her long, thin, gnarled index finger at what Camille and Tristan held in their hands.

"But it don't s'prise me none 'dat nobody wanted to keep 'dat quilt after Clyde died, 'specially his wife. If I was her, knowing what Ms. Carolyn did to get 'dat po' boy kilt, and 'de way her husband fam'bly treat her so bad actin' like 'dey wasn't married, I wouldn' put 'dat quilt on me for nothin' either. Nowhere near me. Naw, suh! No way!

"It don't s'prise me none 'dat 'dat quilt don't feel like it should to peoples, eithuh. I ain't even gonna ask you *how* it don't feel good to 'dem. I been quiltin' for over 70 year. I told you you stitch yo' feelin's right into a quilt. No tellin' how 'dose feelin's come out to 'de person what under 'dat quilt. It don't matter how. What matter is 'dat 'dey know 'dat quilt don't feel right and 'dey needs to get it off 'dem, get it away from 'dem.

"'De Wand'rin' Quilt, you say 'de man tol' you he name it? I *bet* it *wanduh*! I don't even know if 'dat woman—Ms. Carolyn—alive or dead, but eithuh way, I know her soul ain't at rest. An' if she wrote somethin' in 'dat quilt (an' I don't know who else could'a done it) it don't s'prise me none 'dat what feelin's she put in 'dat quilt would be felt till she at peace. I don't know how 'dat gonna happen, so you be careful with 'dat 'ere quilt," she nodded protectively in the direction of Camille and Tristan.

"Ms. Talitha, do you mind if I ask you something?" said Tristan contemplatively as his mind spun with all of her incredible revelations.

"Naw, honey chile, ain't nothing you can ask Ms. Talitha 'dat she scairt' to answer," said Ms. Talitha. She seemed to have gained courage after saying her piece about Carolyn Bryant and the quilt. Like she knew she had done the right thing. "If somebody kill me right now, I had a good, long life. I'm ready to meet my maker any time He want to come for me. I jes' be goin' home. Goin' to Glory." The beatific smile on her face made you think she could actually see in her head the picture of where she was going and it was a very pleasant thought.

"Why did you stay, Ms. Talitha? Why didn't you leave the Delta?" Tristan asked.

"Well, Honey," she said, drawing herself up to her full height and taking in a deep breath, "you ain't got enough time for me to tell you all 'dat. But res' assured, I done thought 'bout it. In fact, more 'dan once. But here I am, eighty-two year ol' on my next birf'day, an' still here in dis' here Mississippi Delta. An' still living on a plantation, at 'dat."

CHAPTER 29

"I can't believe the kids are still asleep in the back seat," said Camille as they quietly opened the doors to get into the car and spoke in low tones. "We only talked to Ms. Talitha about twenty minutes, but it seems like we've just lived a lifetime. I really appreciate you posting up at the door to keep an eye on them while we were in the Community Center. You are such an incredible father. And I love, love, love how you know me so well. You knew to go get that quilt out of the car without me saying a word. Who would have *ever* thought that going into that quilt Community Center would be so productive?!"

Camille took Tristan's hand and squeezed it. He looked at her with pure, unadulterated love in his eyes. He loved this woman so much. It had been her persistence that had brought them to this point. She was so determined. So fearless. So compassionate. So kind. So intelligent. So hardworking. She inspires me to want to be better. To do better, thought Tristan.

"It really is unbelievable, Camille" said Tristan quietly. "I guess sometimes truth really is stranger than fiction. If somebody had told me this had happened, I'm not sure I would have even believed them. What the heck are the chances that we come here to a state to see what we can find out, with not one real lead as to who we're looking for or where to find him or her, and because of a postcard someone gives me at a weird hotel, that has nothing whatsoever to do with what we came for—other than it has quilts you want to see—we end up finding out what we did. Not only who made the quilt, but to actually get to talk to someone who helped her make it. Absolutely unbelievable."

"It truly is, Tristan. One of the things I feel bad about is that all along the way, every time we've found out some helpful piece of this puzzle, it has always left me with questions. It's never just the end of it. Even discovering this incredible piece still leaves questions to be answered. Not the least of which is what we do with what we know. Given who it is who made the quilt, it ought to be easy enough to look on the internet and find out where Carolyn is now, whether she's even still living. I don't know, Tristan. Do you? It happened so very long ago."

"No, I don't know. Of course, I know the story of Emmettt Till's murder and her basic role in it, but I can't say I know a thing about what happened to her afterwards. Outside of it occasionally popping up in the news over the years, I'm not up on it."

"That seemed like such a natural question to ask Ms. Talitha," said Camille. "That is, whether she knew what happened to those folks– Carolyn, her husband, Roy Bryant, and his brother, J.W. Milam, who killed Emmettt Till. But it did not even come into my head. I was so utterly shocked to be able to be sitting there talking to someone who had worked on the quilt and to discover who it is that made the quilt, until I guess I was just mesmerized."

"I guess we both were. It didn't occur to me either. What she said was so totally unexpected, so profound, that I got totally caught up and was only focused on the moment and didn't think to go beyond it."

"You know, Tristan, I totally forgot to tell you about a piece I read in the *L.A. Times* recently. It was a huge, full, 4-column story. It goes right along with what Ms. Talitha said about how when she grew up, Blacks in the Delta still being treated as if they were slaves a hundred years after slavery ended. Only this wasn't even in the Delta. The story was about the 1947 trial of Alfred and Elizabeth Ingalls for holding their maid, Dora Jones, in involuntary servitude for thirty years, ever since she was twelve years old or so. Dora had lived in Boston with them and they took her when they moved to Coronado, California. Dora was forced to perform tasks from morning to night, beaten when she complained, clothed in rags, and paid nothing.

"Not only did they keep her as a slave, but when Elizabeth's first husband got Dora pregant after regularly forcing himself on her for three years, Elizabeth made Dora have an illegal abortion and told her 'You owe me your life now, because you have ruined mine.' Can you imagine?! It was crazy!! Dora died in 1972 at the age of 82, never really having learned to live on her own. The punishment for Dora Jones being held in involuntary servitude for thirty years, Tristan? A $2500 fine and five years probation. Do you believe it? The court also ordered the couple to fork over $6,000 in back pay. $6,000 for working 24/7 for thirty years! It's disgusting. When I think of what the system of slavery did not only during slavery but for years after, especially with Jim Crow, it just makes me sick. And there are so many vestiges from that system, from Confederate flags to our criminal justice system to remaining housing patterns, education, you name it. It is so upsetting that people don't understand the connection and on-going harm these things do."

"Jeez. That is awful!" Tristan replied solemnly. "It really is amazing that this country has had so little in terms of repercussions from all of that, and also an abject avoidance of dealing with the aftermath. Especially since so many vestiges of it linger to this day. I remember that in 2008 and 2009 when Congress and the Senate apologized for slavery, their proclamation did a good job of recognizing that the vestiges of slavery and Jim Crow remain with us in so many ways, including virtually all significant ways we feel such things. You're right. The vestiges remain through jobs, housing, education, healthcare, the criminal justice system, attitudes, and so on. It's so true.

"Whites always want to know why Blacks keep bringing up slavery when it ended over 150 years ago. What they don't seem to realize is how much of what we see today results from concepts, policies, and attitudes set in place during that time. Like attitudes about Blacks' role in society as one of being less than whites. There is not one major indicator I know of that does not reflect those in some way. I read that one of the reasons it took Congress and the Senate so long to even apologize for slavery is the fear of the deadly 'R' word: reparations. They thought if they apologized, the next step would be to have to be accountable for what they had done. That certainly hasn't happened. Except I understand that California is taking a serious look at its role and is looking for real solutions.

"The truth is, I can understand some of the ignorance. Whether we like it or not, people simply don't know what they don't know. Whether we think they should know or not, they often don't. We live in different worlds and my experience has been that often people simply are not operating with the same facts we are; the same experiences that would give them insight. That's totally different than if someone knows of the differences and wants to just treat a group badly based on immutable characteristics. There certainly are those. But, my experience is that, like us, like our family and friends, most people just want to live their lives and go about their day. They don't realize that what they are doing is wrong. That's why education and conversation is so important. How else do you find out?"

"I feel you. We all have work to do, Tristan replied. "But being open to learning is so important. I can sure feel it, even at the hospital with my colleagues. The way they treat non-white patients, staff, even me, at times, in demeaning, dismissive ways, shows me that I'm sure they could benefit from some training about these things. I don't think they do what they do on purpose or even that they are "bad people." They just don't realize they're doing it or why. They need help and don't even realize it.

"As for what we do now about the quilt, given what Ms. Talitha said about Carolyn's involvement, I guess it would only be logical for us to see if she is still alive. If she is, I'm not sure what that would mean for us, but at least we'd have another piece."

"If she's alive, do you think we should contact her, Tristan? See if she wants the quilt back? See if she'd be willing to tell us about the quilt? See if she would be willing to tell us if she put the inscription in it? I mean, it would be silly to deny it, given what it said and that we have a witness who actually helped her make the quilt, so we know they were likely her initials and Emmettt Till's.

"People can be weird. What she did was so heinous that I don't know if she'd even want to revisit it even after so much time has passed. In fact, I'm pretty sure she wouldn't want to. She's managed to keep a low profile all these years. Why wouldn't she? Ms. Talitha said Carolyn Bryant had never spoken to anyone outside her family about the murder until years and years later when she contacted the history man. I can try to find out who that man is. I'll do a search.

"In thinking about this, we also have to think about the issue of us getting into this because a spirit was trying to tell us something. When Tabitha and Paul talked to us, they always acted as if the spirit was of someone who had died. If that's the case, that would mean that if the spirit was, indeed, Carolyn Bryant, then she is no longer alive. But if she is still alive, then what does that do to what Tabitha and Paul told us, what it is they know about spirits?

"Is it possible for people to be alive and feel bad about something and impact it like what happened with the quilt? That is, by making people feel bad under it, pulling it off them, opening up stitches? What a can of worms that would be! If the quilt had been acting weird for at least 30+ years, since before Charlie owned the store, when Sarah first brought it in and it was sold to Gracie Poohks, and only spirits of the dead can do things like make something feel creepy or take out stitches, that would mean Carolyn Bryant died a long time ago.

"But if what Ms. Talitha said about the emotions you stitch into a quilt staying there is true, maybe that's what caused all those things to happen, rather than Carolyn Bryant's dead spirit. Oh, I don't know. I am so confused," Camille said.

"There's another thing we need to think about now that we know this," Tristan said even more quietly, in a voice so low that Camille had to move over closer and strain to hear him.

"What do we tell the kids about any of this? We have always tried to give them the history that we know is real but that they are unlikely to get a good deal of elsewhere. Just like telling them about Jim Crow and The Great Migration, sharecropping and convict leasing on the way here. But this piece is huge.

"Emmett Till's murder is considered the impetus for the energizing of the modern day Civil Rights Movement. His mother, Mamie Till Mobley, refused to be bound by the Mississippi officials' order to not open the box in which his body was sent back to Chicago. She not only opened it, but she insisted on having an open casket funeral so the world could see what Mississippi had done to her beautiful son, now horribly disfigured after he was tortured, shot and left in the river for three days. I saw the photos online a while back. I bet the *Look* magazine article is there too. It was such a violent, brutal killing of such a young boy, until it's hard to know what to tell the kids about it. They're so young. I know we want them to know the reality of history, but I know we also want to give it to them as appropriate for their age. The things we discussed on the way here were historical events about how life was in general for Blacks in the place we are visiting. But this is about a specific fourteen-year-old who was horrifically murdered. There's a difference. They're only six and nine. It's hard to know what to do."

"How in the world did we ever find each other, Tristan? Seriously. Out of nearly eight billion people in the world, we found each other. It was just truly meant to be. We are so incredibly in sync," Camille said, looking into her husband's strong, beautiful face, high cheekbones, firm, well-shaped lips.

"Tristan Wayne Thornton, there is no one in the world I would rather go through this journey of life with than you," she said, looking tenderly at her husband and squeezing his hand, bringing it to her lips, kissing it, then rubbing it on her cheek. "Nobody."

"What in the world brought that on?" Tristan smiled. "That is not the response that I expected out of what it is I just said!" he said, his face showing both confusion and delight.

"Tristan, you know that a big part of what makes our relationship so special is the deep, true, no-holds-barred intimacy between us. It's been there from the very start. I know you know that true intimacy is built on moments exactly like these," Camille said. "Life can be so hard. Having constant reminders that the person you chose to share those hard moments with —and the good times as well— is the right person, is, I think, the true basis for intimacy. True intimacy is built on deep trust. Constant reminders, like the one you just gave about us telling our kids about this, just keep reinforcing that trust, which, in turn, just makes the intimacy deeper and deeper.

"In a way, each time it is added to by acts reinforcing that feeling, it's almost like foreplay. True intimacy is such a turn on. Having my trust in you constantly reinforced by your actions feeds it. Strengthens it. I know it's the same for you. Every kindness, every thoughtful act between us —which we still do all day every day after all these years and never take for granted—becomes an occasion for making us stronger and even more intimate. That's why it's all still so strong even after all this time. It grows. Our attraction to each other is not based on bodies, it's based on our characters, values we share and appreciate about each other. Don't get me wrong now. The body part is awesome. But that is the least of it.

"You are such a good man, Tristan. So decent and ethical, with such integrity and caring and strength. So dedicated and responsible. So compassionate. And so funny! I would trust you with anything, any decision, because even if I didn't agree with it, I'd know you were doing it for the absolutely best reason available. I'd know you know my values, my intelligence, my heart, my concerns, and knowing that they matter to you in the deepest, most profound way. I would also know that in making the decision, you trust me too and know I feel the same way. You love me so. You love the kids so. You love our family so. And you know it's the same for me.

"Your values and mine are so in sync, that me doing what it is you want to do is never me "giving in" to you, it is us deciding together. From the start, being with you never made me feel like there were roles we had to play based on gender. You respected me and what I brought to the table, and I felt the same way about you. But, in a way, it is more valuable to me than you because the default is to men being respected, especially professionally, but that is not necessarily the default with women.

"That's why I appreciated how that was not an issue for you. When I first met you when I was in law school and you were in medical school and we were working together on a university committee representing our respective schools, it was clear that you took me to be an equal. You assumed I was as good and as intelligent as I seemed. That has never changed. Seeing how you operate in the world constantly makes me want to be a better human being. Being with you never drains me; it always fills me up on such a spiritual level, at the heart level. You always make me want to strive to be better, just by being you. Just by the way you go through the world. I absolutely love that. I love that our children get to have that. I couldn't have chosen a better role model for them.

"That's why you are the only man whose name I would have taken in marriage. It didn't matter to you if I wanted to keep my own name. You didn't insist on me taking your name like most men do. But with what you meant to me, the way we were with each other, I *wanted* to do it. I knew that being 'Mrs. Thornton' would not take away at all from me being my own person or represent that I "belonged" to you in some paternalistic, patriarchal way. I knew you understood and respected that. In fact, even appreciated and valued it. You've never let me down. And I love you for it.

"What you said about telling our kids about Emmett Till is precisely how I feel about what to tell the children and when. Let's see how the conversation goes when it comes up and we'll go from there. With those considerations you set out, there's no way we can go wrong."

"Camille," Tristan said softly, "You have always been able to frame things in ways that make so much sense. They are so clear, so comprehensive, so real, so deep. I've never met anyone else in the world who can do that like you can. We're all looking at the same picture, but your framing of it is so incredible, so deep, and so absolutely spot on true when I hear it; but I never would have thought of it that way. It always makes me think about things in such a different, deeper, rather than surface way. It is just one of the very many things I love about you."

Tristan gave Camille an extended, intense look of admiration that could only be safely done on the long, flat, straight Mississippi Delta stretch they were on. Camille returned the look second for second, feeling the tingling in her tummy that always reminded her of the first time Tristan had looked at her with that incredible, incredible smile and she realized she wanted to spend the rest of her life with him, take his last name—something that she had never planned to do upon marrying—and have his babies. She was shocked at her thoughts. They were so unlike her. She'd never felt that way about anyone before. Now, all these years and two kids later, it was all she could do to keep her hands to herself. Her one saving grace was knowing that what she was feeling and knew Tristan was feeling, would not leave, and they would be able to express it later under that beautiful quilt Dora Mae Ikins had made.

CHAPTER 30

"Well, Tristan, I can't say I'm not sorry," said Camille sadly, as she closed out her phone. "I think it really was worth a try to get her to talk to us. After all, we do have a quilt she made. A quilt she likely wrote a secret inscription in that's practically a confession to causing, among other things, a miscarriage of justice and a brutal murder. I wonder if she forgot. But, it doesn't matter. She refuses to talk to us."

"I'm sorry too, Camille," said Tristan. Just our luck that she doesn't want to talk to us. But at least we reached out to her and now we know where she stands. We thought it best to talk to her first so she could verify that the quilt was the one she made and that she wrote the inscription in it. But she doesn't want to speak to anyone regarding the situation. That rules out getting direct evidence of her doing it by her admitting to it. So, what do you think we should do?"

"Well, when I told my mother and sisters on a group cell phone call, they thought the next best thing is to see if we can get in touch with Till's family," said Camille.

"Whoa!" said Tristan. "Really? I'm not sure I would have come up with that. I mean, I know it seems obvious that we would, but somehow, I'd think that was the last thing the family would want."

"Part of me feels the same way, Tristan. I get it. They have lived all these years with the pain of not only what happened to Emmett Till, but also what happened in the criminal justice system. Not only the first time when the all-white jury in Mississippi took less than an hour to return an acquittal, but then what must have been the abject pain of having the defendants be paid for their story of the killing in a well-respected national magazine just a few short months later. Then decades later having the case reopened, having his body exhumed, having the US Department of Justice conduct probes that ultimately went nowhere. Right up to recently, even, with the Department of Justice saying no prosecution was possible just months ago. It's all so much.

"But then, my Mama and sisters were saying that that may be why they would be interested in at least talking to us about it or knowing what it is we discovered, even if they don't want the quilt itself. If they haven't been able to get any sort of justice anywhere else, this might be the only thing they have. This is especially true since they finally located the arrest warrant for Carolyn Bryant in the LeFlore County court basement a few days ago. I couldn't believe the timing. I also couldn't believe they'd never even served the warrant on her in 1955 because they said she had two little kids and they didn't want to bother her. What the hell?!!"

"Yes, I think it does make sense to try to reach out to them," Tristan slowly said contemplatively. "At least they would have a choice. And it would certainly mean more to them than it would to us to have it. But it also means we have to track down the family. Have you come across anything that lets you know whether any of them are still alive now or where they may be living?"

"It should be pretty easy because the news about the arrest warrant being found mentioned family. Everyone in my family said that they would research it and see what they come up with," said Camille. "I'm pretty sure at least several of them are still around because they had been asking for the case to be reopened and then this 'long lost' warrant turns up."

"Even though they're busy preparing for Tess and Renée's wedding?" asked Tristan, surprised.

"Well, they knew I was coming up to finals as well as finishing a research paper I have to present in a few weeks. Besides, you know how Tess has been about this from the moment she told us she and Renée were getting married. She has insisted that they had it all worked out and that it *will* be done their way!" Camille laughed. "If she volunteered to help, I'm not about to say no. Nobody knows better than she does what she has on her plate. She also knows we'll do whatever it is that she needs us to do for the wedding."

"Alllllrighty, then!" Tristan laughed. "I love that Tess's spirit. She is such a force to be reckoned with. Can't wait to see what they come up with! And I'm so, so happy about her being promoted to the offensive coach position at the university. Brian and I can't wait to go to each and every game. We will tease her so bad if they lose a game!" Tristan laughed.

"You'd better not tease her about it! You know what a bear she is when they lose a game. It will be even worse now that she's the offensive coach! As for her wedding format, I can't wait to see what they do either. It's actually sort of exciting," said Camille.

"Tristan, I've been thinking."

"Uh-oh. Should I be worried?" Tristan teased, turning to her to laugh.

"How beautiful she is," he thought. "I am so lucky to have her in my life, to *be* my life. She is extraordinary. So intelligent, kind, loving, passionate, funny, compassionate, intrepid, strong; such a sense of what's right and just; and she knows me better than I know myself. I know there will always be a rib-eye steak from the best butcher in the freezer for me because she knows I enjoy them. She knows there will always be jumbo or colossal shrimp somewhere in the freezer for her, no matter where I have to get them from, just because I love her. It's the little things we do for each other and our family, just because we love them. I am so blessed to have her as the love of my life, the mother of my children. Our children are so blessed. Thank you, Creator."

"No, seriously, Tristan. I've been thinking about the quilt situation. From the very beginning, I've been getting so caught up in the thing itself and looking for answers and trying to figure out the next move, that I don't step back from time to time and really think about what's going on. We actually talked to someone who worked on the quilt. Someone who knew the very woman whose testimony was the cause of one of the most famous murders in the history of this country. We had a darn haunted quilt, for Pete's sake!

"Now we're about to figure out what we can do about all of it. Even if we can't get in contact with Emmettt Till's family, I guess we need to think about what we should do. This quilt is a piece of history and I'm not sure we even have a right to keep it to ourselves like we've been doing. I am a law professor for Pete's sake. My university's motto, its guiding principles are 'To teach, to serve, to inquire into the nature of things.'

"I, of all people, should feel the greater weight of history for what it is we have. If we can't find, and/or get in touch with the family, or even if we can, maybe we should first at least let someone know what it is we have. They can do all sorts of tests to see if what Ms. Talitha said can be verified. They can test the fabrics and batting, and even the ink, to see if it is consistent with the story she told us. We believe her, but there can be corroboration to make her story stronger. They can test the writing in the quilt to see if it matches Carolyn Bryant's. There are people whose whole work lives and professions are devoted to things like this.

"If it really is Carolyn's then this is a huge part of history. Yes, if it's hers, there is still no proof of who the E.T. is that the writing refers to, but they can even eliminate the possibilities of anyone other than Emmett Till by going through her life and figuring out if there were any other significant people she dealt with around the time with the same initials. Making a quilt is a big deal. Putting an inscription in it even bigger. That is, if it is big enough to warrant something permanent like an inscription, then likely there was a situation someone knew about that led to it and others would know about it. Something pointing to that would show up in a person's life.

"I know it sounds far-fetched that there would be someone significant enough for her to put a message in a quilt other than Emmettt Till, with the same initials, but you know how scientists, investigators and academics are. We all like to get as close as we can to the truth. Even eliminating all the other possibilities is a type of proof of sorts."

"You're absolutely right, Camille. Doctors are scientists, you know, and I am a doctor at a teaching and research hospital, so I fit into two of those categories. You're right. No matter what family we find, this is bigger than just Carolyn Bryant, or the Till family. It belongs to history now. Regardless of what we find out about the family, we need to contact someone and let them know about this. My number one candidate for who we should call would be the Smithsonian Institution.

"After all, in 2016, as long-time contributors to the museum-to-be, we were invited to, and went, to the opening of their newest museum, the Museum of African American History and Culture. Decades in the making, it is incredible. Remember, we saw everybody, Oprah; Representative John Lewis who worked so hard to have it come to fruition; President and Michelle Obama; Lonnie Bunch, who was the first director and is now the Secretary of the Smithsonian in charge of all their museums, and all those glorious fellow contributors gathered for the event?

"Talk about exciting. We could even feel it as we were on DC's Metro train going to the Museum. We could tell people were headed there just like we were. That was really something. And the Museum certainly has established itself as the primary repository of all things relating to African American history and culture. This certainly fits into that.

"In fact, remember when we did the donor's sneak preview of the museum that day, we actually went into the Emmett Till exhibit and saw his casket and other things? The exhibit was still so emotional for people to see that they had a recovery space for people to process what they saw."

"I forgot all about us seeing that, Tristan! How could I have forgotten! What you say makes perfect sense," said Camille suddenly slowing down.

"But, I'm wondering if we should go to the Department of Justice or the FBI, even, first. After all, if it's an admission by Carolyn Bryant that she lied about Emmett Till, then it's actually more like a piece of evidence."

"I hadn't even thought of that," Tristan said slowly.

"Of course, as a lawyer, it makes sense that you would. You're right. It's not just an historical artifact. It is even more than that and it has real life implications in the criminal justice realm. But, to tell you the truth, now that I'm thinking about it, given its history and its connection to politics, even though it's not supposed to be political, I don't know that I trust the DOJ to be whose hands we put this in. There has just been too much politicizing of that agency in the past few years.

"I think I'd rather we gave it to the Museum. Things like this are their business and they can figure out the best thing to do about DOJ, the FBI, or even the Mississippi legal authorities. We forgot about them. I don't want us to hand it over to someone who thinks the best thing they can do is act to like it never existed. Remember that even the transcript of Carolyn's testimony went missing. A trial transcript, for Pete's sake! How often does *that* happen?! As did her *unserved* arrest warrant. For 67 years!!"

"Tristan! You're right! I hadn't even thought of that!" Camille replied. "Ooooooh, she groaned, grabbing her head. "I thought we'd had our hands full before trying to figure out how to get to the bottom of this whole quilt saga. But this brings a whole new added dimension. Not only are we dealing with a quilt that was acting weird, we now know who created it and that brings along a whole bushel basket full of other issues, including criminal justice issues. Could we even be determined to be withholding evidence of a criminal case by not turning this over to the police immediately? Obstruction of justice? Tampering with evidence? Aiding and abetting? Accessory after the fact? Do we need to get a lawyer?! I'm a lawyer, but not a criminal lawyer!"

"Whoa, whoa, whoa! Hold on a minute! You're getting way ahead of yourself, Girl!" Tristan said laughing and reaching out and taking Camille's arms and turning her to face him. "There's no reason to panic, since both your sister Dreah and her husband Brian are both excellent lawyers. Even if they don't know the answer, which I can't imagine, in all likelihood they will know someone who does. As for you not being a criminal lawyer, even if you were, even *I* know the saying that a lawyer who represents herself has a fool for a client. So, just relax and take all that worry away.

"But also, just remember where all this started, Camille. All you did was to stop by a little thrift store while we were on vacation and you, a quilter and quilt collector, bought a quilt you liked, and it turned out that the quilt started acting very strangely. Things progressed from there. You had no reason to suspect any connection to Emmettt Till or Carolyn Bryant whatsoever. Once you found out, you still didn't know it for certain, even though you had it on very good authority that there was a connection. No one could accuse you—or us—of trying to obstruct justice, withhold evidence or tamper with evidence about this quilt, or anything else. At least not at this point," Tristan chuckled.

"You're right, Tristan. I just let my imagination run away with me for a moment," Camille said as she breathed deeply and let herself be pulled by him into her favorite place, his arms, his chest, his embrace. In addition to everything else, it was her favorite thinking place too. It always felt so safe there, so reasoned, like whatever came, they could think it through and weather it together because they had each other; and she knew he did not think her weak for leaning on him. She knew it felt the same way for Tristan. One of the things that fueled their intimacy was how Tristan had a way of being completely giving, helpful, interested in people, which made them feel truly connected to him, but they had no idea of how much more was there for Camille alone.

"It was like they had an entirely separate and closed part of their relationship known only to them. Like a lovely secret garden. She was sure all couples experienced some measure of this, but Tristan really was special. He had the often, usual semi-officious air of a physician, but he was also so warm and charismatic. People felt him and they could sense his integrity the moment they met him. All of that was true and real, but, if they only knew how much more there was to him…. But that was for Camille alone.

One of the things Camille absolutely loved about Tristan was that while people were drawn to him because of his strength, when it was just the two of them, he was no less strong, but he was so much more open. She remembered how when they were first together, in their times at the end of the day when he drove her home from campus when she was in law school and he was in medical school, they'd noodle on the porch before she went into her parent's house.

Among other things, he'd murmur into her ear how confused he felt about his feelings for her because he had never felt that way about anyone before and it went against all he knew to let himself feel so open and vulnerable with *anyone*. She loved that. She loved that he trusted her enough to feel it as well as to let her know he felt it. That feeling he had for her had never left him, and Camille could feel it. In fact, it had only grown stronger in their years together. For Camille, that core of who he was with her was like a precious thing to be protected by her at all costs. It made the intimacy based on who they truly were with each other and in the world, that was such a foundation of their time under the quilts, spectacular. They never, ever took it for granted.

"We'll just take it one step at a time for now," Tristan said. "We'll see if there is any of the Till family we can talk to, so we can see what the possibilities even are. Then, after we find that out, we'll figure out what it makes sense to do. As part of that, we can think about whether in contacting them, we want to tell them everything we know about the quilt, or just our conversation with Ms. Talitha.

"Since the quilt doesn't belong to the Till family, but may only refer to Emmettt Till, it's not as if the Till family has a legal claim to it.

Carolyn Bryant made the quilt, but she gave it away as a gift and there is no disputing the fact that the person who received the gift sold it to the store you purchased it from, so she has no claim to it. I'm sure that under contract and commercial law precepts, it belongs to you because you are the purchaser and that is not in question. It is yours. That is civilly.

"Criminally, it may be a different matter if it is determined to be evidence in a criminal case. Based on the conversations we have with whoever we go to to discuss it, we can think about what seems best to do. We don't have to think of this as totally on us. Even if we decide to turn it over to the Smithsonian, the family can always contact the Smithsonian about it, rather than us—you."

"Hey! Who's the lawyer here?" Camille laughed.

"Did you forget that we were together when you were in law school? I picked up things too, you know. With your study group hanging out every week to study, then extra for exams, I couldn't help but hear the conversations, pick up a few things," he grinned.

"Silly man. My law school buddies were more fun than your medical school buddies," she laughed.

"Why do you think I was hanging out with your crew?" he laughed.

"Because they were all males and you wanted to make sure your territory was protected," she teased.

"Well, I certainly can't deny that that may have had a bit to do with it," Tristan laughed.

"But thinking about it like you said is actually a big relief, Tristan. The truth is, we really don't *have* to do anything at all. We can just let it play itself out. I keep thinking I have to take this all on myself. But I don't. I don't *have t*o do anything. In fact, I can always just put the quilt on the bed or in my collection and forget about it."

"Baby Cakes, first of all, you *never* have to take on *anything* all by yourself. I am *always* here for you. Given what we know about the quilt, doing nothing at all wouldn't make an awful lot of sense. But you're right; you don't have to do anything. And again, just so you're clear, you certainly are not in this by yourself," Tristan said, kissing her forehead gently and giving her a squeeze. It had its intended effect. Camille was totally comforted and fortified for whatever was to come.

CHAPTER 31

"Well, I'll be darn! I mean, it makes perfect sense, but who ever thought it would ever mean anything in my very own life to know this? Camille said as Tess gave her the news about Emmettt Till's cousin, Wheeler Parker, Jr., among others, who was still alive. He'd been 16 at the time of the murder of his cousin.

Tess continued. "It was the very cousin who was with Emmett Till on that fateful day in 1955 when Emmett Till, his cousins, and uncle went about three miles away from their Uncle's Mose Wright's farm to Money, Mississippi's Bryant's Grocery & Meat Market owned by Roy and Carolyn Bryant. Hanging out at the store, patronized mainly by Blacks, with its checker players in front, was what mostly everyone did after they got the money from picking cotton in hand. Emmett, known as "Bobo" to his family, was there in Mississippi as a 14-year-old, visiting his mother's family. She had grown up in the south and understood how dangerous it could be for African Americans, especially males."

"Did she grow up in the same place as the death take place?"

"I'm not sure, but it ought to be easy enough to find out."

"No worries. I just wondered."

"Anyway," Tess continued, "from all accounts, Bobo, a much-loved personable, fun-loving, handsome only child doted on by his mother and grandmother, had grown up in Chicago and had never been south. Although his mother gave him stern lessons in southern comportment, he had not grown up learning the rules that would keep a Black person alive there. Little did he know that the whistling he had learned to do in order to stop his pretty severe stuttering, would be interpreted as a wolf whistle that would end up costing him his life.

"Dreah even found the cousin's lawyer he'd been using from time to time as the need arose, and spoke to him.

"Mama found some more relatives as well. She doesn't know how close they all are as a family, but she found them. Since it has been this cousin that has done most of the press that's been found, we're thinking he'd be the best one to approach if you decide to do it. Have you figured out what you're going to do yet?"

"Not yet. This is all so new. Knowing that there actually is family alive makes it so real."

"Well, did you ever think about Carolyn Bryant's family and whether you want to contact them if there is anyone left? I know Carolyn won't talk to you, but I hadn't even thought about her family until Renée mentioned it to me as I was searching for Emmettt Till's family."

"Oh, my gosh, Tess! I hadn't even *thought* about *that* since we first discovered that Carolyn Bryant was the one who made the quilt and she didn't want to talk to us!"

"Well, you might want to give it a think. Of course, you don't have to do anything at all about them, but I just don't want you to be blindsided if the crap hits the whirling blades when this comes out," Tess laughed. "You know that is a distinct possibility in this day and age of social media, specious litigation, everybody wanting their fifteen minutes of fame, yadda, yadda. Everybody also wants their day in court for whatever slight there is, imagined or otherwise. Everybody thinks they've been wronged," she said derisively.

"Geez, Tess! You're making my teeth hurt!" Camille groaned. "Why did I ever even start this?! What a headache! Plus, as the lawyer, that should've been something I thought of!"

"It's entirely possible to be so close to something that you can't see all the angles, lawyer or no. OK, well, I see havoc has been wreaked, so I've done my job. I'm signing off now. I believe I've done enough damage for one call," Tess laughed. "Bye, Baby Girl!" she shouted, and before Camille could reply, Tess was gone.

Camille truly appreciated Tess taking this on, just after being promoted and in the midst of her wedding preparations, to help out her sister who was in a time crunch. In the same moment Tess hung up, Camille's phone rang again and she heard the soothing voice of her mother when she answered. Perfect! No matter how grown you got, you would always need your Mama.

"Camille? Are you OK? You sound stressed," Naomi said calmly.

"Hi, Mama. I'm OK. But this is perfect timing. Tess just called and told me about the Till family members that have been found. Thank you so much for your help. I would not have been able to write my paper, deal with my finals and do this too. At least not so quickly. Finding out that there's family is good news. But now it also means that thinking about what to do with the quilt is really real.

"But then Tess told me that Renée had asked her if we'd thought about seeing if there was any family on Carolyn Bryant's side. I had been so busy with the Till aspect, that I hadn't even thought about finding Carolyn's family. I told Tess I'd think about it. She's right about not wanting to be blindsided. I don't want that. But, I also don't feel like putting a lot of effort into dealing with Carolyn Bryant's family. Or her either, for that matter, since she's still around, but doesn't want to talk to us."

"Well, I think giving it some thought is a good thing," Naomi said slowly." We've mentioned before that this is much bigger than just a quilt you bought from a thrift store. Now that we're pretty sure what it is, we understand that this is a part of history. An important part, if it does what we think it does. Emmettt Till's vicious murder was the foundation for the entire modern day Civil Rights Movement.

"Eight years after he was murdered, the organizers of the 1963 March on Washington for Jobs & Freedom chose the date of his murder for the event. It turned out to be the largest gathering of people on the Mall in Washington, DC, to that date. Even though it was held on, like, a Wednesday rather than a weekend, in the sweltering humid August 28 heat of DC. People from all over the world came to say 'Enough!' Black folks needed to be treated with dignity, respect and equality. And, of course, Dr. Martin Luther King, Jr. delivered his famous 'I Have A Dream' speech."

"You were there, weren't you, Mama?" Camille asked.

"Yes. I was. I was only twelve years old at the time, but I was there. With my father being a Baptist minister, pastor, and Dr. King supporter, there was no way we were not going to be there. Of course, my mother couldn't go because of her heart issues. She wouldn't have been able to stand the heat and crowds, but the rest of us went. All five of the kids and my Dad. I was afraid of my brother going because he was so young, just eight years old. I worried that he would get lost in all those people. But my Dad knew how important this would be.

"I had never seen so many people in my life. And it was so hot! The truth is, I was too young to really understand what this was all about, but I knew it was terribly important. I remember seeing people with those signs and hats that said SNCC and CORE. I had no idea it meant the Student Nonviolent Coordinating Committee and the Congress of Racial Equality. It was so confusing for me. Especially since the hats looked like the same kind that soda fountain servers and hamburger joint servers wore.

"My sister, your Aunt Gale, was pregnant with her first daughter, your cousin, Tracy. I remember that she had on a bright red maternity dress that my Mama had made for her. I was so glad because it made her so much easier to see in that sea of humanity. Between her being so tall, light complexioned, and having on that red dress, I didn't lose her like I feared I would. That was important to me since I loved her so.

"None of us realized that any of us would go on to do work so related to that day, including me being chosen as the recipient of the Dr. Martin Luther King, Jr. Dream Award, the highest award my university gave for those engaging in diversity and inclusion efforts. Or the University even naming an annual monied award for me when I retired, for faculty who engage in Diversity & Inclusion efforts both inside and outside the classroom. Or my brother Bill becoming a pastor like my Dad, as well and doing the impactful, wide-ranging community work he does, or my other sister, your Aunt Brenda helping him with it so closely. Who knew all of that would come from, in part, being on the National Mall on that sweltering hot day of August 28, 1963? The date, eight years before, on which Emmett Till was so viciously murdered.

"That's why I appreciate you exposing your kids to as much as you can as early as possible. That bundle of experiences forms the stuff of their life in ways they can't even begin to imagine, and you never know which experience will be the one that turns on a light for them.

"All of this and we were just talking about the importance of the date of Emmettt Till's death and it leading to the most important march in the history of our country since the next year Congress passed the Civil Rights Act of 1964, which became effective the following year in 1965. For the first time millions of African Americans were freed from the prison of Jim Crow segregation that had been in place for nearly 100 years," Naomi said solemnly.

"Just think, that's only part of what came out of Emmettt Till's death. So much more good has happened that stemmed from it. But, I have to tell you," Mama, Camille said carefully, "When I think about Emmettt Till's death and what it led to, and how this quilt fits into that picture, even though Carolyn Bryant may have made the quilt, the last thing I'm thinking about is searching for, and in some way notifying, Carolyn Bryant's family."

"I certainly understand your position on dealing with Carolyn Bryant's family, Camille," said Naomi. "The good thing is that you don't have to worry about it. You can let it all be someone else's issue to deal with. You've done a great job already. As you well know, everyone who had that quilt for the past nearly four decades chose not to do what you did. They knew something was going on with the quilt, but they chose not to deal with it at all and just gave it back to the thrift shop.

"But, you stepped up to the plate, even though it was a fearful thing you were dealing with. Even when you realized it might be a spirit trying to tell you something, you never hesitated to get to the bottom of it."

"You're right, you're right, Mama" said Camille dismissively. "Sometimes it's so hard for me to step back from whatever it is I'm doing and look at the bigger picture. And you're absolutely right, everyone else did give it a pass and I chose not to.

"Tristan also keeps reminding me that I don't need to take on the stress of figuring this all out. Mama, that man is so good. I don't know what I'd do without him. People say I'm strong, and I suppose they're right, although it just feels like life to me. I just do what seems right to me. The innovative research I do, the causes I care about and advocate for, they're all just what I believe to be the right thing to do, the way to operate in the world. But it really does help to have a strong support system.

"Tristan is my rock. All of you, you and my sisters and our extended family have a piece of what allows me to do what I do in the world. But you know from having Daddy, who Tristan reminds me so much of, how helpful it is to have someone like that who is your partner in life and just gives you whatever it is you need each and every day. It just makes it all so much easier. I know it isn't easy to do that. But I love it that we both feel the very same way about each other and make the effort. It's scary sometimes, because I depend on him so much to be the wind beneath my wings, that I can't imagine ever being without him. I don't know how I'd do it. I know I would, but it would just suck."

"Oh, you'd find a way, believe me," said Naomi slowly, with a tinge of sadness.

It was her mother's tone of voice that made Camille realize how insensitive she had just been. Her mother had felt the same way about their father and she had lost him all too soon. The life they had dreamed of having together, riding off into the sunset, was not to be. Illness had claimed him before they'd even retired. It was always Naomi and Cameron. Until it wasn't.

Camille had been so wrapped up in her own thoughts, that she'd forgotten about her mother having experienced precisely what Camille said she felt was such an unthinkable situation. She and her sisters often discussed their Mama being alone now that their Dad was gone. She didn't seem the least bit interested in dating, but they all felt a measure of guilt about having a partner they cared so much about and their mother being single.

"Mama! I'm so sorry!" Camille exhorted. "What a dunce I am! I was so wrapped up in my thoughts that I totally forgot about you going through losing Daddy, who you felt the same way about! I hope you don't think I was being selfish or thoughtless! I'm so sorry!!"

"No worries! No worries! It's fine! You weren't being selfish! In fact, exactly the opposite. You were talking about your love for Tristan and his for you, which I so admire. I love Tristan and admire him so much. He is such a good man. He is wonderful husband for you and father for my grandchildren. I *totally* understand it! Don't give it a second thought!

I had the privilege of having spent the better part of my life with a very, very good man as well. We were there for each other when we needed to be. This part is easy.

"I miss your father every minute of every day, but at least I'm not in the part of life where I need him the way you do when you're younger and trying to work and establish yourself and your reputation, have a family, have the inevitable issues that come with that—including raising three strong, independent women," she laughed. "I'm just coasting now, enjoying life. We were there for each other when we needed to be and for that I am grateful. Some people go their entire lives never having what we did. We were truly blessed."

"Mama, you make it all sound so reasonable and rational. It's *love!*"

"I know it's love, Darlin'. I've had it. But to everything, there is a season. Your Dad's and my season for that was wonderful. Incredible, even. But, as it turns out, it was only a season. Now life has moved on to another season, and I'm okay with that," Naomi said gently.

Camille left it there.

"Well, Carolyn Bryant's relatives are not going to be a stress point for me, Mama. Between talking to you and Tess and thinking about what this journey has been, I've decided that if they are to be found, if they are to be notified, it won't be by me. Let whoever takes this on do it.

"Tracking down who the initials belonged to is one thing. But because we have the assurance of Ms. Talitha, someone who actually worked on the quilt with Carolyn Bryant, and we therefore know that it was Carolyn Bryant that the initials belonged to and who made the quilt, that's good enough for me. I'm satisfied that it was Carolyn's doing. I'm satisfied that it was an apology she wrote about what she had done to Emmett Till by lying on the witness stand and his death coming out of that. I'm satisfied that it was an apology for the lie she told that got that fourteen-year-old boy horribly tortured and killed simply because of the color of his skin.

"I appreciate her spirit sticking around the quilt to try to make things right, if that's what happened, but I think she'll be satisfied if Till's family knows it. I'm not at all sure she'd care about her own family knowing.

"I don't think she really cared to let her own family know because they supported her husband and his brother and what they did in killing Emmett Till and even telling it unapologetically to a national magazine.

They also treated the wife of their family member that Carolyn gave the quilt to really poorly simply because he chose to marry an African American woman—even though he ended up treating her like crap. The truth is, given what we know, I don't have any reason to believe they would feel particularly good about what Carolyn wrote in that quilt.

"I know people can and do change, but I'm not worried about finding out if these particular people did. What was done to Emmettt Till went far beyond redeemable activity to me. I'm not holding my breath worrying about whether those folks have seen the light and changed their thoughts about Black folks.

"The other day I read a news item that late night show host Trevor Noah had a piece on that was a comedian interviewing people as if the comedian was a news person doing interviews at the National Rifle Association conference. He asked an interviewee who had on a Confederate flag T-shirt, whether he wanted to keep the Confederate flag. The interviewee said yes, he wanted to maintain it for his southern heritage.

"Then the interviewer asked if the interviewee was pro or anti-slavery. The interviewer was visibly stunned when, three times, the interviewee refused to give an answer. He refused to say whether he was for or against slavery in 2022.

"So, while I know people can change, I also know that sometimes they don't. If the interviewee feels that way about something that happened over 150 years ago, I'm not sanguine about something that happened only 67 years ago. I'm OK with not trying to track down that potential hornet's nest and poking it."

"I certainly understand that, Camille, and I stand by whatever decision you make," Naomi said softly.

CHAPTER 32

"Whooohoooooo!!!!!!!!! We're hitched!!" Tess shouted with the biggest smile of her life, sweeping Renée's arms up in the air in a grand gesture as they broke their kiss and turned away from the minister who had just pronounced them spouses. A huge cheer went up from the crowd, with clapping, hand waving, cheering and laughter all around.

"OK, time to get this party started!" Tess shouted loud and long and signed, and led the procession over to the dance floor and food and drink area. The DJ kicked things off with an upbeat selection and the party was on.

Camille surveyed the scene with both amusement and appreciation. Trays were piled high with Renée and Tess's eclectic favorites. There was everything from jumbo seasoned shrimp, jerk chicken, and Chinese pot stickers (with dipping sauce, of course), to their Mama's (and Tess's favorite) manicotti and Monkey Bread and a champagne fountain.

It had been a bit of a trial for their family but Camille appreciated that Tess and Renée had decided that their wedding would be strictly what it is they wanted (with due thought to their family and friends) rather than traditional wedding fare. Camille thought about Tess telling her that anyone who was lucky enough and close enough to get an invitation to her wedding would totally understand what it was they were experiencing, including being touched that her brothers-in-law stood in for her father during the ceremony.

Camille loved the venue, a beautiful, well-kept park, and noted that the weather was perfect. There was fun, great family, friends, food, drink, and upbeat music except for a few sappy love songs Camille knew Tess resisted, but Renée insisted upon. Guests had been told to dress in whatever they felt comfortable in. The food was a buffet rather than a formal sit down meal. It was perfectly fine with Tess and Renée if everyone got totally smashed as long as they had a good time. Let the good times roll.

Camille knew this was Tess and Renée's special day and they wanted everyone to enjoy it as much as they did. Guests were free to bring their kids and Tess and Renée had even hired caretakers to look after them with fun things for them to do, so that the parents could have a good time. At the ready were fully-paid Ubers and hotel rooms at the swank hotel adjacent to the park so that no one would be driving under the influence.

From the looks of it so far, it would be a wedding to remember for every single soul there. They were all having a blast, and no one more than Tess and Renée, thought Camille. Because they had done precisely what they wanted, there was no pre-wedding drama at all. None. Zero. Nada. Zip.

"Remember no-Drama Obama? Well, I'm no-stress Tess!" Tess had kept telling them as things developed.

"Even their wedding vows went off without a hitch," Camille thought. No small feat since Renée was non-hearing and the vows were conducted in American Sign Language. Everyone there knew them well enough to know what to expect and it was flawless. There was not one dry eye in the place after their homemade vows were exchanged, including hers and Tristan's. Tess had told Camille she knew that part of the impact of their heartfelt vow exchange would be that there would be a hot time in the old town tonight for many of those gathered here, as it reminded them of the depth of their feelings for their significant others.

Camille watched as Renée felt the vibrations of the music and she and Tess danced non-stop, right along with all their nearest and dearest friends and family.

Camille and Tristan made sure Luke and Leslie were taken care of and took to the floor to enjoy some infrequent dancing. They'd both initially experienced an awkward moment as they realized that they hadn't danced in so long that they didn't even know what was now popular. They both finally settled on going with the flow and letting the music dictate their movements.

Still, they were relieved when one of Renée's "sappy" slower songs came on. In fact, it was one of their favorites. ConFunkShun's "Love Train" followed immediately by Silk Sonic's cover of it, a cover that ConFunkShun's Mike Cooper and Felton Pilate II greatly appreciated Silk Sonic releasing on the Valentine's Day on the 40th anniversary of the original.

"Mmmmm….." Camille heard Tristan's murmur deep in his throat and felt its vibration on the top of her head as he held her in his arms and they swayed to the music. "This feels so good. So relaxing," Tristan murmured.

"It does, Tristan. It feels absolutely heavenly," Camille murmured back. As always, she loved feeling his arms around her and she could feel the heat where their bodies touched. She made a note to make sure neither of them overindulged in either the food, drinks or fun, so they could have their own fun when they were alone back in the hotel. She could feel it building and knew Tristan felt the same way. Newlyweds weren't the only ones who got to have all the fun on their wedding night!

"I don't think I've felt you this relaxed since, maybe our vacation last summer," Tristan said. "I'd like to say since our Christmas holiday gathering, but that was pretty tense there for a while with the weird quilt, and you've been going pretty hard ever since. Between work, taking care of the kids and me, writing your paper, delivering it, publishing it, finals, and, of course, chasing the quilt situation down, you've been really going at it. I'm *really* glad you've finally let it go."

"Geez, Tristan, when you list it all out like that it sounds *exhausting*. And you're right. It was a *lot*. I am so glad that it's over with. No more stitches coming undone. No need for the quilt to wander anymore. Not only am I glad that it's over with, but I'm glad that I feel so comfortable with what happened with it. I am totally comfortable handing it over to the Smithsonian's National Museum of African American History and Culture and letting them take it from there. Our discussions and meetings with them, and the information we provided them about everything we found out will be a really clear guide to them about where to take it from here.

"I feel much better having *them* deal with the Department of Justice, the FBI, and the Mississippi authorities than *me* doing it. They will fight for justice to be done, whatever that can be under the circumstances. I think that having us go together to see Emmettt Till's family and tell them what we found and show them the quilt and let them know that the Smithsonian was taking it from here was a great idea. They were so grateful for what we did. And so relieved that whatever could be done was going to be done. I was really nervous about their reaction, but they were so grateful. I'm so glad."

"I'm not quite sure I was prepared for all the tears that came with us visiting them and telling them what we discovered," Tristan said. "I mean, I thought it would be emotional, but it was really something."

Camille sighed. "Yeah. It really was rough to watch. Even though they knew we were coming and what we were bringing, I guess it was just even more real when they actually saw it.

"Well, I guess when you've been dealing with it for as long as they have, and you have lost someone, a little bright, loving, fun 14-year-old boy, to a vicious, unimaginable death, and history has fought you all the way about justice, it just is such a relief to finally see proof of what you strongly suspected all the time. I can imagine that those were 67 years worth of tears they were shedding. So many people are still alive who remember it. Books are still being written about it. That was a lot of pent up grief, a lot of tears."

"Well, I guess this will sprout a whole new book or set of books," Tristan heavily sighed. Can you imagine what it will be like when people start to really dig into why it was that you decided to go on a quest to figure out what was going on with this quilt? It's one thing to tell the Smithsonian what happened, but quite another to do it in this day and age of social media.

"You know the vultures will come. I'm not sure there's any real way to prepare for it. Get a publicity agent, media consultant or something, maybe, whatever you call the people who know how to handle things like this. I can't imagine that it won't be huge once it hits. Carolyn Bryant's 'spirit'?! Quilt stitches that kept coming undone?! A quilt that kept creeping off of people?! Oh, my Lord. You're going to have every creep in creation seeking you out.

"As well as the naysayers, Camille," Tristan said with a forlorn sigh of inevitability. "It doesn't take anything for them to just sit at a computer and write utter nonsense and send it off into the social media ether. I don't see how you can avoid it. Even if the Smithsonian doesn't release your name—like if they say the quilt was sent to them anonymously— you've left a trail of people who knew you were looking into the quilt. All it will take is for one of them to spill the beans for their fifteen minutes of fame, or perceived fortune or whatever.

"Especially after all the publicity we just saw when they found in the basement of the Leflore County courthouse the missing 1955 arrest warrant for Carolyn Bryant after all this time—that warrant that wasn't served because the sheriff said not to bother her because she had two young children to care for. I *still* can't get over that. If she'd been Black that wouldn't have even entered their minds. She would have been served. Period.

"Then, having Ms. Talitha's "History Man," Timothy Tyson, the historian Carolyn Bryant contacted and spoke to, giving the FBI the totally self-serving unpublished manuscript Carolyn Bryant wrote about the events, *I Am More Than A Wolf Whistle*. Carolyn Bryant gave Tyson the manuscript and they agreed that the manuscript would be archived at the University of North Carolina and not released for decades. I'm glad Tyson thought the archival agreement should not take precedence over the potential criminal implications and gave it to the FBI during their investigation.

"Then, after all that, having the grand jury in Mississippi decline to indict her. Wow. What a slap in the face for all the people who have been working so hard for justice for Emmett Till for so long. What a horrible message for us all. We like to think that things have changed enough to forget the past, but it keeps popping up. That's what happens when you don't deal with things. Until you do.

"I can't believe the coincidental timing of all of that happening just after your quilt discoveries. What are the chances?! That makes the possibility of this hitting you really intensely even more likely. I hate not being able to protect you from what will come, Camille," Tristan said, the concern for Camille and his family palpable in his voice.

"Tristan, you know what? I'll bet that everything you said is absolutely true. But I am not the least bit worried about it. I did what I thought should be done and that's that. I am sure it will be as annoying as hell for a while when it's the flavor of the week, but it will eventually go away when something else catches the public's attention. Especially when they realize Sarah Marsden is in the picture as the one the quilt was given to by Carolyn Bryant or that Ms. Talitha actually helped make the quilt.

"Tristan, why do you think Sarah didn't tell me who the aunt was that gave her and her husband the quilt? She lived in the Delta. I can't imagine she didn't know that her husband's aunt was Carolyn Bryant and Carolyn's connection to the Emmettt Till murder. It was huge news in that tiny place. Sarah went over to Carolyn's house to thank her for the quilt. Why didn't she just tell me who the aunt was? It would have saved me so much trouble; us so much trouble. We wouldn't have had to go to the Mississippi Delta looking for whoever it was that made the quilt. And what if we hadn't just happened upon Ms. Talitha in that totally random way? As random as buying the quilt in a random little thrift store in another state while on vacation? Ugh!

"I might even have had a hand in Sarah not telling me by trying to be so circumspect in talking to her. When I called her, she asked me why I was looking into this. I didn't want to tell her too much, so I just told her because Charlie had told me about the quilt being brought back by so many buyers who felt uncomfortable with it that he called it The Wandering Quilt. But if I'd told her about the inscription, if I'd told her the letters E.T. and C.B., maybe she would have come clean and told me what she knew, told me who the aunt was. Maybe all this is really my fault."

Tristan sighed deeply. "First of all, Camille, the trip to the Mississippi Delta was awesome and I'm really glad our family went. We learned so much and I'm sure Luke and Leslie will never forget it. What they learned will be so helpful in their lives, so important to their deeper sense of self as they grow and mature. So, I am not sorry that she didn't tell you because if she had it would have meant we wouldn't have taken a family trip that will undoubtedly stick out in all our minds as a memorable one for many reasons.

"Secondly, if you were Sarah and had lived in the Delta and had been through what she'd been through for being Black and had seen what happened to Emmettt Till, or even Mose Wright after he testified, would you go around telling people your connection? I don't think so.

"Thirdly, what you did in speaking with Sarah Marsden, someone you did not know, made perfect sense. Why would you share something like that with her if you had no idea of who she really was, whether you could trust her, or how much she knew?"

"You're so right, Tristan. The trip really was awesome for us all. And Sarah didn't even know me. But she opened up enough to tell me that she'd heard that the quilt made people uncomfortable and had been taken back to the thrift store.

"She even told me she had been beaten by her husband and wondered if it was because of what had been happening in her house with her husband beating her, that it had somehow gotten picked up by the quilt. If she thought about that, I can't see why she didn't think about the possibility of Carolyn Bryant and her relationship to Emmettt Till having something to do with the discomfort of the quilt since Carolyn actually made the quilt, so her energy would be in it."

"Maybe she didn't know when the quilt was made, that it was made during the time of the Emmettt Till murder and its aftermath. If she's not a quilter, I don't know if she would have even thought about the quilter quilting her energy into a quilt.

"But, even if she did know and decided not to tell, decided instead to put all that behind her, I can't say I blame her. That was a lot to deal with that wasn't hers to carry. She did the best she could in getting away from a really painful and harrowing past in the Delta. Dragging it up with you would do her no good."

"You're right. I'm just sorry it's likely to be dragged up now and put on public display in the worst way by the tabloids. I went looking for the quilt's journey. She didn't."

"I'm sorry too. It's not her disaster. She just received a quilt as a wedding gift. But it is what it is," Tristan said with a compassionate firmness.

"So true. I hope she has someone in her life like you that can remind her of that. Speaking of which, back to you protecting me," Camille said in a sultry voice. "Dearest One, you protect me just by being there. As long as I have you by my side in this, Tristan, we can get through it. I know we can. Plus, I have my other family, my support. That's not to say it won't be rough, but together we can do this." Camille stood up on her tiptoes and whispered in his ear "We always do. You. Are. My. Rock," finishing with a tender tiny nip on his lobe. As the DJ moved seamlessly into Ashford and Simpson's oldie but goodie, "I Would Know You Anywhere," Camille felt Tristan pull her even closer as he bent his head down to her ear and whispered into it in crisp, precise, emphatic words brimming with the intimacy she so loved, "*We are each other's.*"

Afterword

Dawn D. Bennett-Alexander

I am writing this, but, like the book, it reflects the joint effort of both my niece/co-author, Renée, and me. We thought long and hard about whether we should include an afterword and finally came down on the side of doing so. Context is soooo important, even in the realm of entertainment, like a cozy mystery. It certainly is in the realm of education, a bit of which we try to provide as well. Since we consider our Quilt Journeys Mystery Series to be both, we believe context will likely be more helpful to our readers than not. Until my 2021 retirement, I taught law at the University of Georgia's Terry College of Business for thirty-three years. Norma Nuñez-Pacheco once came to my class in Global Diversity to speak about Latinx Culture and did such an outstanding job of contextualizing her talk beforehand so my students would know precisely how to interpret what she was saying, that I adopted the policy as my own from then on. In this instance, we decided it would be better to do it afterwards rather than beforehand in order for the reader to come to the novel without context and just take it as a cozy mystery, which it is. But, as it turns out, there is also a twist. We thought readers might want to know why.

This book came out of the blue for Renée and me. It began as a totally random cozy mystery about a quilt and turned into what you have just read (and hopefully, enjoyed!). As it unfolded and took on a life of its own, it became clear that we had lessons we thought valuable to share, totally in context. I had done Diversity Equity, Inclusion & Belonging (DEIB) work for the past forty years, including in 1982, creating and teaching in colleges of business the first Employment Law course dealing with workplace discrimination under Title VII of the 1964 Civil Rights Act; in 1994 co-authoring the first-ever Employment Law textbook that spawned an entire academic discipline, professional organization sub-group, and the foundation for DEIB; had served for three years on the task force that created the international standard for DEIB issued in May 2021 (ISO 30415:21) with 150 signatory countries; had been instrumental in helping launch the first and only online certification program on the planet for certification in the new international standard (through the University of Georgia's Terry College of Business Executive Education/Inclusion Score collaboration); had written the first Grolier encyclopedia entry on sexual harassment and five other encyclopedia entries on discrimination issues; have spoken in-depth with thousands of students and training seminar attendees about the issues and am part of a new cutting-edge effort to bring DEIB to businesses across Europe through a totally online Q&A format (https://www.leqture.com/diversity-and-inclusion/).

Renée had served in the military, been a manager dealing with DEIB issues, became a member of the disabled community later in life, and had a life-long love affair with books, movies and TV that contributed to her having an incredibly active imagination. She also credits the genesis of the latter as the Nancy Drew Book Club membership I gave her as a gift as a child; an extension of the monthly book club her mother/my sister had enrolled me in as a child. We have both been avid mystery book readers for decades. With her Dad serving in the Navy, Renee had grown up internationally. I had lived, taught, and traveled extensively internationally.

Both of us realized that our experience had taught us that people all over the world have the same need for, among other things, love, respect, and acceptance. While our most recent history demonstrates in dramatic ways that there are definitely those who will always reject others not like themselves, we believe the vast majority of people just want to live their lives and not intentionally harm others in the process. We also understood that hurt is hurt, whether unintentional or not, but when it arises from a lack of knowledge, that is fixable. We can do something about that.

We both care deeply about our country and are concerned about the growing negativity we see, oftentimes based on our misunderstanding of who others not like us are. My years of interaction with thousands of people in this context has demonstrated this over and over again. Once people discover something that I take for granted they knew because it is such a part of what is in my head as I go through the world, they are astonished that they didn't know, and lament the difference it would have made if they had. They are happy for the information and use it in their lives thereafter. Hundreds, if not thousands, of emails, letters, texts, phone calls and direct messages I have received bear that out.

That is why we are attempting to fill this gap as part of our cozy mystery series.

The stories are interesting and compelling, but also give readers insight and information about something they may not know that is a basic part of our history and part of why we are where we are today. It makes little sense to say in response to "Black Lives Matter," that all lives matter, if you are looking at the same picture that BLM advocates are. Their picture includes a deep history of unfettered mistreatment of Blacks in this country based on race. An irrefutable fact easily verified. If you do not know this history, you do not understand their picture and will not understand their advocacy. Logically, you are left interpreting the BLM sign on the basis of your own background that may not include information/knowledge of that history. Your response then makes sense. But your response is based on an incomplete picture and does not actually make sense, given their concerns. Turns out the two sides are dealing with two different pictures without even realizing it. Both make sense based on the picture each is working with, but we need to make sure the picture is the same or the disagreement is pointless, unproductive and only increases negative feelings. I have seen this happen over and over again.

To use a contemporary recent example, what happened in the wake of the murder of George Floyd on May 25, 2020, is a perfect demonstration of what happens when we're all dealing with the same picture. A picture of wanting to live in a country whose very Constitution ensures we are treated equally and can all achieve despite race, color, religion, gender, national origin, sexual orientation, gender identity, disabilities, etc., if we are willing to work for our dreams. Millions took to the street to protest what they witnessed in that video's eight minutes, forty-six second fiasco. The truth is, in terms of numbers, most of the millions who took to the streets were white. There were marches in tiny towns that had not one

Black person in it, but they saw the video and hated what it demonstrated. They finally saw for themselves what Blacks had been saying for years, but it was, for the most part dismissed. But at the end of that eight minutes and forty-six seconds, we were finally all looking at the same picture. It was ugly and it moved people to action. BLM finally made sense in a way it had not before. People got it. What folks saw in that video did not reflect the world they wanted to live in, so they made that known. In its wake, public institutions, for-profit corporations, non-profits, schools, churches, etc. moved to do better. This tragic event we all witnessed showed us the importance and power of us all seeing the same picture.

We want to help with getting us to all see and operate from the same picture. We want to provide some of the background and history that allows learning, growth and understanding to take place so that we're looking at the same picture rather than being polarized and divisive without understanding what we are looking at, dealing with, responding to.

All in the form of a cozy quilt mystery story with wonderful, loving characters.

Our book series covers all sorts of categories and issues, not just race. We also use all contexts of storytelling to make for interesting cozy mysteries, from ghostly qualities such as in *The Wandering Quilt*, to everyday living, and everything in between. We go where the story takes us. We're willing to use whatever best gets the job done in an effort to have us get closer to seeing the same picture because as we now know, doing so can be so powerful and enlightening in such a positive way.

Why quilts? Great question!! :-) First of all, who doesn't love a quilt? If cozy mysteries are to be cozy, can you think of anything cozier than a quilt? We think not. I have quilted for the past sixty years or more. I do it to connect me to my Ancestors; like Camille and Ms. Talitha, "to keep me sane" in a chaotic world; and because of the feeling of creating something so beautiful that didn't exist before I created it. But most of all? I do it because of the joy and comfort I know it brings to those I care about. I have never told someone that I quilt without it bringing a delighted and delightful smile to their face and a memory that they are glad to share about the quilt in their life. I don't care who it is, it seems that everyone has a quilt story. I love it. That story always has warm memories attached to it. The person has often never even mentioned that memory to anyone before. They often hadn't even thought of it until I mentioned that I quilt. Quilts mean so much more to us than we realize.

I have even used quilts in my DEIB presentations! They never fail to be memorable for the surprised participants wondering what the connection is between the quilts and DEIB. They are floored when they see that there are so many. Like people, pieces that seem they would never go together fit just fine, thank you very much; colors that seem like they would clash rest comfortable side by side, just like people; little pieces that don't seem to matter turn out to be crucial, like each and every one of us, regardless of race, color, gender, religion, national origin, sexual orientation, gender identity, disabilities, age, etc.; all of the various colors and fabric patterns add to the whole being just what they are, just like all of us, regardless of our various apparent differences; all of the pieces coming together to make a cohesive, beautiful whole, any one of which, if missing, would be immediately missed because the quilt needs them all to be whole, just as society needs all of us varied groups in order to be whole.

But, none of this was in my head as we started on this writing journey. I told you that this book and series came out of the blue because it did. Renée was visiting me and saw the stack of quilts you see on the front of our book. She asked me to tell her about them, so I did. When I got to the purple, white, green and yellow quilt seen on the back cover of the physical book (it is also the first one on the quilt stack of the front cover of all versions of the book) I told her that I had made it to commemorate the 200th birth year of my paternal great-great grandmother. The story that the character Jenniffer Jones tells Charlie, the shop owner about the quilt her mother made is actually a true story about me making the quilt to celebrate my great-great grandmother, Dinah Ratliff. While searching Census records for my grandmother, the 1900 Census showed Dinah lived in the household as well. Born in 1815, she spent the next fifty years of her life in slavery until the Civil War ended it. I did, in fact, work for the 2010 Census as I promised myself I would do and hand pieced the quilt squares as I sat waiting at a table at the public library and the Barnes & Noble bookstore to provide Census forms to those who needed them

Renée's surprising response was, "Wouldn't it be neat if we wrote a book about a quilt?" I'd never really thought about my quilts as having a story and life of their own, but I guess they do.

Renée had never written a book. As a legal textbook author for over thirty years, both with the Employment Law textbook and other legal textbooks, I had no plans to write cozy mystery fiction. They say you should write about what you know and I suppose it was undeniable that quilts fit that bill for me just as law did. Renée may have even been joking. But, in an effort to prove to her that it was possible to begin a project and see it through, the next morning I sat down at my laptop and asked a startled Renée, "So what happens?" Once she realized I was serious, her reply was, "Well, a woman goes into a thrift store and buys a quilt." It grew from there. Renée's idea and my writing. Publishing it was the farthest thing from our minds. Two months later, to the day, we signed the contract for publication.

So, *The Wandering Quilt* began purely as a story about a quilt, but we had no earthly idea it would end up where it did as a cozy mystery series teaching tool for the world. Once we saw how the book was shaping up and what it was doing, we were totally intrigued and realized it needed to be a series. We loved the characters and how they interacted with each other and went through the world and we wanted to see more of them. Especially Camille and Tristan. ;-) We realized how much all of that had to do with lessons for us all about love, family, how we care for each other in the world, how history and today's actions interweave with it all, and so on. For me to be able to blend my love of quilting, history, forty years of DEIB work, romance, family, humor, all in one place was beyond my wildest dreams. Truly. In a matter of several weeks we had finished *The Wandering Quilt* and two other books and another two were well underway. What a stunning surprise.

We were even more surprised when, after writing the book, items began to appear in the news about Emmett Till's case. A bit later, Whoopi Goldberg announced she was releasing "Till," the movie about the murder. What?!! Unbelievable serendipity! Emmett Till was *nowhere* on the horizon when Renée (I think, or was it me?) came up with the idea of including his situation. Out of all the pieces of history we could have chosen, the fact that it was this particular one is pretty amazing.

The Universe at work, as it has been in so many aspects of this work.

We hope that you not only enjoyed the story, but will continue reading the Quilt Journeys Mystery Series and recommend it to your friends. It is an easy way to try to help make the world a better place. A place where we can all not just live, but thrive, as the magnificent humans we were all created to be. We fervently hope you continue learning on your own. It is so easily done. Your favorite search engine is an enormously helpful tool. So much so that we won't even include specific resources for you. Right at your fingertips nowadays are videos, podcasts, books and articles you can use that do an excellent job of teaching you more than the tip of the iceberg we have provided about so many issues in *The Wandering Quilt*.

The basis of my DEIB work is that I believe that most people (especially in the context of the workplace and organizations, where I do the majority of my work) want to do the right thing. Because most of us lead pretty homogeneous lives, they may not realize they are not. We can help with that. This mystery series can help with that.

I believe that the work left to be done is what I call, "Heart Work." In order to make things in the world better, to be less divisive and negative, each of us individually must make a commitment to do what we can to change the one thing we have control over: ourselves. How do we treat others not like us in all the ways we communicate to others? Eye contact, body language, where we go, what we do, who we spend time with, who we don't, how we look at them, how we speak to them. It all sends a message. Is it the message we want to send? Does the message we're sending reflect our values? Is it instead consistent with beliefs we hold without even realizing it, sending negative messages we did not realize or intend?

We must search our hearts and minds and begin the work of being intentional about ridding ourselves of the, often unwitting, scourge of marginalizing others and standing in the way of *all* of us being the best we can be. Each of us is a work in progress and each of us has a part. We just have to have the will to do it. We believe in "space and grace." Space to navigate and explore this new territory, and grace extended to each of us in learning this new landscape, if it is to be sustainable. We're looking at you, cancel culture extremists. We believe teaching to be more productive than immediate canceling over unintentional faux pas. Teachable moments are awesome. They are also very much needed in the rapidly changing society we live in.

For me, my life's motto is "It's ALL about Love..." and I strive to demonstrate that in every way I can in going through the world. We hope you will too. You never know what impact something as simple as that smile you give can have on someone you give it to. Yep, a lawyer talking about love. My decades of experience has proven to me not only that it matters, but it works. Ultimately, what other choice do we have?

Feel free to begin the next step in your journey with my **TED Talk** (https://www.youtube.com/watch?v=ExcDNly1DbI) or my website, **practicaldiversity.com**. It was a gift to humanity after former students, now out in the world, contacted me as the George Floyd fiasco unfolded, wishing they could be back in class with me at such a stressful time in order to be able to process what was going on. They wanted to know if I had resources they could use. The practicaldiversity.com site has now been visited by countless people all over the entire world.

To stay updated on us, we invite you to visit visit quiltedhearts.world

By the way, do you have a personal story to share about the impact of a quilt in your own life? Send it along to us! We'd *love* to see it! Maybe (with your permission, of course) we'll even be able to include one at the end of each book! Wouldn't that be neat?! After all, who doesn't love a great quilt story?! ;-)

Thank you more than words can ever say for reading our book!!!!!!!!!!

DDB-A
October 9, 2022
Athens, GA
dawndba@quiltedhearts.world
reneepatterson@quiltedhearts.world

ACKNOWLEDGEMENTS

DDB-A

*T*he Universe *always* delivers. This is such an incredible demonstration of that. I acknowledge and appreciate that more than words can ever say. Without it, this book and The Quilt Journeys Mystery Series would not exist. But it also would not have been possible without several individuals I'd like to thank. They include my niece, Renée Tracy Harris Patterson, who asked me to tell her about the stack of handmade quilts I made and, when I got to the one I made to commemorate my great great-grandmother, said, "Wouldn't it be neat if we wrote a story about a quilt?" and we did; my parents, Rev. William H. Bennett and Ann P. Liles Benett, for allowing me to be who I am and giving me such great values to live by; my daughters, Jenniffer Dawn Bennett Alexander Jones, Anne Alexis Bennett Alexander and Tess Alexandra Bennett Harrison, for being the incredible, awesome, hilarious, crazy crew you are, bound and determined to make the world a better place and have fun doing it; my delightful grandchildren, Makayla Anne Jones and Christian Edward Alexander Jones, for whom I try hard to create a better world, just like I did for your Mama and Aunties. Nana loves you so!; my BFF, linda f. harrison, aka Pooh/ GrandPooh. Thanks for years of laughter and support. What a run we've had!; Brian Alzue Thompson, much to my utter surprise, truly the great love of my life. Where do I even begin with you, Brian? You have helped me in ways I did not even realize for decades. Without you this series would not even have been possible. You once said, "If you ever wrote a book about your feelings, it would be a bestseller." Thank you for that. I'm sure it never occurred to either of us that that would actually happen. From your lips to God's ears. I know you don't understand how it works. Me either. But for 49 years, it has and I appreciate both the fact that it works as well as you hanging in there with it even though you don't understand it. I can't thank you enough. Who knew we had this work to do together? Thanks so much for the Dora Jones piece!; thank you to my legions of students and Diversity, Equity, Inclusion and Belonging session attendees who, over forty years, have given me the supreme gift of not only be open enough to allow us to have tons of fun while we learn, but also remembering our time together, using it in their everyday lives to make the world a better place and even more incredibly, taking the time to let me know it. Who knew I would be creating, as my extraordinary former student, Eddie Jordahl, creatively put it, "Diversity Warriors"?; I could not leave out of my deepest thanks to Jere W. Morehead, esteemed President of the University of Georgia and my colleague and dear friend of 34 years who I love to pieces, for being such an important, yet hilarious and astute listening post and an incredible and unparalleled leader in all things DEIB and everything else, for the right reasons. I know you well enough to know without a doubt that you will turn beet red when you see this and deny your enormous impact. :-) But we see you. We know better. I love it that you know you are a work in progress and are always willing to be open to continue to learn. A *very* valuable quality in a leader. Thank you so very much; thank you to my beloved siblings, the late Barbara Jean Bennett Bethea, and the living and illustrious Gale C. Bennett Harris Pinson, Brenda B. Watkins, and Rev. Dr. William H. Bennett II and their families. You make my path so much easier because of your love, support and laughs. Thanks for a lifetime of memories to work from; finally, last but *certainly* not least, to our readers, THANK YOU! We wrote this for you. We knew that "if we built it, you would come." We are the ones we have been waiting for. Be the change. We can do this. Feel free to visit my website, ***practicaldiversity.com*** for pointers. Thank you to all those who visit it for inspiration, tips, guidance and just have the heart to browse the subject matter and try to learn.

God, you showed me that life is precious and can easily be taken away. I am very clear, Lord, that you have a purpose for my life. It is my prayer that I am performing in the role you want and that I am making you proud. Auntie Dawnie, you have always been the bomb dot com super hero Auntie to me. It's great all these other people love you and all but at the end of the day you are MY Auntie, ok?! :-) I'm so happy you gave me my Nancy Drew novels encouraging me to read at a young age, which is why I absolutely love a good mystery to this day. Spending time with you and talking together every day has been a pleasure. It is like sitting at your feet and taking a Master Class that produces a series of amazing cozy historical fiction books everyone is sure to love. Attorney Richard Harris and Dr. Gale C. Harris Pinson, or as I like to call them, Mommy and Daddy. I am so very thankful every single day that I can pick up the phone and call you to talk. More importantly, I can get to either one of you in less than an hour. We are taught that the children take care of the parents as we get older. Who would have thought the two of you would be taking care of me in our later years? I love and appreciate you more and more everyday. I am so thankful that you are still with me. My sisters Robin Stanford, Leslie M. Harris Greer and Dawn M. Harris White thank you for being loving, having my nieces and nephews, being inclusive of our blended families and providing them the best possible childhood we could give. My children Dominique C. Harris, Candice N. Patterson, Skylar J. Patterson and Taylor R. Patterson. Although I was the adult raising you, sometimes you all raised me by opening my mind, massaging my heart and caring for my soul. My grandchildren Nia Patterson, Lillianna Vicente and Maia Patterson (Glam Baby) your smiles and living-out-loud lives makes my heart jump for joy! Karla, Karlette & Tiana, Ellen, Nicole, Jerri, Connie, Rot & Ret, my family by choice, your believing in me, literally and figuratively, propelled me into action. All the visits, phone calls, emails, texts, letters, cards, (even the talking about me in hushed tones and behind closed doors), I used it all to reset my outlook in all areas of my life and it motivated me to reinvent myself into a stronger, more capable woman that owns her disability. This is who

I am now, I am proudly part of the world's largest minority. There is a group of people who made a big impact on me, in the most positive way, the people of the medical community. There really is no way that words can cover all that this caring, positive, passionate, dedicated, educated, patient, overworked and [like teachers] underpaid group of human beings bring to an essentially a thankless job. A job that helped me, taught me, bathed me, changed me and still left me with my dignity. Doctors and nurses embody this definition, but I don't ever want to forget the LPN's, LVN's, Dining staff, Housekeeping, Physical Therapist, Occupational Therapist, Speech Therapist, Chaplains, the entire Emergency Rooms staff, local Fire Departments, Paramedics, Imaging staff and those medical staff that touched my life and I mistakenly left out. Please charge it to my head, not my heart. If I had not had you to make my day go okay it's a scary thought to think of. I know it was your influence, support, and help that kept me working to get to the best possible me. You do not go unnoticed. My heart always flutters when I think of all you can, did and will do. I am humbled by all of you. It is my pleasure to use this platform to encourage and challenge all to think about how we can be the change we want to see in the world.